DANIELLE MARCUS

THICK
OF
LOVE

A NOVEL

BLACK
ODYSSEY
MEDIA

WWW.BLACKODYSSEY.NET

Published by
BLACK ODYSSEY MEDIA

www.blackodyssey.net
Email: info@blackodyssey.net

THICK OF LOVE. Copyright © 2023 by DANIELLE MARCUS

Library of Congress Control Number: 2023900477

First Trade Paperback Printing: August 2023
ISBN: 979-8-9855941-3-3
ISBN: 979-8-9855941-4-0 (e-book)

Cover Design by BlackEncryption Designs

10 9 8 7 6 5 4 3 2 1

Manufactured in the United States of America

Distributed by Kensington Publishing Corp.

Dear Reader,

I want to thank you immensely for supporting Black Odyssey Media authors, and our ongoing efforts to spotlight more minority storytellers. The scariest and most challenging task for many writers is getting the story, or characters, out of our heads and onto the page. Having admitted that, with every manuscript that Kreceda and I acquire, we believe that it took talent, discipline, and remarkable courage to construct that story, flesh out those characters, and prepare it for the world. Debut or seasoned, our authors are the real heroes and heroines in OUR story. And for them, we are eternally grateful.

　　Whether you are new to Danielle Marcus or Black Odyssey Media, we hope that you are here to stay. We also welcome your feedback and kindly ask that you leave a review. For upcoming releases, announcements, submission guidelines, etc., please be sure to visit our website at www.blackodyssey.net or scan the QR code below. We can also be found on social media using @iamblackodyssey. Until next time, take care and enjoy the journey!

Joyfully,

Shawanda Williams

Shawanda "N'Tyse" Williams
Founder/Publisher

FROM THE AUTHOR

If you enjoy this read, please be sure to leave a review and tell a friend. I appreciate each and every person who has supported me and my dreams. Thank you, and I pray you continue to rock with me!

Love,
Danielle Marcus

CHAPTER ONE

"**W**HEN YOU TRYING to see me?"

His voice was flirtatious, suggestive. Dallas Avery knew exactly what he was insinuating…sex, and she couldn't believe the audacity.

"Listen, are you coming to get the kids or not, Messiah?" Dallas grumbled, rolling her eyes.

The mere thought of him caused her to cringe these days.

"Didn't I say I was? Why you gotta have an attitude every time I call? Bitter ain't cute on you."

Bitter? Dallas had to repeat the word in her head. He did not get to poke the giant and tuck his tail.

"You know what? Not today, Satan. I will not let you take me out of my element. Bye, asshole," she said, ending the call before he could respond.

Bitter? Hell, yeah, I'm bitter, and I have every right to be.

Fifteen years was a long time to love a man. Dallas Avery had invested everything in him. She gave up her dreams and sacrificed her happiness to make sure their relationship would end the fairytale she had imagined. She gave him the whole gotdamn cow, and he still chose to marry another woman.

A frown tipped the corners of her lips as she thought about Messiah, her sperm donor.

Sorry-ass nigga, she grumbled, snatching a bronze dress from the clothing rack and giving it a once over before hanging it back in place.

Of course, their relationship wasn't perfect, but whose was? Instead of trying to fix it, he found some young hoe who probably

1

still had milk behind her ears and called himself replacing her. Just the thought made Dallas's stomach turn.

She might have accepted their breakup a little better if he had ended things and let her be. However, somehow, he still found his way back to her bed every chance he got, stirring up emotions she was desperately trying to rid herself of. How could she get over him when the familiarity of his touch still sent a shiver up her spine and shot her spiraling on a euphoric high?

Messiah was her drug, and she was addicted to him. But like every other high, it eventually wore off, bringing forth the sobering truth. He left her bed to go home to his fiancée while she hugged a pillow, wishing it was him.

She let out a sigh, thumbing through another rack of expensive dresses at Posh Dior Clothing Boutique. Messiah's wedding to his young hoe was quickly approaching, and Dallas was toying with the idea of crashing the ceremony and opening Pandora's box. Why should they get to have their happily-ever-after while she sat in her room crying herself to sleep every other night? She was tired of being the bigger person when it was obvious no one gave a damn about her feelings.

Mary J. Blige's *Not Gon Cry* had been on repeat on Dallas's playlist for the past three months. When Mary said, "*I should have left yo' ass a thousand times,*" Dallas felt that in her soul. She wished she had left him the first time he broke her heart. Now, he had her questioning why she wasn't woman enough to keep her man. She had to pretend she had everything together and put on the facade of the perfect mother; when the truth was, she was salty. She resented Messiah just as much as she loved him.

Dallas tried her best to push him from her thoughts as she scanned the price tag connected to the sleeves of a gorgeous, peach mermaid-style gown. Her brows creased.

"Eight hundred dollars?" she mumbled, analyzing the dress

again, attempting to tell herself it wasn't all that. But, being honest with herself, she knew she'd kill the game in it. Her body had always been stacked in all the right places.

She studied the price tag again, calculating which bill she could skip to pay for the piece. Messiah Jr.'s basketball camp money was due, the light bill needed to be paid, and Mr. Thomas had already given her an extension on the car loan.

"Here I am robbing Peter to pay Paul while your stankin' ass is out living your best life. And you got the nerve to call me bitter?"

She sucked her teeth, slamming the dress back into its rightful place.

"Dang, what did that dress do to you? I think it would look fly on you."

A deep baritone massaged Dallas's eardrums. His warm breath and the feeling of his presence sent a chill up her spine. She jumped before focusing on him. *Damn, he's fine.*

Dallas snorted. "Not for eight hundred dollars. It better turn me into Beyoncé for that price."

"Beyoncé is overrated. You're not giving yourself enough credit," he added charmingly.

Is he flirting? Dallas took a second to scan him. He was so smooth…and handsome. His chocolate six-foot-two-inch frame was muscular, broad shoulders filled out his blazer, a fresh cut had his waves spinning, and his thick kiss-me lips were inviting. Then, he had the nerve to be dressed GQ in a three-piece suit and a pair of wing-tipped Ferragamos. She knew what they were because Messiah had those same shoes. They'd actually argued over them. However, she couldn't remember Messiah looking that good in them.

"Thanks," Dallas muttered, tucking a stray strand of her chestnut hair behind her ear.

Her gaze landed on the watch on her wrist, causing her eyes to bulge. She only had seven minutes to get back to the office. She had spent more time at the boutique than she'd intended.

"Dallas, right?" He smiled, pointing at her name badge. "I saw you walk in and couldn't let you go without telling you how pretty you are."

Her cheeks stained red. She couldn't remember the last time she received a simple compliment and honestly didn't know how to take it. Her lips curved downward.

"Thank you, but I'm not interested," Dallas responded, studying the dress again, then returning her focus to the stranger.

"Not interested in what? I never made any offers," he corrected her.

Dallas rolled her eyes. She didn't know why she was giving the man such a hard time. She couldn't help it. Messiah left a sour taste in her mouth, and the poor stranger was the easiest to take it out on.

"Whatever. I have to go," she spat, stepping around him and making her way toward the exit.

"You're still beautiful. Mean and all."

Dallas heard him. The half-smile that crept on her face showcased the dimple on her left cheek. She didn't want to be angry anymore. She didn't want to cry over Messiah another night. Why was she finding it so hard to move on? After dealing with Messiah's no-good, cheating ass, dating another man was last on her agenda. He had really done a number on her. They'd been officially broken up for ten months, he engaged for three, and she still hadn't opened herself up to dating again.

"Damnit, Messiah Jr., what did I tell you about leaving this ball in the middle of my floor? And why are your clothes spread all over my living room?" Dallas squalled, bracing herself from falling onto her face. She exhaled, then sucked in a deep breath to calm her nerves.

Dallas loved her kids deeply; she really did. However, she needed a mental break. Mommy time with margaritas and girl talk would be nice or a night of hot, dirty, disrespectful sex with a tall, sexy, chocolate brother who had a nice body and... No, she had to stop herself there. Having random sex wasn't exactly her style.

"Sorry, Ma. My dad is coming to get us today, and he wanted us to dress nice. I was going to ask you which one you wanted me to wear," Messiah Jr. explained, snatching his basketball up and shooting at an imaginary rim. "We're going to dinner with that girl's family. I don't want to meet them, but Dad said I have to."

His peanut-butter face formed a frown. Messiah Jr. was so handsome—the perfect mixture of both parents, from his charcoal-black curly hair inherited through Dallas to having his father's brown eyes and full nose.

Dallas stifled a giggle. "Don't call her *that girl*. She has a name. And don't be like that, son. She's your family now."

Damn, it was hard being the bigger person. It nearly killed Dallas, but she promised herself never to talk down on their *situation* to the children, no matter how much it hurt.

"That's not my family! You're my family, Mom. I'll make a mistake and knock all the drinks on her dress if you want me to." He snickered deviously, causing Dallas to chortle.

"Messiah!" Dallas covered her mouth, unable to hold in her laughter. "It's okay this time, baby. I'll let you know when I need your backup," she added, nudging him and ruffling his curls.

The doorbell chimed before Messiah Jr. could respond. He tossed his basketball in the corner and raced toward the stairs.

"That's Dad. I'll go get Meghan so y'all can *talk*." He made googly eyes at Dallas as he passed her, causing her to shake her head.

Her son was a complete character. He wanted them to get back together so badly. It was almost as if he didn't understand it was over. Their happy family was torn apart because his father decided to marry his mistress, his whore, his homewrecker. Dallas could think of quite a few more names she could have called the girl, but she was trying not to let those ill thoughts consume her.

Dallas let out a husky breath of air, watching her son disappear. Was she ready to come face-to-face with Messiah? No. He'd just broken the news of his engagement and instantaneous wedding, demanding that their children participate as the official flower girl and groomsman. He hadn't even given the wound time to heal, yet there he was, showing up at her doorstep and forcing her to suck it up. She always had to just *suck it up,* no matter what *it* was.

Releasing another husky breath, Dallas tried her best to relax her nerves. It was just Messiah, right? The same tired nigga that went out and proposed to some hoe who he'd only known for months, although she had given him nearly fifteen years.

Fifteen years. Reciting that number almost made her lose her breath. She had given him the whole cow, milked it for him, and his ungrateful ass still went out and got another woman. She gave him the best years of her life, gave him children, and sacrificed her freedom, and he simply said fuck her.

Dallas wanted to hate him, but she couldn't. She just wanted to know why. That question kept repeating in her head. Why would he shoot a bullet right through her heart like that?

Biting her bottom lip, Dallas swung the door open and smoothed the wrinkles out of her top, an attempt to calm her nerves. Standing before her with his hands shoved in his black slacks, the top two buttons of his shirt undone, and his tie loosened, Messiah was perfect.

Dallas loved him. That was something she gave up trying to deny. However, she didn't understand how she could love a man with every fiber of her being and hate him just as much. She had to use all the strength she could muster not to break down at the reality of her broken forever standing in her face.

"Hey, Dally. Are the kids ready?" He pulled his left hand out of his pocket and studied his watch. "We have an hour to make it to the restaurant. Tatiana's people get to acting stupid, and I'm not trying to hear it."

Dallas's face contorted into the sourest frown.

"I don't give a damn what her family do," she spat, pointing her finger at his chest. "You know, you're really an inconsiderate asshole, Messiah. Wait here; I'll send the kids out shortly."

She rolled her eyes, fighting to hold back the tears on the verge of escaping without her permission. She had shed far too many tears over him. He didn't deserve any more.

Messiah frowned. "Damn, I can't come in the house now? I paid for the motherfucka and left it to you, might I add. If I was an asshole, I would have taken it back."

If looks could kill, the mug on Dallas's face would have sent Messiah to an early grave. She could only shake her head at him. He really didn't have a clue.

"No, you're still an asshole. You don't get points for not putting your kids on the street, especially being that *you're* the one who walked away to be with your mistress."

"Come on, Dallas," Messiah groaned, raking a hand across his freshly shaved face. "It's been ten months. How long are you going to keep bringing Tatiana up? It's getting old."

"How dare you cheat on me and decide when I'm supposed to stop hurting? So fifteen years meant nothing to you, huh? I did everything you asked of me, Messiah. I gave you a part of me that no one else had, and this random broad comes along and gets the ring, the horse, and the carriage? Don't you dare tell me how to feel about that!"

Dallas's lips were clenched so tightly that she could barely get the words out. Her heart began to thump hard and fast. The uneasy feeling that settled in her gut almost made her nauseous.

Dallas thought about the little girl that he was supposed to marry. That's what she was to her—a kid. At twenty-three, she couldn't possibly have anything going for herself except a wet ass. Dallas had debated many nights on what the girl had over her that made Messiah propose. She beat herself up trying to figure out what she was doing wrong and how she could fix it. Even after everything he had put her through, a part of her was still hoping he would realize his mistake, apologize for her pain, and they'd live happily ever after. That's what made her sick…the fact that she was willing to take him back. She was weak when it came to him, and she prayed daily for the strength to get over his sorry ass.

"Listen, Dallas," Messiah started, jarring her from her mental debate as he cupped her elbow to make her pay attention to him. Ignoring the grim look plastered across her face, he continued, "You know I'll always have love for you and my children. Me marrying Tatiana will never change that." He ran his hand through his waved hair. "But, in the future, demand what you want from a man. Because I, or shall I say *he*, will only do what you allow him to do. I didn't want a maid. I wanted a partner, Dallas."

Before Dallas could process her actions, her hand landed across Messiah's cheek. She slapped him so hard that the sound echoed through the house.

"Get out!" Dallas screamed, pointing toward the door. "Get the hell out of my house and wait for your children in the car. Go, Messiah!"

Her voice was shaky and a little too loud for her comfort, especially with the kids in the house. But how could Messiah not see that he was breaking her? She felt like his personal prisoner, and he'd given her a life sentence. She had pretended to be strong for far too long, and she couldn't do it anymore. She just couldn't.

CHAPTER TWO

R&B SINGER TANK'S latest hit, "When We," blared through the speakers as Candace swayed her hips from side to side with perfect rhythm. She watched herself in the mirror, her body reacting to each break in the beat. She was in her zone, amazing the onlookers with her style and grace. Dancing was her passion. It was her way of expressing herself. She could watch a move one time and master it, no matter the genre of dance performed.

Tonight, she was teaching an erotic pole dancing class in the back room of her best friend's boutique. Well, one of her best friends. Dallas would have a complete fit if she heard Candace call Sasha her best friend without acknowledging her, too. It had been an ongoing joke since they were in high school. The girls were inseparable, more like sisters than friends.

Candace had a class full, and she was grateful for how quickly the number of attendees had multiplied since her first session. At twenty-nine, she was making a name for herself around the city. Actually, people traveled from all over Michigan to attend her classes. Soon, she would need her own building. That was her dream—to own a dance studio.

After the song ended, Candace whirled around with a big alley-cat grin plastered across her face. The ladies went into a fit of applause and catcalls.

"Alright, y'all, do you have the moves down pat? Let's put them all together now. Imagine your boo is sitting in front of you. This is for him. Get sexy for him," she encouraged, signaling her

9

assistant to restart the song.

"What if I don't do dick? What if I got a whole woman at home?" Tangie, one of her regulars, teased.

Candace let out a small giggle. "Here *you* go. Well, imagine your girl is in front of you then. There's a lot of beautiful women in here tonight. Pick one and dance for her."

She winked as the beat came back on, and the ladies got into position to start the routine.

"Okay, let's move. Work them hips. Twirl, dip, grind on him. Make him hot, ladies," she instructed, watching as the class mirrored her moves. "Uh-uh, Ashley. You got too much booty back there not to know how to work it. Shake that big 'ol thang," she said, causing the ladies to laugh.

Candace had no problem calling underperformers out. She was slick with the tongue, but everyone knew she meant no harm.

The class went over the routine for twenty more minutes before calling it quits for the night. Candace had a date with her man and planned on putting on a private show for him. It always ended in hot, nasty sex that left her center aching with passion. Jaxon fucked her so good that her body began to tingle just thinking about him.

They had been dating for almost two years now. Candace was ready to marry him, but he wasn't ready. She was also ready to give him his first child; he wanted to focus on his career. They were pulling in two totally different directions. One thing was for sure, though; their chemistry was undeniable. The sex was incredible and made Candace ignore several red flags.

A line leader at Ford Motor Company, Jaxon had been on the job since he was nineteen. Thirteen years, no kids, and no wife later, he had a hefty savings account, a 401k, a beautiful home in Rochester Hills, and good credit. It also helped that he was sexy as all hell. The brother had it going on.

They met at the gas station. She didn't know where to pour the antifreeze, and he just happened to be a knight in shining armor. He insisted on taking her number and a lunch date as repayment for helping her, although he could have gotten it for free. Candace had never seen a man so fine in her life. He was tall, honey-glazed, clean-cut, and downright sexy. Plus, when she used the term man, she meant a *real* man. He wasn't into the streets, didn't hang out all night, nor did he wear his pants sagging below his ass. Jaxon had grown man swag, and Candace instantly fell in love with his charm.

"Candace, right? Can I talk to you?"

The voice snapped her out of her thoughts. She turned to face a chocolate beauty with brown hair, big boobs, and a small waist. She was younger, maybe twenty-four or twenty-five, but beautiful. That was undeniable.

Candace smiled. "Yes. Arianna, right? You just started two classes ago?"

Arianna nodded. "That's me, but I wanted to talk to you about private lessons. My man is obsessed with me dancing for him." She playfully rolled her eyes and blushed as if just the thought of him drove her crazy. "Well, when he mentioned that he knew you did these classes, I had to come. You're the shit, girl. I'm going to have his ass begging to taste this by the end of our sessions."

Candace was used to women coming to her and speaking about their private lives. Sometimes, she felt like a relationship doctor. Private lessons weren't unusual, either.

"Of course," Candace replied with a nod. "Just have my assistant set it up. And tell the Mr. thanks for the recommendation."

"Shit, Jaxon will probably be thanking you himself after I finish with his ass," Arianna giggled as she twirled her hair around her finger while blushing.

Candace's face scrunched up in confusion. She knew like hell the bitch couldn't be talking about her perfect Jaxon. He didn't have another woman. He worked entirely too much and spent all his free time with Candace. Their relationship was going so perfectly, and they were making life-altering plans for their future. He loved her; Candace knew he did.

"Jaxon?" Candace finally repeated, squinting her eyes. She must have heard wrong.

Arianna put on her fakest smile. "Yes, girl. Why you say it like that? You know some info on him that I don't? Spill it, girl." She nudged Candace.

Anger instantly surged throughout Candace's body. There were three possible explanations. One, there was another Jaxon who just happened to be Arianna's man. Two, Arianna was a messy jump-off, mad that she and Jaxon were building a solid relationship. Or three, Jaxon was a lying sack of shit. She prayed it wasn't the latter.

Placing her hands on her hips and shifting her weight to one leg, Candace studied the young girl. "Actually, I do know a Jaxon. The only woman he has is me, though. I don't know what you're trying to prove, but I'm not the one, chile. I promise I'm not the one," Candace gritted, shaking her head from side to side.

Her eyes traveled to the door as the other ladies began to file out. She prided herself on conducting a drama-free zone and prayed she didn't have to show her natural black ass before everyone got a chance to leave out. Although she had matured tremendously, Candace still had a wild side that would lay a bitch out, especially a messy bitch.

Arianna's smile turned into a frown Candace wanted to slap clean off her face.

"I think you are the one," Arianna smirked. "I wish you would worry about these whack-ass classes like you worry about my man. I don't appreciate you calling and texting him when he's home with me. He tells me how you're trying to force a baby on him and get married." She rolled her eyes. "I almost feel bad for you, sis. He's just not that into you," Arianna added with a shrug.

Candace didn't know what cut more—the fact that the

little hoodrat was in her face or that Jaxon had the audacity to be pillow-talking with the bitch, giving her ammunition to fire at her. However, she did know she had an ass-whooping to hand out if that's what the young girl wanted.

Stepping closer into Arianna's personal space, Candace stared at her intently, wanting her to see how serious the situation was about to escalate. She pointed an accusing finger.

"Listen, heffa. Don't you dare come checking me about some mess your man created. The way he stays in my bed and makes all these promises to spend a lifetime with me, I'm guessing he's just not that into you, either. Second, bitch, I suggest you carry your soul out of my establishment. Go grab a two-piece and a biscuit because this right here is beef you definitely don't want."

Candace was furious. The lump that had settled in her throat caused her breathing to go ragged and her palms to sweat. All her life, she seemed to have to fight with love. Every single time she thought she had found the one, he turned out to be a loser. Jaxon had lasted the longest out of all her relationships. She thought she was finally going to get her happily ever after. Yet, here this chick was coming into *her* establishment, checking her about *her* man.

Before Candace could blink, Arianna swung, catching her on the right cheek. Candace couldn't believe it. They began to go at it like lionesses over a piece of meat—hair-pulling, fists-swinging, all-out battling.

"Bitch, you tried the right one," Candace gritted, slamming Arianna onto her back and pinning her down. "Ain't nobody ever tell you to check the man, not the broad that knows nothing about you?" she continued to fuss, delivering blow after blow.

Candace released all of the hurt and frustration she was experiencing onto Arianna's face until a set of strong arms pulled her away. They snatched her up as if she only weighed a feather.

"Chill, Candy," the raspy voice whispered into her ear. "Calm that shit down, ma."

He squeezed her tighter as she desperately tried to free herself. She had lost all control. It hurt. Finding out her perfect man wasn't so perfect was like shoving a dagger through her heart and twisting. It was all Arianna's fault.

"Let me go, Diego!" Candace screamed.

Arianna was lucky Candace's best friend's brother saved the day. Diego was huge, and his arms swallowed her. Candace couldn't get loose, no matter how hard she tried.

"Nah, chill that ratchet shit out, Candy. This not even you," he whispered into her ear.

Then, he focused on Arianna as she hopped up and charged toward them. However, the dangerous look that danced across his face stopped her dead in her tracks.

"I put it on my life; you come this way and touch her, I'm knocking yo' ass the fuck out."

He said it with so much venom that Arianna collected her pride and carried her bruised face out of the boutique.

By now, the boutique was completely cleared out. Sasha had hurried the other ladies away while Diego broke up the fight. After her adrenaline died down, Candace broke. She was never a weak woman, nor had she been the type of female to fight over a man. However, Jaxon turned her into someone that she wasn't. He built her up to send her crashing down, and it hurt.

"He lied to me," she whispered as a tear slid down her face. "He sat in my face and lied to me. I didn't ask him to come into my life and make me fall in love with him. I didn't ask for the lies," she cried, looking into Diego's handsome face while he stared back into hers. "Why did he do me like that? I was good to him, Diego," she groaned as more tears cascaded down her cheeks.

The fire that radiated between Diego and Candace nearly burned her. They were so close, and the longing in his eyes made her soul shudder. He was so handsome, and for the first time, she saw Big Bad Diego looking vulnerable. Candace could hear his heart beating inside his chest, and the feeling that ran through her body was so intense that she had to look away.

Their chemistry had been off the Richter scale since she could remember. However, Candace had done everything in her power to ignore the feeling. She couldn't go there with him. Diego was like her best male friend, and their bond was special to her. Whenever she needed solid, unbiased advice from a man, he was there. At night, after her classes, he was also there to protect her and make sure she made it home safely. She could always depend on him when she didn't have anyone else. That's why she wouldn't dare ruin their bond with a disastrous attempt at a relationship. All of her relationships ended in disaster; it never failed.

"Stop crying, girl," Diego whispered against her ear as he gently pulled her face to his.

Using his thumb, Diego wiped the tears away, his gaze boring into her pretty golden face, taking in the way her long lashes fell over her sparkling brown eyes. Candace was beautiful, puffy face and all. Not made up beautiful. She was naturally beautiful.

Diego sighed. "I should beat yo' ass myself. Up in here fighting and crying over a nigga, Candy. Didn't I tell you that you're royalty? Queens do queen shit, baby girl," he explained to her. "If a real man wants you to be in his life, you don't have to fight for a position that's already yours. Stop trying to fit a circle into a square because it will never work, ma."

Candace wrapped her arms around his waist, head pressed against his chest, a pout formed on her lips. She couldn't bear to continue looking into his eyes. She was afraid she'd get lost in him. Being in his arms felt so comforting, and at that moment, she needed comfort.

"But he was supposed to be the one, Diego. We were doing so

good. What am I doing wrong?"

Diego smiled. "Not fucking with me, wasting your time with all these nothing-ass niggas."

Candace giggled. "Seriously, Diego." She tapped him on the chest, purposely ignoring what he said. That was forbidden territory. "I'm a good catch, right? I mean, I own my own business that's doing great. I have a house, car, and bank account. So, it's not like I'm some needy broad. Why do I keep getting the short end of the stick?" she whined.

The smile left Diego's lips. "I just told you. It's because you won't let me have you. I'm about to just gon' ahead and snatch you up."

Candace studied Diego's face to see if he was serious. The realization that she was still in his arms finally settled in, and the electric current that flowed through her body scared her. Diego was serious. Her brows knitted together. Out of all the years they had lightheartedly flirted, he had never blatantly come on to her. Not wanting to process it, she laughed him off.

"Boy, stop playing with me. You're Sasha's brother. I'm not trying to get into it with you and fall out with my best friend, too. You're like my big brother, and our bond is too deep to mess it up with a relationship," she said, trying to convince herself more so than him.

She couldn't date Sasha's brother, right? No. It would be completely wrong to date Sasha's fine-ass, strong-armed, successful-business-having, masculine brother. Damnit. Why did Diego have to push those types of thoughts into her head? Yes, she had joked about the nasty things she would do to him, but seriously considering it never crossed her mind.

"My momma ain't push you out her coochie," Diego chuckled. "And why would we fall out? I'm nothing like these little boys you keep dealing with. I'm a real man, baby girl. I ain't got time to be out here making my chick look stupid. I'm trying to go half on businesses, start a family, and build college funds with my wife. I'm too old for all that kiddie shit."

Candace never got a chance to respond. Sasha came marching back into the room with her face mugged up.

"Who was that, Candy? I swear, she's lucky my brother stopped me," Sasha growled, walking over to the desk that was pushed into the corner for the class and setting her purse down. Then she made her way over to Candace and examined her face. "She didn't get you, did she, boo?" she questioned with genuine concern etched on her face.

Candace swatted Sasha's hand away. She was so dramatic it caused Candace to giggle.

"Girl, you know damn well I was not about to let some young hoe get the best of me. She's lucky your brother's strong ass pulled me off her."

She rolled her eyes, purposely avoiding eye contact with Diego. She didn't know how to respond to him trying to stake claim on her heart. She didn't know how to process it. So, she tried her best not to…yet.

"Let her bring her ass to the next class. Nobody will be able to hold me back. Now, let's lock up. I need to stop by Fat Boy's on my way home and pick Hunt up a steak sub. I will not be doing any cooking tonight."

"Go ahead and leave out. I'll finish locking up and take Candy home," Diego suggested with such finality, as if plans were settled.

Candace thought about being alone with Diego and picking up their conversation where they had left off. Nope, it wasn't happening.

"You don't have to, Diego. I need girl talk with my sister. I'll probably have her drop me off at Dallas's house for drinks while we bash y'all no-good niggas."

Diego frowned. "Don't group me in the same category with no other man, 'cause there ain't another nigga breathing like me. And don't think I'm letting you off that easily. Talk your shit with your homegirls tonight, but I'm on your head, and there ain't nothing you can do about it."

The words flowed from his lips so forceful yet gentle. He was confident, and the rosiness covering Candace's cheeks caused him to smirk.

Diego kissed Sasha on the forehead before making his way to Candace and grabbing her up into a hug. Before whispering in her ear, he savored the scent of her Gucci Guilty perfume.

"Don't have me waiting on you too long. You know I'll come find you."

With that, he pecked her cheek, then walked off toward the door so smoothly that Candace swore her panties were soaking wet.

Sasha's brother better stop playing with me before I fuck him.

The thought caused her to chuckle, but she was dead serious. Diego's sexy ass could get it.

CHAPTER THREE

"BABE, IT LOOKS like we have new neighbors, and he's young and black. There's a baby, too. Aww, she's so adorable," Sasha cooed, watching as the little girl with loose ponytails ran around the yard while a man pulled boxes from his U-Haul.

A pang of hurt flowed through her chest as she watched the little girl. She'd give anything to have a child. She and Hunt had been trying for the past two years, but nothing seemed to work. Everyone kept telling her that she would become pregnant when God was ready for her to reproduce. However, how long was she going to have to wait? She would be thirty in a couple of months, and the years weren't waiting on her. Sasha wanted to enjoy her babies while she was still young, but it was starting to look impossible.

Hunt slid behind her, wrapping his arms around her waist and pressing his growing bulge against her back.

"Why are you so nosey, girl? You're so worried about them when your man is ready to lay you down and pop your own baby in you."

Sasha whirled around to face Hunt. Their eyes connected, and her whole body shuddered. She never thought it was possible to love a man as much as she loved him. He was her whole universe. She couldn't see herself with any man outside of him.

Hunter Barksdale was every bit sexy. At thirty-five, he was tall, chocolate, and had a body created from the heavens above— chiseled to perfection. He had the most gorgeous smile and perfect, straight white teeth. He was rocking a bald head because his hairline

19

had started to recede prematurely, but his baldness made him even sexier. Sasha couldn't get enough of her soon-to-be husband.

She smiled, running a hand through her hair to move it out of her face.

"You're so nasty. I thought you had to be up and out for work."

"Nah, work can wait. I need a little something to hold me over until I get off. Come on." His eyes shifted to the clock on their nightstand and back to Sasha. "I got twenty-two minutes to spare. If you bend over now, we might get two rounds in." He smiled sheepishly, nibbling on her neck.

Sasha leaned her head back a bit to grant him full access as his hands began to explore her body. "'Damn, Hunt."

She arched against him as his lips traveled to her breast, licking around her nipple in a circular motion. Two fingers worked inside her, stirring her juices and preparing her for his entrance. His thumb rubbed around her clit, and the pleasure of the moment caused her eyes to roll to the back of her head. So close. The strength of what was building was mind-blowing. Sasha's body was nearing convulsions. She could feel it. If he stopped, she would die. It was almost too much. Hunt didn't play fair when it came to pleasing her body. She never knew a man who could melt her soul with only his fingers.

With the ease of an expert, Hunt guided her to the bed, shedding their clothes in the process. He wasted no time climbing on top and finding his way inside her slippery cave. She sucked him in like a glove…tight, wet, and warm. His body shuddered before finding his rhythm.

"You feel so perfect," he grunted, pumping into Sasha with a gentle rage.

The length and level of his arousal were almost brutal. He had to taste her lips to keep from screaming out like a little girl. Being inside of her felt that good.

Yanking her legs back, one hand hard on her back, the other

gripping her ass, he let out another grunt. He never slowed the movement, giving her full, hard thrusts. Her breasts bounced as she looked over to the mirror above the headboard, watching his sexy face and the look of pleasure that danced across it. It turned her on to no end.

"Damnit, Hunt," she called out, feeling the wave of her orgasm build up to its highest peak. She was about to cum, for sure. Her body shook with anticipation, every point in her being sparked with need. Her back lifted into a deep arch, and her mouth gaped and opened in an "O" shape. Before she knew it, she lost all control of her senses. Her juices flowed down her legs, coating Hunter's erection. The way she pulsed, squeezing him with her walls as she came, had him releasing with her. They surfed the wave, riding the orgasmic high until they both collapsed, short-winded and thoroughly pleased.

"I think I just put twins in you with that one." Hunter smiled, leaning over and kissing Sasha's forehead before pulling himself from the bed and heading to the bathroom for a second shower.

Sasha laid there with her legs lifted in the air as she read on Google. It helped his soldiers march to her eggs quicker. She hoped like hell this time was it. She wanted a baby so bad that it hurt.

Three hours later…

"I'm so sick of having to see his face. It's like, every time I see him, I think of new ways to murder him," Dallas complained through gritted teeth.

The girls were having a much-needed lunch outing over sandwiches and mimosas. It was rare that they all had the same day off and were able to hang out, especially Dallas. She was the only one out of the crew who had children. There was no question about it; she loved her kids. Yet, lately, she wished she could have waited to have them with another man. If she could, she would throw the whole relationship with Messiah away.

Sasha and Candace let out a giggle. Candace shook her head, feeling Dallas's pain. She didn't want to kill Jaxon, though. She'd be satisfied with punching him in the face.

"Girl, don't go to jail behind that inconsiderate nigga. He ain't worth it. I had to tell myself that, too. Then Jaxon had the nerve to try to downplay the situation as if I'm Boo-Boo the Fool. The girl knows too much for her to just be some crazy stalker chick."

Dallas nodded, agreeing with Candace. "Yeah, that was a little much. Forcing a baby on him? Who the hell does he think he is?" she shot, curling her lips up. "Candy, you can get any man that you want. Don't allow his tired ass to play you," Dallas added, taking a bite of her turkey and Swiss cheese panini.

Candace sighed. "I know, and speaking of any man," she turned to Sasha, "if your brother doesn't stop playing with me, I will fuck him." She giggled at the screwed-up face Sasha gave her. "Seriously, Diego knows his ass is sexy as hell."

"I didn't want to hear that." Sasha frowned. "I don't care what y'all grown-ass humans do. However, please don't mess with my brother if you don't plan to be straight up with him. He's been crushing on you for a long time, and I don't want to see him hurt."

Candace's eyes narrowed on Sasha, and Sasha shrugged. Anyone with vision could see that Diego was feeling Candace, hard. He looked at her with those big puppy dog eyes as if hypnotized by her. Then, the way his face lit up when he spoke about her, Sasha knew her brother was definitely in love with her best friend.

"So, you knew he was interested in me? Why you never told me, hater?" Candace giggled.

Diego was older. He had the girls by four years. He'd been in and out of prison in his teens and early twenties, getting caught up in the streets. But, after the last four-year stretch, he decided to get his life together. He went to school, got his carpentry license, and started his own business. He'd been going strong for six years now and was very successful. Gone was the bad boy who stayed in trouble. Sasha had watched her brother's transformation, and she felt he and Candace would make a great couple.

Sasha rolled her eyes. "First of all, heffa, hate has never been in my blood. Secondly, you were always in a relationship, or he had a girlfriend. Plus, you're my best friend. I didn't want to see either of you get hurt. It's obvious that Diego wants you, and knowing him, you guys will be together soon. So, don't hurt my brother. And, you," Sasha pointed at Dallas, "I think I found your future husband. He just moved in next door. I got a chance to speak to him before heading over here. He's cute, a single parent, and has a little girl who is a few years under Meghan. I'm going to throw a barbecue and invite him over."

She nudged Dallas with her shoulder, giving her googly eyes.

Dallas shook her head. "Uh-uh, I'm not thinking about a man right now. I'm still trying to figure out how to get over asshole and be a mother at the same time. I can't add another headache to the mix."

"How long are you going to drown yourself in misery while he's living life, Dallas? How many times are you going to allow the same man to repeatedly hurt you, when your Prince Charming is out there waiting to put a smile on your face? It's settled; I'm having the barbecue. You will be bringing your fine ass there, and I'm going to hook you two up, even if it's just to have a quickie every now and then. Someone has to knock the cobwebs off that kitty-kat."

Dallas cocked her head to the side. "Don't worry about my kitty-kat. It's taken care of."

Sasha frowned. "By who? Please don't tell me that you're still sleeping with Messiah after all the shit he's put you through."

Dallas swallowed hard, focusing on her chipped nails. "I may have slipped a time or two, or three, but who's counting?" She shrugged. "You do know he was mine for fifteen years. If I want to sit on his dick, I'm entitled to."

"Chile, fuck that entitlement. And fuck Messiah," Sasha said, waving Dallas off.

She was done discussing nonsense. Dallas was a fool, and there was no other way to put it. She could talk to her until she was blue in the face, and the girl would still allow Messiah to treat her like his doormat. Eventually, she'd get fed up. You could only chase a person for so long before your legs got tired.

"Enough about all this depressing stuff." Candace let out a sigh. "Dallas, Messiah has the kids for the weekend. I don't have any classes to teach until next week, and Mrs. Susie Homemaker doesn't have a job because poor Nevea runs the boutiques. What are we getting into? We're thirty, not one hundred. We should be living it up, enjoying ourselves. I'm not too big on the club, but we can do painting with a twist, bowling, or... I know! Tank's sexy ass is supposed to be in concert at the Music Hall. We need to be in attendance. I'm trying to pop a set of twins in him. Have you seen his performances? That body!" Candace gushed.

"Or, I can have a barbecue at my house, invite Diego and my neighbor, and make it a triple date. We could have drinks, play drunken Uno and Spades, and have a good time," Sasha urged, giving them the puppy dog face.

The truth was, Sasha didn't want to hang out anywhere in public. She painted a charade for the outside world. Yes, she had the house and a loving, supportive fiancée who spoiled her with anything her heart desired and gave her the attention she needed, but she was miserable. She wanted to conceive a baby so badly that she was obsessed with the thought.

CHAPTER FOUR

"You PROMISED YOU would keep them the whole weekend, Messiah. I made plans already."

Dallas sighed, leaning against the doorframe as her ex-lover stood before her, sexy as ever. She bit down on her bottom lip, fighting the urge to want to jump his bones. It had been nearly two months since they shared a bed, ever since he told her that he was getting married. She promised herself that she was done with him. Yet, she longed to feel those strong arms gripping her hips and hitting her spots like only he could. She let out a frustrated groan, focusing on his car parked in the driveway with *her* sitting in the front seat.

"I told you, something came up with Tatiana. We have to drive to Ohio to check on her grandmother. I'm going to get them next weekend, I promise."

Dallas watched the way Messiah lustfully took her in. His tongue ran across his thick pink lips, and her center began to ache. She hated him for making her body react to him like that. Self-consciously, she tugged at her crop top, making a futile attempt to hide her belly.

"Besides, where do you think you're about to go lookin' like that? And why are you showing off your stomach? You're a mother, Dallas, not some ratchet hoodrat from the projects."

"If you don't get off my porch and go try to control that girl in your front seat, there's going to be some issues." Dallas frowned, placing her hands on her hips. "I'm still a damn good mother whether I wear crop tops or a nun's uniform. And since your inconsiderate ass wants to put her needs before our children's,

25

I'll just take them with me like I always do. Goodbye, Messiah."

His hand rested against the doorframe as he unapologetically continued to eye-fuck her. Dallas remembered getting that look from him on plenty of occasions right before he fucked her until her legs were wobbly and her center ached.

"So, you gon' let me slide through tonight after the kids go to sleep so I can break you off? I know you been fiending." The rasp in his voice was almost a whisper.

The thought was tempting, but Dallas remembered his statement from two days ago. She was done allowing him to walk all over her.

"Bye, Messiah," she puffed, stepping back and closing the door in his face.

She walked to the living room, where the kids had already started arguing over the remote. Meghan wanted to watch *Descendants*, while Messiah Jr. wanted to catch up on on-demand episodes of wrestling. Dallas let out a sigh.

"Y'all better stop arguing before I cut the TV off, and no one will watch it. We're about to go soon anyways." She plopped down on the couch. "How was your dad's house? Did you guys have fun?"

"No! She wouldn't let us do nothing. All she kept saying was, '*Sit down. Sit down. Y'all can't touch this. I can't wait until y'all go home.*'" Meghan mimicked Tatiana in a whiny voice, instantly causing Dallas's face to contort into a frown.

"No, she didn't." Dallas shook her head.

"Yes, Tati-ugly did, Ma. She be trying to play us. She be all nice when my dad around, but be mean when he's not," Messiah Jr. cut in, causing Dallas to stifle a laugh. He was too grown for his own good.

"That is not her name, boy. And I'm going to have a talk with your father. That's unacceptable. In the meantime, go upstairs and change so we can go to your aunt Sasha's house."

Both of the kids hopped up. Meghan took off to her room, but Messiah Jr. stood there studying his mother.

"What, boy?" Dallas wondered out loud.

"Dad and that girl don't really have nothing to do, Mom. They got into it, and she made him bring us home. I hate her. I can't wait until y'all get back together."

Dallas didn't know how to respond. She wondered if Messiah Sr. knew that his decisions were affecting his kids. He lit the match, leaving her to put out the flame. She was tired of acting like a damn firefighter.

Three hours later, Messiah Sr. was the least of Dallas' worries. Sasha never knew how to have a simple party. She always went over the top, and today was no different. She had a spread of food laid out like it was Thanksgiving in July: chicken, ribs, shish kabobs, grilled shrimp, grilled crab legs, potato salad, and the list went on. She also had a cooler for the kids with juices and an adult cooler with adult drinks. Sasha had even rented a bounce house for the children to play in.

Dallas took in the scene as the kids ran wild and adults kicked it. She needed the escape. Her life had resorted to the robotic routine of going to work and coming home to motherly duties. If she didn't have to sit through a basketball game with Messiah Jr., she was at cheer practice with Meghan.

It was just after five o'clock, and the party was in full swing. The music was going, playing a mixture of early 2000s R&B and new school hits, Cardi B included. Those sitting at the spades table were engaged in a serious game of rise and fly and shit-talking, while the kids were running around and hopping in the bounce house. On top of the couples, Hunter had invited a few friends and family members over. He turned the event into a full-fledged party.

"Ma!" Messiah Jr. ran up to Dallas with a smile plastered across his face. "Hunt said me and Dominic could go play his

PlayStation 4. I'm about to go in the house. Cool? Cool," he told her more than asked, then ran off before she could respond.

Dallas watched as he disappeared with Hunter's cousin's son. She wondered how she ended up with such a character. He was getting so big and full of personality. A pout formed on her lips. She and Messiah were supposed to enjoy watching the kids grow up together. They planned it that way, and now all of their plans were ruined.

"Ms. Beyoncé, you feeling better today? I ain't trying to have to duck or dodge no bullets for speaking to you."

She recognized that voice. He had been on her mind for the past week, and she hoped she would run into him again to apologize. However, she never would have imagined running into him at Sasha's get-together. Dallas didn't mean to be such a bitch. Messiah did that to her sometimes.

A smile creased her lips as she took him in. Still chocolate, still too damn handsome for his own good, even while dressed down in blue jean shorts, a tank, and a pair of Jordans. He was definitely a man who could be both sophisticated and street.

Dallas used her hand to block the blazing sun from her face as she stared up at him.

"Let me find out you're stalking me."

He let out a chuckle. "Nah, never that." His gaze analyzed her entire body and stopped at her face. "But the way you're looking today, I just might reconsider the thought."

Dallas's cheeks stained red. She had to get used to being complimented again.

"Whatever. How'd you end up here? Don't tell me you're the neighbor Sasha insists on hooking me up with."

"Nah, that's not me, sweetheart, but homeboy missed his shot. This all me right here, and you don't even know it." He winked cockily. His confidence was sexy to Dallas.

"First, let me apologize for the way things went the other

day. I wasn't in the best mood. Second, how do you know I'm even interested in you…" She paused, realizing she didn't have his name.

"Trenton," he told her, glaring into her eyes. It was long and calculated. "You can call me Trent. And you don't have a choice. You gave me permission to have your heart when you smiled at me, and I took it."

That line caused Dallas to let out a girlish giggle. He was too much. Trenton was going to be a problem, and she knew it.

"Uh-uh, Trent. I know you are not over here pushing up on my sister," Sasha giggled, grabbing Dallas's arm. "Ignore him. That's Hunt's cousin. He just got back from the military. He was over in Iraq, and you know how them army men be traveling all over the world, leaving kids in every country."

Sasha rolled her eyes. She didn't know much about Trenton. He may have even been a good man, but she was dead set on hooking Dallas up with the neighbor. Once she got her mind set on something, she locked in like a pit bull.

The heat from the hot July day caused Trenton's skin to perspire as his lips curved down into a frown. "So, you just gon' judge me like that, Sash? I'm the best thing that's ever going to happen to sis. Look at the way she's blushing. She already knows it. Ain't that right, Beyoncé?" he teased.

"Beyoncé?" Sasha's brows knitted together.

Dallas snickered. "It's an inside joke. I actually ran into him last week at the boutique when I was looking for a dress for Messiah's wedding. We're fine. He's not bothering me."

"But what about Devaughn? The neighbor?" Sasha made a poor attempt to whisper.

"She ain't fucking with homeboy. It's a wrap." Trenton let out a small laugh. "Y'all too old to be playing matchmaker and shit anyways." He turned to Dallas. "You play spades?"

She nodded.

"Come on, let's whip some ass and talk shit."

Dallas bit into her lip skeptically. She liked him…more than she cared to admit.

"I'm in a bad space right now. My kids are here. The last thing I need to be doing is trying to date a man."

"Date?" Trenton's brows furrowed. "Slow down, beautiful. I just want to steal a little of your time. Date is a strong word. You might be crazy or something." He smirked charmingly, causing Dallas to smile. "See, that's what I want. Smile. You're too pretty to be mugged up all day."

CHAPTER FIVE

As SHE TOOK in the scene unfolding in her backyard, Sasha's face tightened into a frown. The guest list had surpassed the expected number of attendees. It was supposed to be a little intimate get-together, but Hunter had invited half the city of Detroit, and quite frankly, Sasha was annoyed. A pang of jealousy washed over her as she watched her man and his cousin, Alicia, laughing it up like two old friends. They were close, and she understood that. But, there was a problem when her man showed another woman more attention than he did her.

Sasha rolled her eyes as tiny hands wrapped around her knees and an adorable giggle escaped the mouth of the most beautiful little girl she had ever seen. The neighbor's daughter was gorgeous. She had beautiful, long sandy brown hair, bluish green eyes, creamy vanilla skin, and a little smile that made you fall in love with her.

"Zion, let her go, silly girl," Devaughn chuckled, sweeping up her petite frame and lifting her into the air. "Where are you going to run to now?" he teased, tickling her as she got giddy with laughter. Sasha laughed, too.

"She's so adorable," she cooed.

"Yeah, adorable and busy." Devaughn smiled, lowering his daughter onto the ground and watching as she took off running toward the bounce house with the other kids. He stuffed his hands into his pockets and rocked back and forth. "Thanks for inviting us over. Zion has been taking the move pretty hard. So, it's been cool to get her around kids," he said, squinting over at Sasha, appreciating her beauty.

"We're neighbors. I figured it could be an icebreaker," Sasha said with a shrug.

Her eyes focused on Hunter again, who was rolling over the ground with one of Alicia's twins. He'd make such a good father. She rubbed her belly, praying the last time they made love was it, and miraculously she became pregnant.

"Yeah," Devaughn responded, following Sasha's gaze to Hunter. "He seems like a good dude. He's lucky to have you," he shot.

It was the way he said it. *He's lucky to have you.* She wondered if there was a deeper meaning behind his words. Of course, Hunter was lucky to have her. She was lucky to have him, as well. Her man had been nothing short of amazing. She beamed with pride, thinking about their relationship.

Sasha bit on the folds of her cheek. "Yeah, I guess he is." She shrugged. "So, what brings you to the neighborhood? Where's your wife? I highly doubt you're single."

Devaughn's expression darkened, then his face relaxed into that handsome smile of his.

"Why is that? I told you, no wife. I'm still waiting on Zion's mom to get her life together. She's back in Chicago, and I'm focusing on myself at the moment. We came to Michigan because my job offered a better position, and we needed a fresh start. So, here we are."

"Well, I hope she gets herself together soon. Zion is a great kid, and you don't seem too bad yourself."

They both chuckled.

"Thanks, I guess."

Sasha watched his mouth as he spoke. She knew she was wrong for the tiny spark of interest that piqued inside of her, so she diverted her eyes back on Hunter and the kids.

"How's the neighborhood? Where's all the kids? I thought this was a good family-oriented neighborhood for Zion to grow up in.

I'll always love Chi-town, but the violence was getting ridiculous." Devaughn laughed, causing Sasha to focus on him again.

She looked into Devaughn's eyes. She saw pain, but she also saw a strong man who was wary. Devaughn had a story, and she wanted to know what it was. His genuineness drew her in.

Sasha shrugged. "I mean, Kathy and Leon have two kids; they're four houses down. Angie has a son Zion's age, but he's into so many activities. There's actually a few kids in the neighborhood. And, of course, Zion is welcomed here. I always wanted a little girl to play in her hair, go shopping, and get our nails polished together."

Sasha giggled, but there was no mistaking the longing in her eyes.

Devaughn didn't miss it. His eyes traveled back to Hunter, now rolling around in the grass with both twins. "So, why don't you just have a baby?"

"We've been trying for two years. It hasn't happened yet. I'm starting to think it's not meant for me to have kids."

Devaughn never got a chance to respond. In a sense, he didn't want to. Obviously, she was hurting. He knew the feeling all too well. It was a miserable feeling to want something so bad—to deserve the one thing you want and not be able to have it.

"Sasha, girl. Your fiancé said go make him a drink." Alicia smiled, taking Devaughn in.

She made no attempt to hide the fact that she was fucking him with her eyes. Sasha's nose crinkled. She didn't care too much for the girl. She was a horrible mother, spoiled, and had a lot of growing up to do. She tolerated her for the sake of Hunter, though.

Sasha sighed. "You couldn't make it, Alicia?"

"No. You know how your fiancé likes his drinks. Plus, he wanted you to make it, not me."

Alicia smirked before walking off. Sasha watched her saunter away. Alicia had curves for days, a body most women would pay top dollar for, and she didn't mind flaunting it. Sasha rolled her eyes, sucking her teeth as Devaughn chuckled.

"It's okay. I need to check on Zion anyway. It was nice talking to you. Sometimes it's good for the soul to talk and have someone just listen."

"Yes, I guess it is," Sasha agreed. "Well, go check on Zion, and if you need anything, I'm here," Sasha offered before walking off, her sundress swaying with the bounce of her hips.

Her thoughts traveled back to Devaughn. He was a fine piece of man, and whatever woman let him go was stupid.

"You gon' stop dancing like that, Candy," Diego whispered into Candace's ear as she did a routine to SZA's "Love Galore."

She kept it PG since there were children around, but the way she moved with such style and grace, he had no choice but to be drawn to her. She rocked to the beat, never missing a drop. Her runs were smooth and sensual. Candace could easily be a dancer for Beyoncé, Rihanna, or any of the top entertainers.

She giggled, rotating her hips against his tall, masculine frame. Diego towered over her by at least eleven inches and was thick. He swallowed Candace's five-foot, three-inch frame with no effort.

"Boy, and if I don't?" She whirled around to face him, continuing to move to the beat.

Ever since Diego declared that she belonged to him, it was as if his looks had multiplied by one thousand percent. Diego was so sexy that it had Candace's center aching. She tried her best not to imagine the sinful thoughts flowing through her head about him, but Sasha's brother could get it any way he wanted it, any time he wanted it.

"I'm going to have to show yo' little ass I'm not the one to be teasing. But, then again, you ain't ready for all that. I'm addictive, Candy. You gon' lose your fucking mind once I get a hold of you."

"You so damn cocky, boy." Candace giggled, biting down on her bottom lip.

She wanted him to show her. She was a single woman. Having sex with Diego wouldn't be a crime...or would it?

"Nah, I'm just confident. What you doing when you leave here?" he asked.

"Going home. It's already ten o'clock. You know I'm an old woman now. I don't party, and I'm in bed by eleven."

Diego pulled on the hairs of his chin as he stared at Candace. Her jeans hugged her ass just right, and the belly top she sported showcased her flat abs. She was fly. There was no denying that. He wished he could take her to one of the empty bedrooms in the house and fuck her until she came to her senses, realizing he held the keys to her soul.

"That ain't being old; that's what grownups do. Ain't shit in the clubs but niggas looking to fuck and broads trying to get fucked."

"Your mouth is so crass, Diego."

"It is what it is." Diego shrugged. "Yo', ride with me to make a run right quick."

"A run where?"

"To see a man about a dog. Does it matter?"

"Yes, it does, smartass. Why I got to ride with you?" Candace planted her hands on her thick hips, pretending to give him attitude.

Diego smirked. He was used to Candace's feistiness. That was part of what drew him to her.

"Because I said so," was the only reason he offered as he gripped her slender hand, guiding her toward his cocaine-white Range Rover.

Candace had ridden in Diego's car a thousand times, but this ride felt different. A contented peace washed over her as she took in his side profile. Diego was so damn sexy to her. He was thugged out, but when he showcased his sense of humor while remaining confident and carefree, she had no choice but to be drawn to him like bees to honey.

"You stay watching me. What's going through your head?" Diego asked as he coolly pulled out into traffic with his body cocked to the side, one hand holding the steering wheel.

Candace fixated on the passing buildings. "You remember when I barely had money to buy myself something to eat, and you would always look out for me?" Her shoulders straightened as her brows knitted, mocking Diego. "Here, little girl. A woman always supposed to keep money in her pocket."

Diego chuckled. He did remember it. He remembered a lot about her. He watched, amused as she continued.

"I used to be so embarrassed. I hated my mother for making us struggle while everybody around me had the fly clothes and stuff."

"Embarrassed for what?"

"Because I was the charity case. That's my biggest fear, Diego. I don't want to struggle. I don't want to be her anymore. That's why I'm scared of you." Her voice lowered to a whisper as she revealed her last statement.

Diego's brow raised. "Scared of me? Get the fuck out of here. I should be the least of your worries. I wouldn't fuck with you if I wasn't trying to be official with you. You ain't just some broad, Candy. You my ma'fuckin' baby."

"I hear you talkin'." Candace smiled on the inside.

They rode up the John C. Lodge expressway until it ended on Jefferson Avenue. Detroit's downtown was busy with the hustle and bustle of the nightlife. Cars raced past them blasting their music of choice. The skyline was lit from the Renaissance Center across the river to Canada's border.

"Don't just hear me." Diego winked as he turned left onto St. Aubin Street and pulled into the parking structure of some condos right off the water.

"Where are we?" Candace frowned.

"Making a run. Stop asking so many questions."

Diego pulled into the first spot he found, silenced the engine, and hopped out, leaving Candace no choice but to follow his lead.

The condo belonged to Brian, one of Diego's childhood friends. Candace remembered him because they were like two peas in a pod growing up. Whenever you saw Diego, Brian wasn't too far behind. He welcomed them in, and there were a few other people inside, as well—a man and women, half-naked women.

Diego kept Candace close to him, and she basked in the closeness. As much as she tried not to create a situation in her head, she couldn't help it. She had already started to embrace the idea of giving Diego her heart.

"What's up, bro?" Brian greeted Diego with a five and then focused on Candace. "Man, get the fuck out of here. Little Candace?" He squinted, holding his hand out as if to mock how short she used to be. "I knew y'all ma'fuckas was creeping."

Diego waved him off, guiding Candace to a seat on the couch. He sat next to her, his hand landing on Candace's thigh. "This just the homie. She playing."

Candace tapped Diego's shoulder. "Really? I could have stayed at the party if you're just going to insult me."

Her lips puckered, and when Diego leaned over and kissed them, Candace almost jumped at the electrical current that traveled between them.

"Don't be kissing me like that," she whispered breathlessly.

"Don't be poking them out, asking me to kiss 'em," Diego challenged as Brian shook his head.

"Y'all crazy. Look, come talk to me in the back. I got that for you," he told Diego as he smacked some caramel-complexioned woman on her ass as she walked by.

The girl giggled, and Candace took in the scene. Something wasn't right. Brian had a wife, and neither of the women in attendance was her.

Candace began to wonder what Diego wanted from her. He lived his life in the fast lane for the majority of it. She knew what came with the fast life, and that was something she wasn't willing to deal with—the late nights and cheating. Diego wasn't some average Joe. Women would flock to him whether he was pushing drugs or managing a legitimate construction company. It was his persona. His magnetism just drew women in.

She watched his back as his thick, muscular frame disappeared. *Damn, he's sexy.* Her kitty began to purr, wanting him to touch her in places he had no business exploring.

"So, how long you and Nino been fucking?"

The voice snapped Candace out of her daze. Her eyes slanted toward the platinum blonde weave-wearing, wannabe video vixen.

"Since I was fifteen, why?" Candace lied just because she knew the girl planned to start drama.

"Hmmph." The girl smirked. "That's crazy. I was just with him a few weeks ago. So, I'm trying to figure out how he trying to have his cake and eat it, too."

Candace shrugged while eyeing the door to the room Diego and Brian went inside. She was past ready to go. Slapping the taste out of one of his hoes wasn't how she expected the night to go.

"And you felt the need to tell me that because?"

"I don't know about you, but I don't like to be played. So, I'm letting you know. Woman to woman."

Woman to woman gon' get yo' ass fucked up, Candace thought with a roll of her eyes.

"Listen, sweetie. Woman to woman, whatever you thought this was, it ain't. So, don't speak to me. It looks like I'm going to have to talk to him about keeping his whores in check."

"Hoe?" the girl yelped.

"No, I called you a whore. Not a hoe," Candace corrected her.

"Oh, this bitch think she cute. Slap her, Diamond," the girl's friend coerced.

She has to be the flunky, Candace imagined. Her clothes were too tight for her rolls of fat, and the blonde hair she wore wasn't as fitting as Diamond's. *Definitely the flunky,* Candace mused.

"Yeah, come slap me, and I promise, Big Bird will be picking you up off the floor."

Why did Candace say that? The girls began screaming at Candace like Chihuahuas. Neither of them touched her, but they were barking.

"Man, what the fuck?" Diego frowned as he and Brian exited the backroom.

He pulled the backpack Brian tossed him securely over his shoulder and marched toward the ladies. His eyes never left Candace. He would show them who the real Nino was if anybody touched her. He left that part of him in the streets, but for the right situation, he'd come out of retirement.

"You better get ya' little hoe," Candace growled, throwing daggers at Diego. "What, you thought we was supposed to have a kumbaya moment? Like we were gonna sit around and make girl talk about your dick?"

Diego chuckled, too calm for Candace's liking. "How y'all gon' trade dick stories, and neither of y'all seen it? I ain't never touched that girl." He stepped into Candace's personal space. "What I tell you about being a queen? You keep taking off that crown."

Candace's lips twisted. "So you didn't fuck her a couple of weeks ago? That's what she said."

"No, I didn't," Diamond quickly lied. "I said I was with him a couple of weeks ago. I thought we had a good time."

Diego shook his head. "We kicked it at a party. I was with a lot of people," Diego confirmed, and Candace didn't miss the look of embarrassment in Diamond's eyes. "Let's go, Candace."

Candace didn't protest. She was more than ready to be gone. She waited for them to get into the car before firing off questions.

"So, you had me ride with you to pick up drugs? You back to your old tricks."

Diego cut his eyes at Candace, but he didn't speak. He snapped his seatbelt on and pulled off.

"Seriously, I don't have time to be arguing with your hoes and dealing with you running in and out at all times," she added.

"You won't even fuck with me. So, how you have to deal with that?"

"I'm with you now," Candace challenged.

"For how long?"

"What's in the bag?"

She was deflecting. He knew it.

"Look in there and see."

He didn't have to tell her twice. She needed to know if he was into illegal activity. That would determine how she proceeded with him. Much to her surprise, the bag only contained a Gucci belt, some fly Christian Louboutin loafers, and jeans.

Diego smirked. "Find what you looking for?"

"Whatever," Candace muttered.

"Nah, it's not whatever. I worked hard as hell to be a changed man. You know me better than anybody, Candy. I wouldn't have you chilling in the same room as somebody I'm fucking, and I definitely wouldn't bring the streets into my personal life. Give me more credit."

"I'm trying to. This is new for me. I've been hurt so much, Diego."

"Well, I won't be the one to add more pain. Let me in."

Candace didn't respond. She wanted to let him in so badly, but she was tired of jumping into situation after situation.

CHAPTER SIX

"DAMN IT, DALLAS. Slow down, babe," Messiah Sr. groaned as he watched her body rotate on top of his shaft.

His manhood disappeared inside of her, then reappeared glistening with her juices. The sexual high was euphoric. It had been entirely too long since Dallas felt a man inside of her, and Messiah knew exactly how to get her juices flowing while making her body hot. She missed him so much, even when she didn't want to. He had her bound and shackled mentally. She would never be able to move on with him stroking her pussy so precisely.

Dallas closed her eyes tightly, biting down on her bottom lip. She needed the release brewing inside of her to calm her hot ass down. She thought of sexy-ass Trent. In fact, she wasn't having sex with Messiah. In her head, she was straight giving Trenton the business.

"Dallas," Messiah cried out, steadying her hips. "I'm about to bust. You better slow down if you want to get yours," he warned, feeling the tingling in the tip of his shaft.

Dallas let out a groan. Hearing Messiah's voice was messing up her groove. It wasn't nearly as sexy as Trenton's.

"Shhh." She hushed him, placing one finger on his lips. "Don't talk. Just fuck me back, Trenton."

The moment she finished her sentence, her eyes flew open, her hands shooting to her mouth as Messiah sent her body flying to the other side of the bed.

Shit. Dallas couldn't believe she had slipped and called Messiah another man's name.

"Messiah, I—"

"Who the fuck is Trenton?" he growled as a menacing scowl danced across his face.

He was pissed, and Dallas knew it. She watched the veins in his neck bulge as his chest heaved up and down.

Dallas's heart rate began to accelerate. She had to ask herself why she was so scared when it was Messiah who picked up and left. He opened the door for another man to share her bed. Even though she hadn't allowed one to do so, it was in her right to share it.

She cocked her head to the side. "Really, Messiah? I know you're not questioning *me*. You're getting married in two months. I apologize for calling you his name, but please keep your questions to yourself, and I'll do the same. As a matter of fact," Dallas grabbed the sheets to cover her exposed body and began to stand, "I think you should leave. This was a bad idea. I had a weak moment, and I shouldn't have."

Messiah pulled her back down before she could get up. He stared intently into her eyes. He had too much pride to admit he fucked up. He missed her. He missed waking up to his family.

"Who is Trenton?" Messiah mumbled. "Did you fuck him? Did you give my pussy away to him? You know this is always going to be mine, right?"

Those words would have caused Dallas's heart to melt just a couple of months ago. Now, her skin began to crawl. She had done it again. She allowed the devil into her bed and between her legs. She cursed herself for being so weak.

"You're so damn selfish." Dallas frowned, trying to release herself from Messiah's embrace, but he wrapped his arms tighter around her waist.

"Calm down, Dally," he whispered into her ear. "Who is he? I know it's selfish of me to feel this way, but I would be more comfortable if you got rid of him. I don't like that you're dealing with me still and calling out another man's name. I would never call you Tatiana."

Dallas's face screwed up so hard that it hurt. She snatched herself from his arms, standing in front of Messiah with her hands fastened on her hips. Now, she was mad. She was past mad; she was livid.

"How dare you fix your lips to tell me what you're comfortable with, Messiah? You're marrying your mistress! I don't give a damn if you call me Boo-Boo the Fool. Nothing will ever hurt worse than you leaving our family for some young hoe that probably still has milk behind her ears! I gave you the best of me, and I can't get that back. You ruined me!" Dallas screamed. "You know what. Leave, Messiah. Go home to her. The kids will be home soon, and I do not want to confuse Messiah Jr. And, while we're talking about the kids, if I hear that your fiancée is disrespecting my children one more time, I'm going to whip her little ass."

"Tatiana doesn't disrespect our kids. What type of man would I be to allow that?"

Dallas smirked. What type of man was he? An ignorant, lying, cheating, disrespectful bastard.

"The same type of man that up and left his family for another woman, only to find his way back into my bed every chance he gets. Now you tell me what kind of man you are."

Messiah sighed in annoyance as his cell phone began to ring.

"What's up?" he answered, holding up his index finger to silence Dallas.

She had to tilt her head to the side to see if it would help her get a clearer picture of what was going on. She just knew he wasn't talking to that girl.

"Stop tripping, Tati. I told you I was chilling with the fellas tonight," he muttered.

Lies. He was good at that. Dallas began to wonder how many times he'd told her those same lies while she sat around waiting for him to come home.

"Look, let me call you when I'm on my way."

After ending the call, Messiah reached out to grab Dallas. His touch disgusted her. He used to excuse himself before speaking with his hoe. She didn't even get that much respect anymore.

Dallas snatched away. "Let me go. Just go home to her. I had a weak moment."

Messiah's brows creased. "Fucking me isn't having a weak moment. You got my kids. We have history. No matter who I'm with, I'll always find my way home."

"No…"

Boom!

The bang was so loud that Dallas fell to the ground, protecting her head.

"What the fuck?" she yelped, hearing the crashing noise again.

It sounded like something or someone was colliding with glass. Simultaneously, their eyes bulged, realizing one of their cars was losing a fight.

"Oh, hell nah!" Dallas shrieked. "I bet it's your little hoe! If she touched my car, Messiah, I swear I will beat her little ass tonight."

"Just chill out." Messiah sighed, adjusting his jeans while stepping into his shoes. "It's probably *Trenton,*" he mocked, wincing when he heard another bang.

"No, unlike her, he's mature. She doesn't even like my kids, and you're marrying her."

"So, are you going to argue, or are we going to figure out what's going on?" Messiah grumbled, making his way through the house and to the front door. As soon as he swung it open, he cursed his luck. "Fuck!" he hollered, running his hand through his hair.

It was her. Dallas studied the whore that stole her man. She looked like a deranged woman as she stood there—chest heaving, tears flowing. However, there was no denying that Messiah's fiancée was beautiful. A pang of jealousy rushed through Dallas, causing her anger to stir.

"I knew you was here! I knew it! Bring your ass out here! I saw you!" Tatiana cried as she swung her Louisville slugger at Messiah's Impala, striking it again.

She had busted the windshield along with the back windows. The dents would cost a fortune to repair, but most importantly, her heart was shattered.

After accessing the damage, Dallas realized Messiah's hoe hadn't touched her car. So, she stood off to the side, watching as the scene unfolded. Tatiana had turned her bat on Messiah, and they were making a complete spectacle of themselves. Secretly, Dallas was glad she caught them.

"And what yo' big-face ass looking at? You just couldn't lose in peace. I got the ring. He comes home to me every night!" Tatiana spat, waving the bat at Dallas.

Dallas burst out into laughter. For the first time since the breakup, she realized she didn't lose at all. Both Tatiana and Messiah were pathetic.

"My big-face ass is going to sleep good as hell knowing I don't have to wake up to a lying, pussy-eating, cheating, dog-ass nigga. Yes, boo. You win all the heartache, sleepless nights, and pain he gave me."

Dallas began to walk toward her front door, dismissing herself from the situation. She heard Tatiana shuffling toward her, and Lord knows she wanted the girl to hit her. She was going to knock her the fuck out. She'd been itching to do it.

"By the way," she added, "make sure he washes his face before kissing you goodnight."

Dallas knew she was wrong as two left shoes, but she was tired of being the bigger person. She wanted Tatiana to hurt as badly as she did for ripping her family apart.

The next day…

Sawyer Credit Union wasn't exactly her dream job, but it paid the bills. Honestly, Dallas didn't know what her dream job would be. She tried getting her CNA license and working at a retirement home. However, after two days of wiping asses, she quit. Then, she went to school and received her Early Childhood Education Associate's Degree. Four months in, she realized taking care of someone else's child wasn't the job for her either. Actually, Dallas had tested quite a few careers. Things so weren't the way she imagined them to be at the age of thirty. She was unmarried, a single parent, and hated her job. Messiah ruined everything. Dallas prayed she'd be able to break the chains he had her shackled to…and soon.

A pout formed on her lips as she closed the file she had been studying and began tapping her pen against her desk. The disagreement she had with Messiah replayed in her head. He must have really thought she was a fool. She concluded he had every reason to, scolding herself for sleeping with him again.

"Dallas…" Her coworker, Cassandra, leaned into her cubicle with an alley-cat grin plastered across her face, interrupting her train of thought. "You have a visitor, and the man is sexy as ever," she gushed. "I think it's your break time. Don't be too fast."

Cassandra winked at Dallas before disappearing.

Leaning over her desk, Dallas stared into the lobby. It was Trenton, and boy, did he look good all dressed up in his suit and tie. He had a bouquet of roses, too. Dallas blushed, then let out a sigh to release her nerves. She hadn't given him her number, nor had they talked since the barbecue, but he had been on her mind since that night. She giggled, remembering how she called Messiah by Trenton's name. It was funny after the fact.

Making her way through the office and past the teller line, Dallas found herself in the lobby face-to-face with Trenton. He smiled, and she smiled back, accepting the roses.

"Thanks." She paused. "How did you know I'd be at work?"

Trenton shrugged, staring into her sparkling browns. He didn't know, but he remembered reading her name badge and decided to show up at her job to let her know he was thinking of her. They had so much fun that he forgot to get her contact information. He needed more of her. He was always a straightforward man. If he wanted it, he was going after it. So, there he was.

"Because I'm psychic." Trenton winked, displaying a dimple on his left cheek that Dallas hadn't noticed before. He ran his tongue across his full lips. "You look beautiful. How's your day going?"

Dallas shrugged. "It's going pretty good, but I'm hungry and only have forty-five minutes for lunch. There's a seafood spot across the street if you want to walk me over there," she instructed, advancing toward the door to avoid the stares of nosey coworkers.

"Does that mean we're about to have our first official date?" Trenton quizzed, leaning forward and holding the door open for her.

The heat from his body's closeness and the scent of his cologne caused Dallas to shudder. He looked good, smelled good, and had charm.

"No. It's more like you showed up at my job, I was hungry, and now on top of flowers, you have to buy me lunch." She turned and smiled at him.

Trenton let out a chuckle. "Sounds like you're trying to hustle the hustler. If I buy you lunch, that means it's a date, and you have to let me take you to dinner, too."

The offer was tempting. Dallas took a second to consider. She could call her mother to keep the children. However, it was a school night, and they were on a strict schedule. Then, there was Messiah. She thought about their fallout and chuckled. Nope, not an option. Dallas sighed, cursing Messiah. He got to live his life freely while she had to consider her children in every step she made. It wasn't fair. But, as always, she had to suck it up.

"I don't know about dinner, Trenton. I do have kids," she reminded him. "But, you can take my phone number, and *maybe* we can go out this weekend. It's their father's weekend to get them."

Trenton rubbed the hairs on his chin, pondering the thought. He knew a measly thirty minutes with her wasn't enough, but if that's the way it had to be, he'd accept it.

"Or how about I take the whole crew to dinner at Zap Zone? Pizza and games on me?"

"I don't think so. I barely know you enough to be bringing my kids around you."

Dallas giggled, but she was dead serious. As much as she complained, she didn't play when it came to her children. Trenton was cool; however, it was a little early to involve the kids. They didn't even know if they'd make it past a couple of occasional fucks. Yes, he had met her children at the get-together, but as far as the kids knew, he was just some random guy at the party.

Trenton smirked. "Understandable, but that's temporary. I plan to be around for a long time, Ms. Lady. And I want you to know I'm fully aware that you come as a packaged deal. I would never mistreat or do anything to harm your babies. I can't love you without loving the kids."

Dallas's nose crinkled. "So, you're talking about love after spending just one evening with me. I'd hate to see how you act if you got a chance to get inside my panties."

"Nah." Trenton's face grew serious. "You wouldn't hate it at all. In fact, I guarantee your pretty ass would be the one stalking me like a lovesick puppy. It's more than physical with me, baby. I'm going to make love to your mind, your body, and snatch your soul while I'm at it."

"You're so cocky." Dallas blushed. "Anyways, I'm not about to go there with you."

She playfully rolled her eyes as they made their way into the restaurant. She had to change the subject. If she didn't, they would end up in the bathroom with her challenging him to make good on his threats.

"So, why every time I see you, you have on a suit? Sasha says you just got out of the military. What do you do now?"

"Nothing," Trenton replied with a shrug. "I had a couple of interviews at the security joint up the street."

"You're currently unemployed?" Dallas asked, trying her best not to sound disappointed.

The last thing she needed was to be taking care of a grown man. Her children already had that spot secured.

"No. I didn't say nothing about being broke." He smirked as if he had read her mind. "I was discharged from the army honorably with full benefits. I'm just not the one to sit around and do nothing. Too much idle time on your hands is dangerous," Trenton corrected her as the waitress guided them to their seats.

He opted to leave out the fact that the army destroyed him mentally. He didn't speak on those issues. He tried his best to forget all those innocent lives lost as a casualty of war. Women, children, babies…it was sickening.

"Okay, don't be snapping at me, boy," she giggled.

"I wasn't snapping. We're just talking, right?" Trenton quipped, leaning back in his seat.

Dallas was gorgeous. He liked the relaxed feeling he got when he was around her. It was her energy. She put positive vibes all through his atmosphere, with her fake mean ass.

"But, how long your homegirl been with Hunt? She's a trooper if she can deal with that situation," he added.

Dallas frowned. "What situation?"

Trenton stared into her eyes, realizing that Dallas genuinely didn't know what he was talking about, so he opted to backtrack.

It wasn't his place to speak on it.

"Nothing. I just know my cousin can be a lot sometimes. I see they're happy, though. So that's all that matters."

"Yeah, I like Hunt for Sasha. He treats her really good. I wish I could have found myself a Hunt before I decided to waste so much time with an asshole. But I'm not going to get into all that," Dallas complained, refusing to allow Messiah to ruin her lunch date.

Speaking about him was still a touchy subject for her and probably would be for a long time.

"The grass ain't always greener," Trenton warned. "So, tell me about your situation. What made him so bad?"

"He's marrying his side hoe in two months." Dallas rolled her eyes.

"Damn. Sorry to hear that." Trenton gave her a sympathetic glare. "I see anger when you speak on him. You still love him?" he asked.

Dallas smiled as the waitress approached for their order. "I'll take the shrimp scampi with extra alfredo sauce and a strawberry lemonade to go."

When the waitress focused on Trenton, he held his hand up. "I'm fine. Allergic to seafood."

Dallas shrunk in her seat. "I'm sorry. Why didn't you say anything? I could have grabbed McDonald's or something."

"Nah, you're good. If seafood is what you want, then I wanted to make sure you got it. Plus, I needed to steal a little of your time. As long as I don't eat none, we won't have any problems," Trenton informed her, studying Dallas for the thousandth time, appreciating her beauty. "And don't think you're off the hook. Do you still love him? Let me know what it is now before I waste my time."

"We were together for fifteen years. We have two kids together. How can I not love him? But, will I ever go back to him?" Dallas paused, thinking about that answer thoroughly. Could she take Messiah back after everything he put her through? "I honestly can't answer that. The kids love him. I know they would love to see us as a family again, but he hurt me so bad."

"You do know you don't have to be together to raise them babies. You don't have to accept being treated like anything less than a queen. A real man ain't got time to cheat; he's going to be too busy trying to find a million different ways to make you smile."

"Thank you. I keep trying to tell myself that I deserve better. I'm slowly learning to love Dallas more than a trifling man," she sneered, checking the time on her watch.

There were still twenty-eight minutes left of her break. She wished she could take the rest of the day off and hang with him, but her job was more important than being up under a man.

"Don't go grouping all men in the same category. I'm no saint, but I'm still not about to have my girl out here looking stupid. All I need you to do is keep it real with me, and I'll be one hundred with you. I like you, Dallas. I don't know why, but I do. I'm looking forward to Friday so I can pick your brain a little more. Thirty minutes ain't enough."

Dallas blushed. "I'm going to have to get used to you. You talk really good, but I don't know if you're bullshitting me or if you're my knight in shining armor."

"I guess time will tell."

Trenton smiled that dimpled smile that Dallas swore she could watch forever. Her lips tightened into a pout when the waitress came back with her bagged food. It meant their *date* was over, but she needed more of him.

CHAPTER SEVEN

"WHY AM I even here?" Candace sighed as her eyes roamed the hotel room. "I know you're on some bullshit, and my retarded ass is just sitting here eating it up." Her lip pulled between her teeth, feeling foolish.

When Jaxon called her to meet him, she had every intention of telling him to kiss her ass and close his chapter with dignity. However, here she was sitting in a five-star hotel room, allowing the champagne and lies to kiss the heartache away.

"You're not crazy for loving me, Candace. You're here because you know I'm the best thing that's ever going to happen to you. We have something here." Jaxon sighed, feeling frustrated as his manhood began to soften.

Arguing was the last thing he wanted to do. Candace was supposed to be his peace. She didn't complain much, and he took care of her. That's how their relationship went.

Candace sucked her teeth. "A whole female approached me, Jaxon, and she had the nerve to come with receipts! You gave another woman the fuel to fire at me, and you didn't have enough decency to give me the option to decide if I wanted to deal with it."

She didn't like for her emotions to be toyed with. He played her like a violin, and the more she thought about it, the angrier she became.

"I can't do this, Jaxon. I'm not the side bitch type of chick."

Jaxon licked his thick lips, staring at Candace. "Have I ever carried you like a side bitch? I know Arianna is vindictive, and her delusional ass can sound very convincing, but it's been over for a long time. Me and her have history, so I look out for her."

"Look out for her how?" Candace frowned.

"She held me down when I was down, trying to find my way around life. She's been through a lot, Candy. So, I look out. Pay a few phone bills and stuff like that," Jaxon tried explaining.

Candace let out a small laugh. "But you didn't find it important enough to tell me about her in the entire two years we've been together? And apparently, she knows *everything* about me. Fuck you, Jaxon."

She was so outdone with him that she snatched the pillow from the bed, chucking it at his head. Then, she pulled herself up, deciding it was time to go. She felt her chest burning. Why did she always have to get the short end when it came to men?

"Candace, wait." Jaxon grabbed her arm. "I love you. You're my heart, babe. Do you really think I would sit up and make fun of something that important? She knows about you because her crazy ass somehow got into my text messages. She knows a lot of shit that she shouldn't know." Jaxon frowned.

"And what did you do about it?"

"I realized that my relationship with you is more important than her. So, she's a dead issue."

Jaxon reached into his pocket, pulling out a crushed velvet box. He held it out, causing Candace's heart to race. He was about to do it. Jaxon was about to propose to her, and butterflies filled her stomach.

"This is me promising to get my shit together for you. I promise that one day I will be the man to give you everything your heart desires. What you think about that?"

He smiled as he popped the box open, showcasing a beautiful gold diamond-studded ring. Candace's hands shot to her mouth as tears formed in her eyes.

"Wait, are you asking me to marry you?"

"One day," Jaxon corrected her. "This is more like a promise to you. Don't give up on me," he begged.

A gotdamn promise ring? Candace couldn't believe it, but she tried not to be disappointed. *Well, I guess it's a start.*

A week later, Candace watched as Jaxon's jaw muscles flexed and loosened as he chomped down on a piece of gum. He had perfect bone structure. Jaxon wasn't exactly the finest man in the world, but he may have been runner-up. Candace loved that they could just kick back and do normal people's stuff. They could work on goals and build a future together. It was rare to find a good man with his priorities together these days.

She thought about Diego. She'd been avoiding him, and a twinge of guilt filled her heart. She prayed she wasn't making the wrong decision by leaving him alone. Candace couldn't risk possibly losing her happily ever after for the unknown. Jaxon was safe.

She had been with the street dude who didn't have goals past being the biggest dope boy and riding around in the flyest cars. He was cool until they were pulled over with a trunk full of drugs. Luckily for her, he took all of his own charges. It was that day she decided she was nobody's *ride-or-die.* Then, she dated the momma's boy, who couldn't take a shit without his mother's approval. She didn't know if she was dating Calvin or his mother. Finally, her favorite—Rodney's fine, deadbeat ass with the good dick. He almost got over on her until she realized he was eating up her food, burning through her gas, and helping to spend her hard-earned money with nothing in return to give her but a wet ass. She got rid of his tired ass with the quickness. Then, Jaxon came along, painting the perfect fairytale. He had to be the one. Men like him only came once in a lifetime.

"I just need to stop by the house right quick, beautiful. Then we can go to the concert." A seductive grin curved Jaxon's lips as he focused on Candace. "I missed seeing that beautiful smile so much, Candy Girl. I'm not letting you get away. So, stop trying to run from me."

Candace wanted her heart to flutter like it used to. However, Diego had ruined the way she looked at him.

"Well, get your past situations in check. That girl had no business coming to my job with that bullshit. And you had no business still paying her cell phone bill, especially after being with me for two years. Anything from your past should be a distant memory."

"Are we still talking about that?" Jaxon groaned.

"Whatever, Jaxon. I know it's her calling my phone private. She is so childish." Candace rolled her eyes. "Are you sure y'all not fucking?"

Jaxon let out a sigh. "No, Candace. I wish you would stop asking me about that girl. I barely have time for us. With the way I work, where do I have time to fit her in?"

"People make time for what they want," she muttered, staring out the window. Lately, she was starting to realize Jaxon always had excuses.

"What was that, Candy?" Jaxon raised a brow.

"Nothing. Whose concert are we going to again? I didn't hear about any major concerts on the radio or anything like that."

Jaxon smiled as he twisted the wheel, making a right onto his block inside the Rookery Woods Subdivision in Rochester Hills. His house was an immaculate brick colonial with a rare first-floor master suite, large walk-in closets, and a dramatic two-story family room with a fireplace and large floor-to-ceiling windows. The upstairs featured an open loft space overlooking the living room and a private library. And the basement, Candace loved it. It was fully equipped with a wet bar, exercise room, and full bath. Jaxon had the perfect family home and lived in that big house all by himself.

He hit the button to lift the automatic garage, then smiled

over at Candace.

"Just relax, Candy. It's a surprise. I'll be right back. I would tell you to come in with me, but I know we wouldn't make it to this concert if you did. I have a few days of backup you need to take care of," he flirted, and Candace's center tingled.

"Nothing's wrong with being a little late," Candace responded with a shrug. "Especially when you're talking about breaking me off with some good dick. Don't play with me, Jaxon."

Jaxon's eyes traveled toward the door as if he was debating the idea. His mouth parted to say something but closed immediately. Leaning over, he popped a kiss onto her forehead.

"Tonight, Candy Girl. I have a surprise for you. So, behave."

Candace watched him disappear into the house. She loved him; she really did. So, she didn't understand why Diego crossed her mind. He was no good for her, right? Jaxon was perfect. Diego had a felony record, which included armed robbery and drug charges, and he was still very much hood. Given, he had calmed down a lot since his days of hanging in the streets. He even owned a successful business, but he was still hood. There wasn't any security in dating a felon.

Candace didn't consider herself a gold digger, but she was a woman who liked stability. She needed to know that if she failed, her significant other would be there to catch her. Growing up, she bounced from house to house because her mother could never keep the rent paid. Her clothes were so terrible that she had to survive high school by borrowing designer outfits from Sasha and Dallas. When it was time to do teenage things, she never had any money. It bothered Candace—the fact that she lived in poverty while everyone around her seemed to be living good, enjoying life. The thought of having to go back to being that girl frightened her. Therefore, she now sought security, and Jaxon was secure. She fell in love with his stability before actually loving him.

Candace pulled out her cell phone and began to scroll Instagram. She liked a few of her dance idols' pictures and watched a couple of videos. By the time she snapped and posted a selfie of herself, Jaxon was making his way back to the car. His face was set in a hard frown, and the way he slammed the door as he got back into the vehicle caused a worry line to form on Candace's forehead.

"What's wrong, babe?" she wondered out loud.

Jaxon sighed. "I hate to even do this, but I got to take a raincheck, babe. The job just called me. We had mandatory overtime tonight, and I knew nothing about it. They're trying to write me up even though it's a miscommunication on *their* part." He shook his head, starting the car and backing out of the driveway. "You know what? Call up one of your friends and have fun on me," he suggested, handing her the invites and a couple of hundred-dollar bills.

It took everything in Candace not to be mad. She wanted to tell him how she didn't know a person alive who worked as much overtime as he did. Then again, she couldn't get mad at him for working. His lavish lifestyle was proof of the fruits of his labor.

"I guess I'll see if Sasha wants to go with me. You can drop me off there."

She sighed, and Jaxon didn't miss how her bottom lip puckered. He let out a small laugh.

"Don't start that pouting. You know I'm going to make it up to you."

Candace forced a smile. "You better."

Candace didn't understand how she ended up at the concert

with Diego instead of Sasha, but she was glad she asked him to accompany her because she was having the time of her life. It tickled her that Diego could keep up with her dance moves and keep a smile on her face at the same time. He was such a manly man, and their chemistry was almost impossible to ignore.

Diego stood firm behind her as they jammed to a little Kash Doll, Neisha Neshae, and she went absolutely nuts when her favorite singer, Kendall, walked onto the stage and began crooning those slow jams she loved dancing to. Candace was in heaven.

"Yo, don't be looking at that man like that," Diego whispered in her ear. "I was going to take you backstage to meet homeboy, but I'm not feeling the way you staring at that man and shaking your little booty."

Candace turned to look Diego in the face. Her lips lifted as if to say she didn't believe him.

"Boy, stop." She kissed her teeth. "You couldn't get me back there anyway. And stop hating because Kendall can sing the panties right off my ass, and you can't." She stuck her tongue out, teasing him.

The concert was a private show for invites only. However, the arena was still packed. The music was loud, and despite everything that was going on around them, it didn't take away from the intimate feeling of them being so close, their body heat sharing the same space, and that chemistry...damn, it was undeniable.

Diego stared into Candace's brown eyes. There was so much he wanted to confess to her, so many emotions he was uncertain of. He wished she understood just how deep his feelings ran for her, but he was afraid of rejection. Nothing in life ever scared him, yet he didn't think he could handle the idea of little Candace brushing his feeling off like they were nothing. That was funny to him.

"What are you laughing at, Diego?" Candace playfully rolled her eyes. "You know your lil' ugly self don't have that much pull."

"So I'm ugly now? The way you be staring at me when you

think I'm not looking tells me that's a gotdamn lie." He chuckled, focusing on the stage, then brought his attention back to Candace. "As a matter of fact, come on." He tugged at her arm.

"Come where, Diego?"

"Stop asking so many questions and come on," he muttered, wrapping her slender hand into his and being careful not to pull her along too fast since she had on a pair of six-inch heels.

As they made their way through the thick maze of concertgoers and a set of metal doors, Candace's brows twitched with amusement. She just knew Diego could not get them backstage. However, her theory was proven wrong when Diego knocked on a set of doors, and Hunter's cousin, Trenton, swung it open.

The two men slapped fives, and Candace's mouth nearly hung to the ground as they were guided into the back area where all the who's who were in attendance. She recognized a few local celebs: Glam Beauty, who owned the beauty bar in Southfield and serviced a host of celebrities and influential Michiganders; Versatile, the famous choreographer who worked with Chris Brown and Usher; then there was Cornell Ervin, the big-time clothing designer who styled a long list of stars. Of course, there were other entertainers and artists, but those three were who mattered to Candace. She followed them and studied their stories. They were young, successful, and grew up in poverty, just as she had. Yet, they made a way out of no way, and Candace admired them for that. She was banking on her exercise dance classes jumping off the ground, becoming a rags-to-riches story, too.

Candace tapped Diego's shoulder as they began to make their way around the big open room. A few people waved at him; others stopped him to speak. Candace was thoroughly impressed by the respect people automatically gave him.

Diego stopped walking to face Candace. He smirked, holding a hand to his ear as if attempting to hear her better.

"What was that you were saying about not getting back here? Stop trying to play me like I'm not the man." He chuckled, watching the way her nose crinkled.

"Whatever, only because your sister's boyfriend's cousin was security. How did you know he would be here anyway?"

Diego shook his head, realizing that Candace underestimated his stature. When he was out in the streets, living on the edge, he rubbed elbows with a lot of important people. He wasn't just some knucklehead selling drugs. He gained contacts and obtained buildings and houses. Diego was a businessman by nature, whether the business was legal or illegal. Unfortunately, he crossed paths with the wrong person and had to give the system four years of his life. Never again. He realized he was entirely too smart and talented to waste his time throwing bricks at a penitentiary and looking over his shoulder for stick-up kids and enemies.

"You really don't know who I am, do you?" His expression steadied as he gave Candace a penetrating glare.

"Nino! What's up, my brother?"

The voice caused Candace to whip around as a smile instantly creased her lips. Kendall walked over to Diego with his hand outstretched for a shake. For the second time that night, her mouth hung to the ground. Kendall knew Diego by his street name—like he *knew him, knew him.*

"Nothing much, bro. Trying to enjoy the concert with my lady friend, and she's acting like a groupie over your pretty boy, singing ass." Diego chuckled as he watched Candace's cheeks turn rosy red.

"Whatever! I am not acting like a groupie." She placed her hands on her hips, focusing on Kendall. "I just happen to love your music. It goes well with my dance classes."

"Dance classes?" Kendall's brows furrowed.

He was the perfect shade of vanilla with a curly half-Mohawk and straight white teeth. He still had on his performance outfit—a button-up with the buttons unfastened, showing off his chest, and a pair of designer jeans. He was almost flawless. Candace took in how fine he was, but she wasn't into pretty boys. Diego was more her type—no, Jaxon. Yes, Jaxon was her type, she reminded herself.

Diego spoke up for her. "Yes, my baby puts Janet Jackson to shame. I'm talking, make Ciara go sit her skinny ass in the corner," he boasted, truly proud of Candace.

Kendall smiled at her, his glare taking in her entire frame. Candace was sexy to him. Her body was tight, and her black thigh-length dress showcased just enough of her thighs for him to wonder if they were as soft as they looked.

"I don't believe she's that good," Kendall challenged, pulling out his cell phone and playing his latest hit, "Making Love." "Let me see what you're working with."

When it came to her passion, Candace threw her nerves out the window. Dancing was everything to her. That's why when she closed her eyes and allowed the rhythm to guide her, she moved with such ferocity and grace that no one could deny her. She connected to every word, her hips rolling and dipping to every beat. By the time she finished, half of the people in the room were mesmerized. She was only brought out of her zone by the sound of applause.

The first person Candace locked eyes with was Diego when she reopened hers. He nodded his head in approval, and the way he winked at her caused her heart to thump faster. Their attraction was getting out of hand.

"Well, I'll be damned. Look at you. You just put the whole room under your spell. Where's your card? I'm going to have management contact you. I may have something for you," Kendall assured her.

He had a big alley-cat grin plastered across his face. Although disappointed she belonged to Diego, he couldn't deny that she had an amazing talent.

Candace reached into her bag. It took everything in her not

to scream. Soul Train Award-winning, Sony recording artist, big-time Kendall was taking her business card. This was the moment she had been waiting for, and she prayed all her hard work was finally about to pay off.

Diego watched as Candace handed Kendall her card. He was happy to be able to connect the dots between Candace and her dreams. He only had one stipulation. Candace needed to remember who her heart belonged to, even if she didn't realize it yet.

Diego pointed an accusing finger at Kendall. "Use that number for business. I act a fool about my baby," he warned.

His voice was playful, but Kendall understood him loud and clear.

"No doubt, bro." Kendall nodded his head. "It was nice meeting you, Ms. Candace. I'll be having my management contact you. I have to make my rounds."

Candace watched her favorite singer as he walked off. Without warning, her arms wrapped around Diego's neck, and she let out her excitement with a squeal.

"Thank you so much, Diego! Thank you! Thank you!" she gushed. "I'm going to love you forever for this."

Diego's arms found their way around her waist. She fit so perfectly.

"You were going to do that anyway, Candy," he told her confidently. "But, no thanks needed. You deserve it."

Shit. His words flowed from his lips so cockily. They felt good to her soul, but she couldn't fully indulge in him. *Jaxon.* She had accepted his ring, promising not to give up on him.

"You know you need to quit," Candace blushed, deciding she needed a drink. Their energy was crazy.

"Nah, you're the one that needs to quit. Why was you avoiding me? You owe me some time. Where we going after we leave here?" Diego asked, watching as Candace fidgeted with her purse strap.

Candace was perfect to him. She had her hair pulled up into a taut bun, showing off the features of her delicate face. The freckles just under her eyes were unique. She hated them, but they were beautiful to him, and her lips were full and soft-looking. *Soon*, Diego vowed. Soon he'd be able to taste them whenever he wanted to.

Candace couldn't look at Diego. She knew what she was about to say would shift the dynamics of their relationship.

"Diego, honestly, I never looked at you as anything more than a brother. I mean, of course, I joked about sitting on your face."

She laughed, but he didn't find it funny. If she sat her pretty ass on his face, he was going to suck the soul straight out of her pussy.

When Diego didn't laugh, Candace cleared her throat and straightened up.

"Anyways, I'm saying, I never looked at you like that, and now I'm so attracted to you that I'm nervous. And you know me—I've never been scared of nothing. But I don't want to take it there with you because I know I'm not done with Jaxon. I don't want to damage the bond we already have." She lifted her hand to flash the promise ring. "He proposed," she said, only telling half the truth.

In her eyes, a promise ring was an engagement ring. He promised to marry her when the time was right. That meant it was an engagement.

Diego's face screwed up into the sourest frown. "And you said yes?" he questioned.

Candace nodded. "I did. That girl was lying. He showed me proof."

Candace almost felt stupid repeating Jaxon's words. Deep down, she knew he was telling a lie. However, believing him felt so much better.

Diego stepped into Candace's personal space, his chest pressed against her, the heat from his body giving her an electric charge.

"I bet you don't marry him. I don't know when you're going to realize that I already got your soul right here." He patted his chest, the area where his heart was located. "I might allow you to play with that nigga until I get everything settled. But when I come for you, it's a wrap for him and any other dude in this world. So, figure that shit out, Candy. I don't give a fuck what you have to do. Get rid of him."

Suddenly, the room became a little too hot, and Candace wondered if anyone else could hear how loud her heart began to thump as she took Diego in. She quickly pulled away, adjusting her dress.

"You're too much for your own good. You know that, right?" She smiled. "Let's go. I'm hungry. I provided the concert tickets, so you got the dinner."

Diego smirked. "Nah, your ex-man provided the tickets and got his girl snatched. I guess I'll do dinner, only because I'm not done stealing your time. I still have to figure out how I'm going to tell you that you're stuck with me for the rest of the night."

"What?" Candace giggled.

Diego nodded. "Yeah, I'm not taking you home tonight. We don't have to touch. I can make love to your mental without being inside you, so don't get it twisted. I'm tired of you treating me like a peon. I'm not playing by your rules no more."

"I think that's called kidnapping." Candace giggled again.

"Nah, it's called putting my foot down."

Candace didn't respond. She allowed Diego to think he put his foot down. The truth was, if he had simply asked for them to spend the night together, she would have agreed. She didn't want to be alone. Lord knows, she could never just wake up to Jaxon and enjoy him.

Candace rolled her eyes. It was rare that Jaxon stayed the entire night with her. He'd stay late, but she almost never got to wake up in his arms. It was crazy to Candace, but she understood he worked early and liked to sleep in his own bed. Her eyes traveled to Diego as they glided out of the concert, hand in hand. She wondered if *he* would like waking up to her.

CHAPTER EIGHT

"**S**HE'S TAKING ADVANTAGE of you, Hunt," Sasha said, sighing as she snatched up one of the twins' shoes and tossed it in the corner.

The twins were four, and although she enjoyed having them around, she still wanted alone time with her man. It seemed as if every chance Alicia got, she was using Hunter to babysit her children. She was starting to act like he was her children's father instead of a cousin.

Hunter narrowed his eyes as he looked over to Sasha while helping Turner put a puzzle together. "No, she isn't. I offered, figuring it would be therapeutic for you to have the kids around since we've been so stressed with having our own." His brows twitched. "You don't enjoy having the kids here?"

"Of course," Sasha replied, nodding.

It was the truth. The twins, Turner and Taneisha, were wonderful kids. So was their older sister, Tasia. It did help to fill the void a little. But she needed the comfort of her man with no distractions. She was going through a state of depression that had her antisocial and moody. Hunter didn't seem to get that.

Hunter smiled. "Good. Now come over here and help us figure this stupid puzzle out. Either I'm getting old, or I'm getting old."

He chuckled, pulling Sasha over to him as she kneeled to their level. He wrapped her in his strong arms and pecked her cheek.

Turner turned his little nose up at them. "Nasty!" He frowned, then let out a baby giggle, causing them both to laugh.

"I'm not nasty, little boy." Sasha chuckled, studying the puzzle and guiding Turner's hands, placing the pieces into their rightful place.

"Are you guys hungry? Did your mommy feed you before you came?"

"No," Tasia answered, walking into the den with them.

She was seven, and Sasha took a liking to her most.

"Can we cook some spaghetti and meatballs?" she suggested with a smile growing on her face.

That was how they bonded. Tasia loved to be in the kitchen while Sasha cooked. She was a chef in the making. Under Sasha's guidance, the little girl could fry chicken, bake a cake, and boil rice. Before the twins were born, Sasha practically raised Tasia. She always had her, and they'd go on play dates with Dallas and Meghan. It was the closest thing to being a mother, and now that Tasia was older and they were starting to grow apart, Sasha wished she had her own daughter.

"Of course," Sasha smiled, pulling herself up from the floor.

Hunter shook his head. "That's okay, babe. I'm going to take them to grab something when Alicia gets back here with my car. I have to drop them off at home. Then, Trenton and I are going to meet up for drinks."

Sasha grimaced. "I thought we were going to spend the day together. Before the kids came, that was our plan, Hunter."

Hunter sighed. "I know, Sasha. But I figured since you didn't want to leave out to go anywhere, I'd just get a little air with my cousin. Then, when I got back, we could watch a movie and have a little us time."

Hunter didn't have the heart to tell her that her negative spirit was starting to depress him. All she wanted to do was mope around the house and have sex. He loved Sasha wholeheartedly and would do anything for her, but her obsession with having a child was starting to drive a wedge between them. Sometimes, he would make up something to do to keep from having to come home. He didn't know how to tell Sasha to suck it up and move on. That was too insensitive, and Sasha was so fragile.

"Can I talk to you in the kitchen, please?"

Hunter let out a sigh and ran his hand along his face. "Let me get them settled right quick, Sash. I'll be in there in a second."

Sasha could tell he wasn't in the mood to argue, but she was. She felt him pulling away from her, and now wasn't the time. Lately, she had been questioning herself as a woman. Hunter loved children. He would make such a good father. What type of woman couldn't reproduce for her man? Sasha feared Hunter would eventually go out and find a woman who could give him what he wanted. That would completely shatter her soul.

After pacing the floor for what seemed like forever, he finally made his way into the kitchen, where Sasha was chewing on her jaw to calm her nerves. She took her man in—his freshly shaved head, his dark brown eyes, and the way his muscles looked in his wife beater. Lord knows Hunter was the sexiest man on Earth to her. He was a *real* man, a provider, a companion. She had prayed for him, and the thought of losing him scared her to death.

"What's up, beautiful?" He spoke in that deep rasp while leaning against the counter and staring at Sasha.

"Are you cheating?" she blurted out.

Hunter exhaled heavily. "No, Sasha. Please don't start that. When do I have time to cheat? If I'm not at work, I'm here with you. You have access to my phones, my emails, my Facebook."

Sasha started to contest him, but he held a finger up to silence her.

"Before you say anything, it's not because you asked. I allow you access so you won't have a reason to question me. I damn sure don't have nothing to hide."

Sasha focused on the floor. She knew Hunter was right and cursed herself for allowing her issues to become his.

"I know, babe. I'm sorry. I'll probably sit on the porch and get a little fresh air. Then finish redecorating the guest room. I'll be ready for that movie and quality time when you get back."

Hunter shook his head. "No work, Sasha. Relax and just

enjoy you. Do whatever you need to do. I want my woman back." Hunter stepped into her personal space, cupping her chin and lifting it until she was looking into his eyes. "Is that possible? Can I have my wife back?"

A smile tipped at the corners of Sasha's lips. "I never left. Plus, you haven't made me your wife yet, Hunter."

He pecked her bottom lip, then deepened the kiss, savoring the taste of her mouth.

"Soon enough, beautiful. Soon enough," he promised, placing the last kiss on her forehead.

Sasha melted. She loved her man so much.

After Hunter and the kids left, Sasha decided to sit on the porch and write in her journal. Poems had become her therapy. Some were full of anger and pain, others full of love. Either way, they always seemed to give her relief.

Sasha and Hunter shared a four-bedroom ranch with a large shaded porch. A swing in the right corner looked out onto the street, her meditation spot. The neighborhood was peaceful. Not much activity took place, and Sasha liked it that way.

"Zion, get back over here."

That deep rasp caused Sasha to smile. She heard the tiny giggle before she saw the adorable face appear over the top step. The toddler raced to the swing and fell into Sasha's legs, holding her hands out to be picked up. Sasha lifted Zion, placing her on the swing next to her.

"Hey, pretty girl. You must have been waiting for me to come outside."

She smiled, watching as Zion relaxed and began to rock the swing back and forth.

"I'm sorry," Devaughn apologized, making his way onto the porch.

Sasha noticed how handsome he looked, casually dressed in a pair of shorts and a T-shirt.

"This little girl thinks you want to be bothered with her every time she sees you. I think inviting her over to play the other day was a bad idea." He chuckled, focusing on Sasha.

There was something about her that intrigued him. He just couldn't place his finger on it.

Sasha shrugged. "Actually, I don't mind her company. Zion is a good kid, and she's welcome anytime. Quiet as it's kept, we don't need you around to hang." Sasha playfully rolled her eyes at him, causing him to smile.

There was a long pause before either spoke. They both studied Zion. She was so content that Devaughn decided to let her be. He knew it was hard not having her mother around. The move altogether must have been a challenge for Zion, and Devaughn appreciated Sasha for her willingness to accept his daughter.

"Thank you," Devaughn finally sighed.

He scooped Zion up and placed her onto his lap as he sat down. Sasha watched him get comfortable without her permission. Well, she didn't mind his company. She actually needed a companion at the moment.

"Thanks for what?" she questioned.

Devaughn shrugged. "Being you. I mean, this whole move has been a strain on both of us. I never factored in the fact that we wouldn't have anybody here in this big city. I got the job offer and took it without thinking things through. I start work again next week, and it terrifies me to have to put Zion in a daycare center with complete strangers."

Sasha's lips formed a pout. She saw the genuine level of stress in his wary eyes. She knew the look all too well.

"Zion is welcome to stay here with me while you work. I mean, I've only known her for a couple of weeks, but I'm not a total stranger."

Devaughn shook his head. "I couldn't do that to you. I didn't mean to vent. For some reason, it's easy to talk to you."

"And I'm here to listen. We're neighbors," she said, then nudged him.

Sasha picked up one of Zion's ponytails. She had beautiful hair, but it was styled awfully. The lopsided ponies were definitely a man's handiwork. Sasha chuckled.

"You know what, I think Zion and I need to have a little girl's time. Whoever did her hair sucks," she teased, causing Devaughn to burst into a fit of laughter. Staring at his daughter's hair made him laugh harder.

Devaughn ran his hand over his beard. "I guess it wouldn't hurt for you to do her hair. I need to run to a few stores, if it's okay with you."

"Bye, Devaughn." Sasha giggled. "Zion, can you stay with me while your daddy goes bye-bye?"

Sasha barely got her sentence out before Zion was climbing off his lap.

"Bye, Daddy," she said in her baby voice, sitting in Sasha's lap.

Devaughn pretended to pout. "So, you're going to diss Daddy like that?"

"See you later, Daddy," Zion replied with a wave.

"Don't be jealous," Sasha teased. "Jealousy isn't very flattering on you."

A brow raised. "So, you find me flattering?" Devaughn countered.

"Not like that. I mean, you're okay. But, I wasn't—"

Devaughn laughed at her nervousness. It was cute.

"I was only teasing, Sasha. I know you're happily married."

She *was* happily engaged to Hunter, right? For the first time in their six-year relationship, she found herself questioning it, and that scared her. Hunter was perfect. He didn't deserve her second-guessing that fact.

CHAPTER NINE

DALLAS HAD CHANGED her outfit a million times before settling on a simple pair of ripped jeans, an embroidered white tank, and cute four-inch heeled sandals. Her look could be dressed up or dressed down, depending on where Trenton planned on taking her. She smiled while thinking of him. It was time to move on and free herself, especially after their last fiasco. Messiah's young hoe was pissed. She tried saying the kids couldn't come back over, but that didn't last long. Messiah was a dog, but he loved his kids.

For the past three days, Dallas and Trenton had been talking on the phone; their conversations were deep and intriguing. Trenton was very opinionated, but he had lots of wisdom and spoke with a certain confidence that made Dallas feel as if she had to listen to him and soak up everything he said.

At thirty-four, Trenton had a story to tell. He'd been in the army since he was nineteen and had traveled the world, creating his fair share of memories. He experienced pain, found love and lost it, and was today trying to pick up the pieces and rediscover Trenton. Dallas loved that he made himself an open book. He wasn't afraid to express his feelings, and she admired his level of maturity and confidence.

"You looking cute, Mom. Who you getting dressed up for? My daddy?" Messiah Jr. asked, making his way into Dallas's room and plopping down on her bed. He leaned back a bit, taking his mother in. "I can't wait until y'all get back together. I don't like that girl, and you're always sad, Momma. I don't want you to be sad no more."

Dallas's brows twitched with concern. "I'm not sad, Messiah.

Sometimes parents grow apart. We still love you, and we're both still going to take care of you, but it's not a good idea for us to be together anymore."

Messiah Jr. rubbed his chin, deep in thought. "So, y'all don't love each other no more?"

"Of course, we love each other still. We just aren't in love with each other anymore. Daddy has moved on, and Mommy has to move on, too."

Messiah Jr. shook his head. "If you're not with my daddy, I don't want you with nobody else. Daddy says I'm the man of the house now. I'll protect you and Meghan. You don't need no other boyfriend."

Dallas chuckled at the way her son's chest poked out. He was so serious.

"I know. You're my big man, Messiah, but Momma got to have a life, too. Your daddy is getting married, so why can't I have a friend?"

Messiah Jr. frowned as if that was the most foolish question in the world.

"I don't want him getting married, and I'm your friend, Momma. You don't need no other friends."

"Boy, if you don't go and get your bag together. Your dad should be here any minute. I'm going to call him to see where he is. I have somewhere to be in the next hour."

Dallas decided to leave out that Trenton would be there to pick her up. Messiah Jr. didn't seem too receptive to the idea of her dating. He had already been dealing with enough, so she didn't want to add on any extra stress.

An hour later, Dallas stood nervously as Messiah Sr. and the kids seemed to drag around the house. If she didn't know any better, she'd say he was doing it on purpose. He had been extremely friendly since he got busted at her house. Apparently, he was on the outs with his fiancée.

Trenton was due to pull up any minute, and she wasn't ready for their worlds to collide. Messiah didn't need to know that she was starting to fall for another man, and Trenton didn't need to meet the asshole who had broken her heart and still had his chains wrapped around it. A part of her felt like she was cheating on Messiah, and as much as she tried to talk herself out of feeling that way, it wouldn't go away.

"Do you guys have everything? Come on, Meghan, grab your bag so your father can leave. I'm sure he does not want to sit up here all day," Dallas fussed, pulling the shades back and peeking outside.

Trenton texted her fifteen minutes prior and said he'd be pulling up in twenty. Messiah had five minutes to leave, and the way he sat comfortably on her couch annoyed her. She would have never allowed Trenton to pick her up had she known her child's father would be late.

"Actually, I don't mind, Dally. I figured we could kick it here for a second like old times. Where was you about to go?" Messiah questioned, taking in the way her curves filled out her jeans.

Her hair was pressed straight with a part down the middle, and her face was set in a light coat of MAC foundation. Dallas was beautiful, and she knew it. She rolled her eyes at the way Messiah ogled her. She hoped he was smoking with jealousy. She wanted him to realize what he was missing. Messiah needed to hurt as much as she did.

"I have a date, Messiah. He should be here any minute, and I would like you to leave before he comes. There is no doing anything like old times anymore. By the way, how is Tatiana? Has she recovered from the last time you called yourself sneaking in my bed? Aren't you getting married?" Dallas muttered, pressing her hands to her hips.

Messiah chuckled. "The other night, you were screaming

another story. We were doing a lot of things we used to do," he hinted suggestively, a frown creasing his lips. "Damn, I'm finally about to meet Trenton. Since you're calling me his name and shit, I wonder if he knows I still make your body cum?"

"Messiah, that is so petty. Why does it matter when you're about to get married? Did you break it down to your fiancée what you still be trying to do? I'm sure she wouldn't like that. And for your information, Trenton and I are going on our first date tonight. So, what we did the other night is irrelevant. It won't happen again."

Messiah let out a hearty laugh. "You know damn well that's a lie. That's mine right there. It always will be, no matter who you *think* you moved on with."

Dallas rolled her eyes at his cockiness. He was an egotistical bastard. She prayed she could finally get over him and his bullshit.

"Whatever, Messiah." She waved him off. "You take me out of my character, and I hate it. Stop fucking with me. It took everything in me not to beat your young hoe's ass the other day. Seeing her so worked up over your lying, cheating ass actually makes me feel sorry for her. I used to be her. There isn't that much love in the world. I'm doing me now. You had your shot," Dallas sassed, marching to the stairs. "Messiah Jr. and Meghan, get down here now so you guys can go. Do not make me come up there!" she boomed as her cell phone began ringing.

Pulling it out of her pocket, she felt her heart start to race when she looked at the screen. It was Trenton.

"Hello," she answered, letting out a sigh.

Her eyes traveled to Messiah, who was staring at her intently. His gaze was scrutinizing. For the first time, Dallas realized he was jealous even though he'd been the one to break up their happy home to be with his side hoe.

"I'm outside, beautiful. Are you ready?" Trenton asked.

"Umm, I am, but the kids' father is still here getting them

together to leave. If you want, you can go to the store right quick, and I'll be ready in five more minutes."

Trenton chuckled. "Why would I do that? I plan to be around, so we have to meet anyways. We might as well get that out the way now. I'm sure that was his intention."

Dallas closed her eyes tightly. "Are you sure?"

"Yep. Open the door, Dallas. I'm on the porch," Trenton told her, then hung up before she could object.

Dallas raked her hands across her face. Both men were alpha males, and she prayed they behaved, especially with the kids present.

She pointed an accusing finger at Messiah. "You have your situation, Messiah. Do not be an asshole, messing up mine. I deserve happiness just as you do," she warned.

Messiah shrugged. "What if I'm not happy and want you back? This *is* your first date, right? I'm willing to forgive you if you're willing to forgive me."

If looks could kill, Messiah would most certainly be dead. Dallas couldn't believe his audacity.

"Forgive me for what?" she practically yelled. "You know what? I'm not going there with you tonight. Get your kids and get the hell out of my house," she spat, marching to the door.

She tried her best to erase the frown on her face, but the truth was, Messiah had gotten under her skin, deeply. How could he toy with her like that? He didn't want her. However, as soon as he saw that she was attempting to move on, he wanted to come confusing things. She refused to fall for his trap. She couldn't.

Taking a deep breath, she swung the door open. Seeing Trenton standing there with flowers and a smile caused her nerves to relax slightly.

"I don't have to tell you how amazing you look. I'm sure you already know it," Trenton complimented, extending his hand for her to take the flowers. Then, he pulled her in for a quick hug and peck on the cheek. His head nodded behind Dallas. "What's up, fam? Trenton," he said, introducing himself and extending a hand for Messiah to shake.

When Messiah didn't return the gesture, Trenton allowed his hand to drop back to his side, and he let out a small laugh. He pulled on the hairs of his beard, looking off to the side. Then, he focused back on Messiah Sr.

"I see it's one of those type of situations. First, I'm going to let you know that I have Dallas's best interest at heart, as well as the kids'. So, no worries. Second, I'll also let you know that I don't give a damn about anything you two had going on before me. As long as you respect me and my space from this day forward, I'm good." Trenton turned toward Dallas. "I'm going to wait in the car now, beautiful. I want to respect you and the kids." With that, he turned to walk away, but not before mumbling over his shoulder, "I didn't want to shake your punk-ass hand anyway."

Dallas fought the urge to giggle. Trenton had checked Messiah so maturely that Messiah was left speechless. She knew he was burnt up about it.

He let out a loud huff. "So, that's the type of man you want? A ghetto, ignorant asshole?"

"Actually, Trenton was in the military, has a Bachelor's in psychology, and is very intelligent, Messiah. You started it. All you had to do was shake his hand." Dallas shrugged before focusing on the kids as they scrambled to the door. "Be good for Daddy, babies."

Messiah waited for the kids to make it out of the door. Despite the tough guy role Dallas was trying to put on, he knew the mother of his children. They had history. She loved him. She always would.

"You can't get rid of me that easily, Dallas. I really don't like the fact that you're inviting him to the house where my kids lay their heads."

Dallas shrugged. "And I didn't like you leaving our family, but

I had to deal with it. Just go home to your young hoe and make it right before she pops up again and gets popped in her mouth for disrespecting my house."

"Here *you* go." Messiah released a sigh. "I'll call you later so we can talk," he added, leaning in for a kiss, but Dallas stopped him.

"Please don't. I'm done. Respect it."

She held her ground, and it felt damn good.

Flood's Bar & Grille was relaxed. Jazz music played by a live band hummed through the building, a sophisticated thirty-five and up crowd filled the room, and Dallas couldn't believe she allowed Trenton to have her on the dancefloor. She hadn't been out dancing since before she had kids. Messiah had stopped courting her long ago.

"People are looking at us," Dallas whispered as Trenton lifted one arm, spinning her and pulling her back in. He was a smooth dancer, much to her surprise.

"So? You're here with me. That's all that matters." His baritone was deep and husky.

Lord knows it felt good to be pressed against him. Dallas tried her damnedest not to enjoy him as much as she was, but how could she not? Trenton had no problem giving her the attention she missed. He was witty and intelligent. He made her feel wanted and beautiful. She was a sea of emotions, and it scared Dallas shitless.

Clearing her throat, she released a breath of air, pushing space between them. "I need to go to the bathroom," Dallas said, then darted off before he could respond.

She couldn't do it. There was no way in hell she would allow herself to be set up for failure.

The ladies' room was packed. Dallas had to squeeze her way in front of the mirror. She stared at her reflection and let out a sigh.

What is wrong with me? Relax, Dallas. Enjoy yourself. You deserve to be happy again, she coached herself, running a hand through her hair to fix the stray hairs.

She remembered that warm fuzzy feeling. Dallas loved Messiah. He made her feel like she was the most important woman in his life. He cherished her at one point. Now, she didn't mean shit to him. She couldn't go through that pain again. Trenton was shooting hard for her heart, and she wasn't ready to allow him to have it.

After getting her emotions in check, Dallas pulled herself from the bathroom, finding Trenton at the bar. He smiled at her once they caught eyes. She looked away. *Damn, this man is sexy.*

"Are you good?" Trenton leaned over and spoke into her ear as soon as she was close enough.

Dallas nodded.

"Hungry? The food is good here."

She nodded again, not really knowing what to say. Things were awkward.

"Look," Trent cupped her elbow, forcing her to look at him, "I'm not him."

"What is that supposed to mean?"

"It means relax. I know you've been through some shit, but don't make me pay for it. I like you. Give me a chance to show you who I am and not what you're used to."

Dallas's heart tugged at her chest. She was conflicted. How could she relax when she had Trenton's fine ass chipping away at the walls she desperately put up? How could she forget giving a man fifteen years, only for him to go out and marry some young bitch he barely knew?

She sighed. "Baby steps. I'll try. I've been broken, Trenton."

He smiled. "Let me help put you back together again, Dallas."

CHAPTER TEN

"So, TELL ME again how you ended up at the concert I gave you tickets for with Sasha's brother? It's not making sense, Candace," Jaxon complained into the phone as Candace swatted Diego's hand away from touching her thighs.

"Will you stop," she whispered, covering the mouthpiece so Jaxon wouldn't hear her.

Diego and Candace had been hanging out tough ever since the concert. She was surprised by how easy it was to be around him. She could let her hair down and be herself. They could laugh together, not to mention it was refreshing to have a man *want* to be with her. Candace didn't have to fight for Diego's attention; he automatically gave it to her.

"Sasha didn't want to go. He did. It's no big deal. Diego is like my brother," Candace lied smoothly, forgetting that Sasha's brother was a complete asshole.

She tried to hold in her laughter as Diego cocked his head to the side and gave her the screw face.

"Brother?" he mouthed with a sneaky grin.

Before Candace could react, Diego pounced on top of her, pinning her down. He was careful to be quiet, but Candace was finding it terribly hard not to giggle, moan, or whatever her body needed to do as Diego's soft lips sucked on her neck, his hands exploring her curves.

"Listen, I can't argue with you right now, Jaxon. I'll call you when I get back to the house."

Candace abruptly ended the call, punching Diego's strong arm.

"Why would you do that, boy? He's already mad that I went to the concert with you," she fussed.

Diego smirked. "Because you sitting there lying to that man. I'm not your gotdamn brother, and you know you're where you need to be. So, why play with him?"

"Whatever, Diego Antonio Riley. Don't be doing that type of stuff. He is my boyfriend."

"Not for long, Candace Marie Riley," Diego challenged, giving her his last name. "Your heart doesn't belong to you anymore. So, you no longer have control over who you give it to. As a matter of fact, I'm giving you a week to figure that out. I'm not about to continue investing my time in you just to be your little secret when he ain't around. I'm selfish, Candy. If we're trying to build together, I can't do it."

Candace frowned. Was he giving her an ultimatum? Of course, she enjoyed Diego's company, but she wasn't willing to give up her security for the unknown.

"That's not fair, Diego," she whined.

He laughed, pecking her juicy lips. "What's not fair? Wanting to give you the world, but at the same time, watching you go home to the next man? Or having to think about you all the fucking time, wishing I could wake up next to you every morning and kiss your crusty lips but having to settle for a good morning text? I think that's real unfair, and I'm not about to set myself up for failure."

Candace blushed. The intensity in Diego's voice caused her to shudder. Yes, she wanted the same things he wanted. She wanted to be loved on just like the next woman. But love didn't pay the bills.

"My lips aren't crusty," she muttered, causing them to burst into laughter.

Diego shook his head. "After all I just said, that's the only thing you took from it?" He intently stared into her eyes as he lay on top of her, his hands running through her hair.

Candace sighed. "No, I heard you loud and clear, Diego. You scare me, though. Where were you when I was going through all these dead-end relationships and getting my heart broken?"

He shrugged. "Experiencing life. Fucking up so I could grow into the man you need me to be. Plus, you had to go through that bullshit. How else would you be able to appreciate being treated how a woman is supposed to be treated by her man?"

Candace scrunched her nose up. "Ewww, why are you so smooth?"

"Because I'm Diego, the smoothest rock on the block," he teased, kissing her lips again.

Candace savored the taste of his kiss. It felt good to finally feel genuine affection from a man. It didn't matter that they hadn't gone all the way yet. She didn't think they were ready for that, at least not mentally. If Candace let him inside her walls, there would be no mistaking the fact that she belonged to him, and another man would end up dead violating what was his. So, Candace definitely needed to get her life together before they took it there.

Later that night, Candace was booked for a private ladies' night out, pole dance edition. If it were up to Candace, she would have stayed with Diego and hung out all day. It was becoming her favorite pastime. She wasn't ready to admit it to him yet, but she would leave Jaxon in a heartbeat with the proper amount of prodding.

A smile creased the corners of her mouth as the MapQuest voice announced that she had reached her destination. It was an old brick building on the west side of Detroit off Seven Mile and Livernois. She studied the address from her phone, then focused on the building again. It definitely wasn't in any shape to be used.

Boards lined what looked like windows, and the doors were gated and secured by a padlock.

Candace let out a huff, snatching her cell phone from the passenger seat to recheck her email for the address. Either she made a mistake, or she had been scammed. That was the downside of being an entrepreneur. Her income depended on her workload, and unfortunately, many *clients* didn't value other folks' time.

After confirming she had the correct address, Candace rolled her eyes while dialing the phone number from the client intake form in her email. She had a few choice words for them. However, two phone calls went unanswered. So, Candace decided to leave a nasty voicemail.

Just as she revved the engine to pull off, a knock on her driver's side window nearly caused her heart to jump out of her chest. She loved her city, but Detroit wasn't the safest place. The murder rate had skyrocketed, and the muggings were ridiculous.

It took a second to process that Diego had followed her to the job, and he seemed to think sneaking up on her was funny. It wasn't. She was beyond annoyed.

Rolling down her window, Candace snarled at him. "What's so funny? And why are you here? I'm not in the mood right now, Diego," she grumbled.

"Shut up and get out." He was rude, yet sexy.

Candace wanted to contest, but the finality in his voice made her comply. Pushing her door open, she stepped out, adjusting the leotard that was riding her ass. It had her curves fully displayed, and Diego would be a complete lie if he said he wasn't aching to explore her inner goddess, to navigate her ocean and figure out which spot made her waves flood the gates of euphoria quickest.

"Seriously, Diego, I'm irritated. I can't believe this inconsiderate bitch scheduled a whole appointment with me and then doesn't show up. I think it was Jaxon's ex, and if she wants to play these types of games, we can go there. I am not the one to play with. My time means money. Every second counts."

As Candace went off on a rant, Diego couldn't help but laugh at how her nose crinkled and the slits of her eyes tightened.

"You talk too much." He shook his head, pointing at the weathered building. "What do you think?"

"Think of what? This ugly, broken down, raggedy building?"

Diego dragged his hand down his face. "Yes, Candace." He sighed. "*I* scheduled the session. Damn. I don't have money for the session, but if you like it, I got this building. We can gut it out, fix it up, and turn it into a little dance studio."

This was a joke. Candace couldn't believe Diego would up and buy her a building. Chills began to run through her body as she shook her head from side to side.

"Uh-uh, I know you're not trying to say what I think you're saying, Diego. Do not play with me like that." She felt the tears welling up in her eyes.

He smiled. "Play with you for what? I mean, I had this building just sitting here, and since I wasn't doing nothing with it but wasting money on paying the taxes, I figured I'd give it to somebody who could put it to use. But, if you don't want it, it's cool." He shrugged nonchalantly.

Candace let out a squeal, jumping into Diego's arms. She kissed him repeatedly—his lips, nose, forehead. She had wrapped her arms around his neck so tight that he almost couldn't breathe. With the way her body fit so perfectly in his arms, she didn't want to let go. He would go out and buy her two more buildings if it kept that smile on her face.

"I can't believe you're giving me my own dance studio, Diego." Her face wrinkled as tears seeped from the creases of her eyes and slid down her cheeks. "Why? What did I do to deserve this?"

She gazed at the building and back into Diego's face. She

had men that spoiled her, but she never had a man to invest in her dreams. Diego had been nothing but supportive, from being at her dance sessions every night to lock up and make sure she made it home safely to introducing her and her dance skills to Kendall. Now he had given her a whole studio. His actions had more value than any dollar amount.

Diego used one hand to balance her and the other to wipe the tears from her face. He kissed her. "You deserve it because you're you. I see your passion, Candace. This isn't about getting into your pants. Although, I want to put it on record that I plan to fuck you silly," he chuckled. "But, yeah, this is about me wanting you to be the best Candace that you can be. You're about to take off, Candy. And what type of man would I be not to help when I know I can? Even if you decide a relationship is not for us, I want you to have it."

Candace's heart melted. Her brows knitted together.

"Boy, don't play with me. We go together now. You're stuck with me."

Diego laughed. "I figured you would see it my way. Seriously, though, can I get a little private dance or something? I ain't got no money."

Candace pecked his lips again.

"You can have whatever you want," she told him, and she meant it.

No one else mattered. Diego was the total package, the real thing, and she felt foolish for ignoring him for so long.

CHAPTER ELEVEN

"**Y**OU'RE JUST GREEDY." Sasha chuckled, rolling her eyes at Hunter as he handed her his plate for a second helping of taco salad.

They were having an intimate get-together, engaged in a serious game of spades—Hunter's idea. On the guest list were Dallas and Trenton, along with Candace and Diego, who were due to pull up at any minute.

"He always has been greedy. That's Hunt, though," Trenton countered. He threw the big joker onto the table, phishing for trumps.

Hunter squinted his eyes toward Trenton, a deep frown forming on his face. "What is that supposed to mean?"

No one else thought anything of it, but Hunter obviously took offense, and Sasha didn't understand why. She knew her man, and the way his jaw flexed was a sure sign that he was about to get ugly.

Trenton looked up from the table, staring his cousin directly in the eye. "It means just what I said. You always been greedy. Why am I feeling like your chest is swelling up, though?" he challenged, letting out a small laugh.

"Alright, y'all. I was only kidding. It's not that serious," Sasha said, trying to defuse the conversation.

They all were a little tipsy from the wine and Cîroc that had been passed around for most of the night. So, she figured they were just tripping.

Hunter held his hand up to silence Sasha. "No, obviously, he got something to say. I've been getting fucked up vibes since this man got back. What is it, *cousin*? You've been jealous since we were

85

kids. I know you want to be me, but there's only one Hunt."

Trenton burst into a fit of laughter. "Be you? Nigga, please. I don't even think you want to be you." He shook his head, tossing the cards onto the table, then focused on Dallas. "You ready, babe? I see he a little in his feelings tonight, and I'm not trying to end up doing something *he's* going to regret in the morning."

Trenton's voice was calm, but it had a dangerous ferocity.

"Seriously, y'all? Don't leave." Sasha turned to Hunter. "What happened? It's not even that serious."

Hunter shook his head. "Let them leave, Sasha. He probably didn't take them crazy pills tonight. His mind fucked up," Hunter shot, delivering a low blow.

The old Trenton would have knocked his head clean off, but the new Trenton gave him a pass. Trenton stood from his seat and pointed at Dallas.

"Let's go, Dallas. I think he had too much to drink, and if I was a bitch, I'd lay all his shit on the table. Luckily, I *did* take my medicine today." He smiled over at Hunter. "If I had a problem with you, you'd know it. You might want to clean your closet, though. Maybe you wouldn't be so tight." He focused on Sasha. "Thanks for the hospitality, Sash. You're a good woman."

Trenton stared at her, biting back his words. Sasha would figure out she deserved better in due time.

After Trenton left with Dallas, Hunter pushed himself from the table, snatching up his car keys. Sasha followed him as he trudged to the door. She let out a deep sigh.

"Where are you going, Hunter? What's going on?" she asked as he pushed the door open and made his way outside.

"Go back inside the house, Sasha," he ordered.

"No. Where are you going? What's wrong with you tonight?"

Hunter whipped around to face Sasha, shooting daggers at her with his eyes.

"Go in the house! I need some air. I'll be back. You need to call your friend and tell her to leave that crazy-ass nigga alone."

Sasha had never seen Hunter so upset, and it scared her. What he and Trenton had going on was deeper than what met the eye, and she didn't know what to do. She liked Trenton for Dallas. He didn't seem all that bad. Then again, with the way things had gone left so quickly, she didn't know what to think.

"Is everything okay?"

As Hunter's car sped out of the driveway, Sasha's eyes slanted over to her neighbor's house. Devaughn was leaning against the gate, peering over at her. It was just after nine o'clock, and the sky was ash with tiny stars that looked like dots. The breeze was nice—not too chilly and not too hot. It was the perfect night to lay on top of the hood of your car and stare up into the sky.

Sasha let out a sigh, placing one hand on her hip and using the other to kneed at her temple, then shrugged.

"I don't know what just happened. It feels like everything is falling apart."

Her shoulders dropped as she swallowed down a jittery lump of anxiety.

"You want to talk about it? You've been a blessing to Zion and me. The least I can do is offer a listening ear." Devaughn looked back toward his house. "Zion is down for the night, so I have nothing but time."

Sasha bit down on her bottom lip. Their vulnerability was creating a bond that neither of them saw unfolding. Making her way over to the gate beside Devaughn, Sasha leaned in, staring up at the sky.

"I mean, how can you have everything and still feel like you have nothing? I should be happy right now. I don't have anything to complain about, yet here I am complaining."

"You're human, Sasha. You're entitled to feel however you

are feeling. Now you just have to figure out a resolution. What's making you feel empty? That's where you need to start."

Sasha took a second to ponder the thought. She knew exactly what it was that was depressing her. She wanted a baby. She figured it would give her purpose in life. At the moment, she felt worthless. Candace owned the successful dance class business, Dallas was a loan underwriter and super mom, and of course, Sasha owned the boutique. However, it wasn't her passion. Hunter sort of gave it to her as something to do with her time.

She shrugged. "I guess it's the whole baby situation. I think I'm stressing about it too much. I feel like it's driving me insane. Two years and nothing. I'm tired of getting my hopes up."

"Have you tried the fertility clinic to make sure everything is okay with the both of you?"

Sasha looked at Devaughn as if he had suggested something foreign. She shook her head from side to side.

"No, Hunter would never go for it. He says he doesn't need any human to tell him if and when we will have a baby. They're not God according to him." She rolled her brown eyes.

"Well, what about adoption?" Devaughn posed.

"Not the same. I mean, if I ended up with a pretty little girl like Zion, then yes. But, I'll pass," she giggled, meaning it as a joke.

Devaughn didn't take it lightly. He'd be a liar if he said the thought of them being a couple and raising Zion together didn't cross his mind. Sasha was perfect. He didn't know everything about her, but what he knew of her was perfect.

"How about you keep Zion's busy self Monday through Thursday, and I'll take her on the weekend?" he chuckled.

Sasha cut her eyes over at Devaughn. "I'd do that in a heartbeat. Zion and I would be everywhere. I'd turn her into a real-life diva baby."

Devaughn paused for a second. He had his official first day of work in the morning, and Zion was set to go to the daycare up the road from his job. But Sasha seemed serious about caring for his daughter, and it would make him feel much more comfortable to have someone familiar protecting his princess.

"Well, if the offer is still on the table, I'd love for you to look after Zion—just until Kindergarten starts in September. I start work tomorrow. Maybe it will give her time to get comfortable without too much stress on her."

Sasha smiled. "You know that's not a problem. You can bring her in the morning. I don't have any plans," she informed him as bright lights lit up her driveway.

She squinted. Diego's Dodge Challenger came to a stop, and the lights shut off. Pushing herself from the gate, she dusted her pants off and studied Devaughn again.

"Whelp, that's my cue to leave. Bring Zion in the morning. I'd love to keep her."

Devaughn nodded. He wanted to say much more but opted to tell her a simple goodbye. He felt slighted by their time being cut prematurely. Sasha didn't know it; however, she had become the only friend he had in their big world, and he needed the companionship more than she may have realized.

CHAPTER TWELVE

"I'M FOR REAL. Ninety-nine percent of what happens to you, you attract. What you focus on becomes your reality, Dallas. Like you keep telling me you hate having to go to your job. So, of course, you're not going to have a good day. Wake up and say, 'Today is going to be a good day," then I bet you'll have a good day," Trenton said, pointing at Dallas as he sat across from her, biting into his double cheeseburger.

They were at McDonald's having lunch for Dallas's break. As much as Dallas tried not to like him, Trenton made it impossible not to. He had begun to make it a habit to meet her for lunch so he could steal as much of her time as possible. Being that Dallas had children, she couldn't go out with him regularly. She wasn't ready to bring him around the kids, and Trenton respected it.

Dallas sucked her teeth. "Yeah, right. It's not that simple. If it were, I'd be a millionaire, married, and traveling the world," she giggled, adding an eye roll.

Trenton didn't return her smile. "Seriously, think about it. What have you been thinking about the most in the past few months? What has your every thought been about?"

Dallas took a second to think about the answer.

"I guess moving on from asshole and finding my happiness again."

Trenton smiled. "So, are you happy again? Have you moved on?" he questioned with a raised brow.

"Yes, I can honestly say I am happy and so over that asshole," she chuckled.

Dallas didn't have to think about that. Of course, she was happy.

"Exactly. You attracted that energy into your life. You wanted to move on. You wanted your happiness back, and you got me." He flashed her a charming smile. "That's that law of attraction, baby. And keep dreaming about it. We'll be millionaires, married, and traveling the world soon." He winked, then checked his watch. "It looks like we have ten minutes to get you back to the office, beautiful. We need to wrap this up."

Dallas folded her arms across her chest, pretending to be sad. "I'm not ready to leave you."

Trenton leaned forward, popping a kiss onto her lips. "Stop acting like we don't have forever to be together. You know you're stuck with me, right?" he told her more than asked.

"Whatever. We'll see when you get to know the real me and my little monsters," she snorted with that same girlish giggle she had been doing their whole lunch date.

"I thought I was getting to know the real you. What? You wearing a mask? Are you really the feds pretending to be this bad-ass chick who's stealing my heart?" Trenton challenged, causing Dallas to blush. He always knew the right things to say.

Dallas shook her head as she pulled herself from the booth. They were at McDonald's, yet she felt like she was leaving an expensive date of lobster, steak, and shrimp. Trenton could make the simplest things mean a lot.

"You're such the charmer." She sighed, reaching out her hand for him to grab it as they made it out of the restaurant. Once outside, she stared into Trenton's charcoal eyes and asked, "What was that about between you and Hunt the other night? What happened? He went ballistic over nothing."

Trenton shrugged. "He's a bitch, and he's scared of me calling him out on his bitch-ass-ness, but that's not my style."

"Well, is there something my friend should know? Hunt seems like such a stand-up guy, and he treats Sasha so well. I just hate that they're going through infertility issues. They want a baby so bad, and it's starting to ruin my friend."

Trenton let out a small laugh, shaking his head. "That's his business. I'm honestly not concerned about what he does in his free time. I only have eight minutes left of your time, and I'm not about to spend it on them."

Dallas began to toy with her curls. "Well, how about you come over tonight, and we watch a movie? I agree, these little thirty-minute meetings aren't enough," she suggested, deciding to break her rule of keeping her kids and her relationships separate.

Trenton raised a brow. "What about the kids?" he asked.

Dallas smiled. "You did say we had forever to spend together, right?" Trenton nodded, and Dallas continued. "So, I think it's time to figure out if you can deal with my kids and me before I fully allow you to have my heart and have to dropkick you in the head for playing with it."

He laughed. "They kicked me out the band because I wouldn't play, baby. That should be the least of your worries," he assured her.

Deep down, Dallas believed him.

Later that night...

"Ma, I'm hungry," Messiah Jr. complained, causing Dallas to roll her eyes to the ceiling and sigh.

It was just past nine-thirty, and Dallas made sure the kids were already fed, bathed, and in bed for school the next day. She knew he was only being difficult because she had company. He wasn't hardly hungry.

"Messiah, if you don't go lay your butt down, it's going to be a problem. Since when do you eat after nine?" she questioned, looking over the couch at her son.

He was such a big boy, but he would forever be her baby, especially wearing the army fatigue onesie that he had on.

"But I'm hungry. Can you make me a sandwich, please?" he begged, focusing on Trenton, then back on his mother.

He was appalled. How dare she bring this man into their home.

Trenton let out a small laugh. "It's okay. You can make little man a sandwich. I'll pause the movie," he offered.

Reluctantly, Dallas pulled herself from the couch and pointed toward the kitchen for Messiah Jr. to follow. He trudged behind her slowly, allowing his gaze to land back on Trenton before making his full exit.

"What is your problem, Messiah? Why aren't you laying down? You know good and well I'm not about to give you nothing to eat this late. Don't get in trouble on this good Thursday night," she fussed through clenched teeth.

Messiah Jr.'s face tightened. "You didn't ask me if he could come in my house and watch my TV, Mom. Y'all said I'm the man of the house, and I don't want him here," he spat.

Dallas tried her best not to laugh despite finding her son's statement utterly comical. Messiah Jr. was serious, though.

"Boy," Dallas stifled a giggle, "this is not your house. You haven't paid for one thing in this place. Go to bed before I whoop your ass, Messiah," she scolded, giving him a stern glare. "And don't bring your ass back down those stairs again tonight," she added, watching as he stomped off.

"I'm telling my dad," he muttered over his shoulder.

"I don't give a damn. Go to bed!" she howled, watching him disappear up the stairs.

She fixed her face, then returned to the living room with

Trenton, plopping down on the couch next to him.

"I'm sorry about that. He is getting too grown for his own good." She sighed.

"Did you get him his sandwich?" Trenton questioned, turning to face Dallas.

He heard the whole conversation and was willing to leave if it made the kids more comfortable. He knew their feelings were factored into how far the relationship with Dallas would go.

Dallas shook her head. "No. That boy didn't want a sandwich. He called himself checking me about having company. Messiah Jr. has to accept that his father and I are done. He has it made up in his little head that we're getting back together."

"Do you think about getting back together with him? Even for the kids?"

Dallas's brows furrowed as she pondered the thought. "Sometimes. But, honestly, there's so much damage that it's irreparable. I actually haven't thought about Messiah since we've been dating."

Trenton leaned over and pecked her lips. "Good," he said, then smiled, "because anything you thought y'all still had is over. It's my turn now, and I'm selfish. Remember that, Dallas. And, if you feel the need to backtrack for whatever reason, let me know. Don't string me along."

Dallas brought their lips together again, but this wasn't a peck. She kissed him deep and hard. She had been waiting to kiss her man like that for a long time.

"No worries this way," she assured him before connecting their lips again.

Messiah was just a memory, at least, that's what she convinced herself to believe. She desperately wanted to be free.

CHAPTER THIRTEEN

CANDACE DIPPED LOW, rolling her body, and turned onto her back. Long legs lifted in the air as she moved sensually, rolling into the splits. Kendall's album *Savage Lovin'* played through the speakers, serenading the room, and as always, she had everyone in awe. Dancing was her God-given talent. It came to her with the same ease as breathing.

After finishing her routine, Candace stood to her feet and took in her class. The numbers had risen again, from forty ladies to sixty-two. With the rate it was growing, she couldn't wait until Diego finished her studio. Just the thought sent jitters up her spine.

Two weeks had passed since he announced he was building her a studio, and for two weeks, they had been together every single free moment they could spare. Diego quickly became her second favorite pastime and was a strong contender for number one. Surprisingly, she even put him before Jaxon.

Poor Jaxon. He'd been calling Candace, dropping by, and texting her like crazy. She didn't have the heart to tell him that it was over and that she couldn't go through with her promise to marry him. Sasha's brother stole her heart. So, she avoided Jaxon. It was easier that way.

"Why Candy always got to show out?" Tangie playfully rolled her eyes. "I'm not hopping my big ass on that pole. Y'all are liable to have to call the fire marshal to pick me up," she added, placing her hands on her hips.

Tangie was what most considered a BBW, a big beautiful woman. She was genuine and curvy with her weight. She wasn't the smallest, but she wasn't sloppily overweight either. She carried it in all the right places and flaunted it tastefully. She had bright eyes and a smile that was contagious.

A few ladies snickered; the others got in formation.

Candace shook her head. "Here *you* go. Just do what you can, Tangela. Why you got to always give me a hard time?" she added with a giggle.

Before she could start the routine over, the bell for the boutique chimed, alerting Candace that someone was waiting out front. Her brows furrowed. They were well into her class, and she wasn't expecting any more ladies. Everyone who reserved their spots for the class was in attendance.

Candace walked over to her bag on the desk and grabbed the taser that Diego bought her a few months back. It wasn't a gun, but it was better than being empty-handed. If Jaxon's ex-girlfriend was there to start problems, Candace was fully prepared to solve them for her.

"One second, guys," Candace called out, making her way to the front of the boutique.

The shadow standing on the other side of the glass doors caused her to let out a sigh. It was Jaxon. She should have known he would be showing up soon, forcing her to deal with him.

This was bad. Diego would be pulling up at any minute. He was an asshole, and there was no doubt in Candace's mind there would be a confrontation. Pulling the door to her, then unlocking it, she stepped outside to face the music.

The night was cool for August, and as the breeze caused Candace's hair to blow, Jaxon peered down at her. She was beautiful. He missed her. He didn't understand what he had done wrong. They were doing so good, and then they weren't.

"Jaxon," Candace started, looking off into the night sky. Cars zoomed by, and horns blew, but overall, it was pretty quiet. "Why are you here? You know I have a class to run."

Jaxon's tongue ran across his full lips as he stared at her

intently. "How else was I supposed to reach you? I don't understand what's going on between us. Why are you avoiding me?"

His eyes traveled to the ring sitting on her finger. She was still walking around with his promise of forever. That was a relief.

"Is it Arianna? I told you, I'm not messing with that girl. If she said something else to you, I'll handle it."

Candace shook her head, biting down on her bottom lip. "It's not that, Jaxon."

She paused for a second, wondering if leaving him was as great an idea as she thought. She closed her eyes.

"I think we need to take a break so I can figure out where I want to be in life."

"What is there to figure out, Candace? We said we were going to get married one day. I'm going to start helping you with your studio, and we will start our family. I know you're not tripping because I don't want those things at this moment."

The frown on his face caused Candace to shake her head. Diego was ready and willing to give her everything she dreamed of. However, Jaxon was standing there feeding her bullshit, and for the first time, she smelled it. He was never going to fully commit to her. Jaxon fed her what she needed to hear to be content.

"When is one day going to happen, Jaxon? If you know you want to marry me and start a family, why give me a *promise ring* instead of the real thing? Why can't we move in together, or you at least stay the night with me? Two years, Jaxon? I'm not getting any younger. I'll be thirty in December."

Jaxon raked his hands across his face as his gaze landed on the figure walking up the sidewalk toward them. It was Diego, and he stopped right beside Candace as if he belonged there. Jaxon didn't like him, never did. He was too attentive to *his* woman. It was the vibe that he gave off.

"Excuse me. Can me and my woman have a little privacy? Why

would you just stand there if you see we're talking?" Jaxon shot.

The aggression in his voice caused Candace to let out a husky breath of air. Things could get really bad…really, really bad.

Diego chuckled. "Because I'm trying to figure out when you gon' realize she ain't your woman no more and take your loss with a little dignity. This all me right here."

He smiled as he wrapped his arm around Candace's waist. It was petty, and Candace knew Diego was trying to get under Jaxon's skin.

"Diego!" Candace tapped his arm. "Now is not the time for that. Please let me handle this situation on my own."

"What is there to handle? You're not rocking with him anymore. Give him back that bullshit, bubble gum ring, and tell him to click his heels and disappear back to wherever them ma'fuckas take him."

Candace had to try her best to stifle a giggle. Diego was so rude.

Jaxon's face was a mixture of anger, shock, and annoyance. Candace took him in, and her eyes traveled to the ground. She didn't want to hurt him, and a part of her even felt bad about it. However, the heart wanted what the heart desired. Diego was who she needed. Their chemistry was so strong that she was afraid to be without him.

Jaxon pointed an accusing finger. "I should have known you were no different than the rest of the sluts that—"

He never got a chance to finish his sentence. Diego's fist connected with Jaxon's jaw so fast that he didn't see it coming. The scene was too much for Candace. Diego was like an animal. His eyes were dark, and his blows were harsh.

"Stop it, Diego!" Candace squealed, pulling at his arm. "You're going to kill him! Stop!" she cried out.

It was total chaos. The ladies came running out of the boutique to watch. Some tried to help break up the brawl, and cars offered a honk of the horn as they drove past. This was not how she wanted things to go. Diego and Jaxon should not have been fighting.

"Diego!" Candace called out to him again, watching in horror as Jaxon balled himself into the fetal position, protecting his head from the blows. "Please, stop. He doesn't want to fight you," Candace added once she saw that she had finally gotten to him.

Diego's eyes slanted toward Jaxon, then to Candace. Damn. He had lost himself somewhere between realizing that Jaxon was speaking to his woman and the slut comment. He knew he had two strikes against him, and murdering Jaxon wasn't worth permanently losing his freedom. He cursed himself for snapping the way he did, but Jaxon had asked for it.

"If you rolling with me, cut this class thing short and let's go, Candy," he growled, traipsing into the night toward his car. He needed to cool off. "And you bet not help him up, or there's going to be some problems," Diego rumbled over his shoulder.

Candace ran her hands through her hair. She took everyone in, feeling as if she would break down and cry. This was too much. Diego was too much. Before she could speak, Tangie stepped up and began barking orders, taking control of the entire scene. She helped Jaxon up, cleared the ladies out, went back inside the boutique to fix the furniture, and then made her way over to Candace before leaving.

"Girl, why are you looking all crazy? You heard Diego's fine ass. Get your stuff and meet him in that car," Tangie chuckled.

Candace shook her head. "I didn't like that, Tangie. We're all adults. He had no business putting his hands on Jaxon. That scares me. You know Diego isn't good with that temper. I don't want to fall in love with him and end up having to hold him down because he went and got himself locked up again."

"Girl, you are thinking entirely too much. Diego is a good man, Candy. He's a little rough around the edges, but he's a catch. Don't think I forgot about that little skinny heffa you had to whip the other week. Jaxon isn't all that either."

"But, Jaxon said she was an ex—"

"Ex, my ass, Candy! Do not be naïve. Homegirl was fighting

for her man." Tangie nudged Candace's shoulder. "Your boo is waiting for you. Go express your feelings to him, and ride him extra good for me. Diego looks like he can put it down in the bedroom."

Candace cut her eyes at Tangie. "Alright now, heffa. Don't be looking at how he does nothing," she playfully fussed as they headed out of the boutique.

Tangie sucked her teeth. "Girl, bye. He a'ight, but I am happily married, and I'm sure he can't light a candle to Jermaine. Maine be having my fat ass thinking I'm an acrobat."

Both ladies had to laugh as they made their way to their separate cars, Candace hopping in with Diego.

Neither of them spoke on the ride back to Candace's house. They allowed their thoughts to do the talking for them. Diego knew he had gone too far, and Candace wondered if they could actually have that happily ever after that she dreamed of having. It was kind of sexy how he stood up for her, though. Now that the commotion had died down, Candace figured Jaxon needed his ass whipped for disrespecting her like that.

Jazmine Sullivan's "Insecure" played on the radio as Candace and Diego sat in her living room, talking. As soon as they got to her house, they fell back into their routine, as though the chaos with Jaxon had never happened. Neither of them wanted to speak on it.

The mood was so relaxed. Diego sat on the living room floor, his back against the couch, and Candace snuggled in the warmth of his arms. They found themselves doing that a lot—enjoying the closeness of being with each other. Candace felt she belonged right where she was, and Diego wouldn't have it any other way.

He clasped one hand inside of Candace's and used his other to tuck stray strands of wavy hair behind her ear. Then he kissed her cheek softly.

"You know how long I've been waiting for this, Candy?"

Candace's head tilted up so she could look into his handsome face. Diego had distinct features. His eyes were a coal-black maze that she could get lost in, his skin a rich chocolate complexion, and the thick onyx goatee hid his juicy kiss-me lips a bit. Even the freckles that lined just under his eyes were sexy. He was gorgeous to Candace.

Her lips smiled playfully. "You weren't checking for me, Diego. I was a little poor, clothes-sharing girl to you. You were too busy chasing those big booty hoochie mommas and running the streets." She rolled her eyes.

Diego's stare intensified, and his expression grew serious.

"That's a lie, Candy. You probably don't remember it, but I do. I know I was a wild-ass hothead back in the day. I did stupid shit just because I could."

He shrugged, remembering all the senseless trouble he'd gotten into over the years.

"Everybody used to tell me how I wasn't gon' be shit and was going to end up dead or in jail," he continued. "My own momma put that shit in my head. But I remember this one night in particular. I had just gotten into it with my old bird and was madder than a ma'fucka. Probably about to go out and get into some bullshit. Then you stopped me on the porch. You looked me dead in the eyes and told me that I was going to be somebody and was too smart to end up a statistic."

Diego let out a small laugh as he allowed his memory to go back to that night. He smiled as he envisioned her innocent face down to the black and pink jogging suit she had on.

"It wasn't what you said. I appreciated that when everybody had given up on me and broads were just after my money, little ass Candace believed in me. I got locked up two days later. And guess who held me down, visiting and sending me letters and shit?" He paused, pecking her cheek again. "Little-ass Candace. You don't know how much that meant to me, baby. That's why being at this point right now feels so good. I want to be here for you like you was there for me. If it's in my power, I want you to have everything that makes you smile. I want you to have that dance studio because I believe in you like you believed in me."

Candace placed a finger to his lips to silence him. She replaced her finger with her lips, pressing deep and allowing her tongue to do a sacred dance with his. She didn't know how to respond to his revelation with words, so she let her tongue do the talking.

Diego's hands roamed her body. His manhood was so stiff that it felt as if it would break if he didn't find his way inside of Candace soon. She couldn't kiss him the way she was doing. He didn't have full control of his desires when it came to her.

"Stop before we end up going half on a baby," he whispered against her lips.

Candace smiled. "You gon' stop pushing me off. I've been trying to throw it at you for a month now." She twisted her body to face his, pulling her shirt over her head. "So, are you going to give it up? Or do I have to take it myself?"

Diego didn't take too kindly to threats, especially *those* types of threats from *her*. He was being a gentleman. However, he had been planning to suck her entire soul out of her pussy like it was a neckbone. Then, when she thought she was at the point of no return, he planned to push her over the edge with deep, hard, slow, calculated strokes until his name was etched inside her walls.

"Lay back," he commanded.

Not giving her a chance to do it herself, his strong arms swooped around her, flipping her over to her back. His presence was smoldering. Candace wondered if he could feel how much she needed his touch from the heat radiating from her body.

"You know once you let me inside, it ain't no backtracking,

right?" Diego whispered against her lips as his hands greedily explored her curves. "Don't take all this good dick if you ain't ready for what comes with it," he added, pressing his lips deeper into hers.

"Shut up and fuck me, boy. You just make sure you got your end covered," she growled, nearly delirious with drunken lust.

She needed to feel him, to hear his grunts of satisfaction, and to release the powerful orgasm she knew was bound to come.

Diego smiled deviously. He knew she didn't fully understand what she'd just committed to, and it made his manhood rock up even more at the thought of what he was about to do.

Yanking her panties off in one swift motion, Diego slid down so he could be eye-level with his dinner. She had a pretty pussy with a neat line of hair traveling down the middle. He appreciated the sight; he even said his grace before devouring his meal.

Candace's leg swung over his shoulder, and his hands gripped her hips, pulling her closer to his face. The smell of her was hypnotizing, and the taste was...indescribable. As Diego's lips made contact with her clit and his tongue covered it, he savored the taste.

"Shit," she mumbled as her hands connected with his head, rubbing his waves, coercing him to continue to make her feel good. "Diego, baby."

Her words caught between another moan as her body tensed from the sensation of pleasure.

"Diego, what? Didn't you say shut up and fuck you?" he growled, gripping her hips tighter and sucking harder on her bud, earning a delirious moan. "Now you shut up and get fucked."

If he didn't send her body on an orgasmic high that took complete control of her mind, body, and soul, his name wasn't Diego Riley. His oral was amazing, but the way he filled her walls, giving her slow strokes while gently suckling on her toes, was an experience for the books.

Diego was the shit.

There was no other way to put it.

CHAPTER FOURTEEN

THEY WERE FALLING apart, and Sasha could feel it deep in her soul. He was changing. Their energy was usually perfectly balanced. Now, it was off. Sex wasn't as steamy and spell-bounding as it usually was, and his late nights at the job were becoming more frequent. He didn't even smile at her the way he used to, making her feel as if she was the only one that mattered anymore.

Sasha solemnly stared as she poured herself a fresh cup of coffee. She had to fix it. Hunter was the most valuable thing she had going for herself. His love was everything, and she would be lost without it. Sometimes, she found herself questioning what had happened to them. Why was she so unhappy when she had everything at her fingertips? Women would kill to be in her position.

A sigh escaped her pursed lips as her gaze traveled over to Zion, sleeping peacefully on their leather sectional. The poor baby had played herself right into a nap. They raced, played house, went out for lunch at Chili's, and before she passed out, Zion had given Sasha a complete makeover—hair and nails included.

Sasha had been keeping Zion for an entire month now. They had become buddies. She was so adorable, charming, and loving that you had no choice but to fall in love with the toddler. Sasha felt their bond was growing deep from the lack of female presence in Zion's life.

Sasha wondered what had gone so wrong with Devaughn and his ex. He was an amazing, hardworking, and extremely handsome man with lots of wisdom. He was easy to talk to and offered a shoulder much different than what Dallas and Candace had to lean on. He gave honest, unbiased advice from a male's perspective. He made the simplest things seem easy. For example, he was the one who made Sasha realize Hunter might have been dealing with his own demons. She had disregarded his feelings without meaning to do so.

Throughout the whole relationship, Hunter was always the strong one. He had an answer for everything and took the lead as a man should. She never considered that he might have been stressed about their inability to conceive or about keeping them put up in that big home in Bingham Farms. Not to mention he made sure all the bills were paid. Hunter took on the weight of the world while she had fallen into her own pity party, ignoring his needs.

Sasha made her way to the dining room table and sat down with her coffee. She pulled out her cell phone and shot Hunter a text, telling him how much she loved him and was grateful to have him. Then she stared off, looking at nothing in particular, lost in thought.

"Sasha! Where you at, babe?" Hunter's voice could be heard as if on cue.

The front door slammed, locks turned. Sasha heard his footsteps as he came around the corner, the wooden floors creaking with each step.

"Sasha!" he called out again just as he came into view.

She put a slender finger to her lips for him to lower his voice, then pointed to the couch.

"Shhh, you're going to wake Zion," Sasha said, then pushed herself up from the table while taking her man in.

Hunter's head was freshly shaved and shining; his peanut butter skin and amazingly crafted bone structure were perfect. Dressed down in a pair of designer jeans and a simple fitted T-shirt, Hunter still had a classic GQ flair that never seemed to go away. He was impeccable. There was no other way to put it. She knew it, he knew it, and anyone with perfect 20/20 vision could see it, as well.

Hunter's thick lips traveled downward as his eyes landed on the toddler fast asleep on the couch. Quite frankly, he wasn't feeling the relationship that Sasha was forming with the neighbor. He most definitely wasn't feeling having to come home to another man's child every day while he busted his ass on a twelve-hour shift, sometimes longer depending on the workload and architect layout. If Sasha wanted to do something with herself, she could have picked up a part-time job, volunteered at a daycare, or done something more productive.

"I'm not about to be walking on eggshells in my own house, Sasha. Why every time I come home, I have to deal with another man's child? I got off early, thinking we could go out and celebrate this new business deal, but we can't do nothing because you got his kid. I'm starting to feel a certain way about you two, Sasha. I don't like it."

Sasha shifted her weight to one hip and crossed her arms over her chest. Her forehead creased in contempt.

"What is that supposed to mean, Hunter? We can still go out. Her father should be here in the next half hour. And what are you insinuating? Feeling a certain way about what? Devaughn is a friend, our neighbor. I'm just helping out until school starts in a couple of weeks."

"Personally, I don't think a woman who's happily engaged should have male friends. So, stop using that term so loosely. You know what? Never mind."

Frustrated, he let out a husky breath of air and trudged toward their bedroom. Sasha went after him. She felt her sanity slipping away. The merry-go-round of emotions was surely going to drive her mad.

"Hunt," she called after him. "Hunter, don't walk away from me. I want you to say how you feel. Hunt…stop walking, damnit! Now, listen to me. I don't know what the hell is going on between us. One minute you love me, and the next, you're trying to find every excuse to be away from me. I love you with all my heart, and it's killing me to see us falling apart and know I can't do anything about it. I'm sorry I can't have your kids. Don't you think that kills me? I—"

Her words became choked in her tears. All the emotions she had been holding in, allowing to build up, came spilling over. Big crocodile tears flowed down her cheeks.

Stepping into her personal space, Hunter wrapped her in his strong arms. His head rested on top of hers, and they both soaked in the feeling of being close. They allowed their energies to transfer to each other, communicating an unspoken language. He needed Sasha, and Sasha needed him just as much, if not more.

"Calm down, baby. My bad," he whispered, squeezing her tightly. "Shhh, I didn't mean to come at you like that. I love you, Sasha. I trust you, too," he assured her, cupping her chin to make her look up at him. "I apologize, okay?"

Sasha nodded through a sniffle. "It's so hard, Hunt. I know you want kids. I see how you are with the twins, and it messes with my head that I can't give you that. It scares me. I don't want you to leave me for a woman who can."

A smile of pure and masculine amusement spread across his face, causing his eyes to crinkle.

"Picture that. I love you, Sash. I'm not going nowhere. If we don't end up with a child of our own, it wasn't meant to be, and I'm fine with that. Stop beating yourself up over something you can't change."

"But—" Candace started.

Hunter cut her off, pressing his lips to hers. It began as a light peck but grew into a deep, tantalizing "I-need-you-right-now" kiss. When Sasha came up for air, dizzy and breathless, her lips twitched into a smug grin.

"Don't be kissing me like that, Hunter," she blushed.

"I'm going to do more than kiss you. I'll tell you what. I'll run to the grocery store, get us some dinner to cook together, and we can retire with a movie and me deep, deep inside of you. How does that sound?"

"It sounds much needed. Thank you, Hunter."

He pecked her lips again while staring into her sparkling browns.

"No, thank you for never giving up on us. We'll get it together," he promised.

He said it with such sincerity that she believed they'd find their happily ever after again.

Two hours later...

"Sorry I'm late, Sash. We had five extra trucks and two call-offs. You know it's mandatory I stay over to pick up the slack," Devaughn explained, trying his best to ignore the way her chestnut skin glowed.

Sasha was beautiful, inside and out. He hated that he was so attracted to her, especially since she was somebody else's perfect woman.

"It's fine. You know Zion isn't a problem. Hunt hasn't gotten back from the grocery store yet anyway," she responded, waving him off.

Stepping to the side, she allowed Devaughn to make his way inside the house. Zion was engaged in an episode of *Mickey Mouse Clubhouse*, equipped with a snack plate of fresh oranges and carrots.

"So, how are things with you two? Good?" he wondered with a raised brow.

Sasha smiled, thinking of Hunter and the moment they shared before he left for the store.

"Yes, and you were right. We just needed to talk. Our

communication was horrible." She let out a deep breath.

Devaughn couldn't afford to divulge himself in emotions that would only lead to disaster. However, he still felt a bit slighted to hear that they were getting back on track. Was he wrong for wishing Sasha and Hunter would separate? For wanting her for himself? He needed her far more than Hunter did. Zion, too.

Life for Devaughn wasn't exactly flowers and candy. Growing up in Chicago was a struggle in itself. Fighting the statistic of becoming another black man who fell victim to poverty was torture. There was violence in the streets, violence at home, and nowhere to turn. He definitely couldn't walk into the police station and expect to be protected. He had a better chance of surviving in the streets. And that's what he did.

He worked two jobs while finishing college and paid his mother's bills until he moved into his place. When he met Zion's mother, the beautiful Latina with an amazing personality, he thought his life was coming together. However, moving in together with her was his worst mistake ever, and the only good thing that came out of it was Zion. Christina, Zion's mother, was a monster. She was the devil disguised as a woman. She was a liar, manipulator, thief, and the real reason he got the hell away from Chicago.

Devaughn cleared his throat. "Well, let me get Zion and get out of you guys' hair. If I haven't told you lately, thank you, Sasha. I appreciate having a friend like you."

Sasha's nose crinkled. "Friend? We're almost family. I'm ready to take Zion for myself and give you visitation rights."

She giggled. He didn't. Sasha's expression straightened.

"Seriously, she's no problem. Thanks for trusting me with her."

"Yeah, you shouldn't be so perfect. Let me grab Zion. It's getting late. Oh yeah, and before I forget, I found a church a few weeks ago. I remember you saying you're trying to find your way back. I'd love for you and Hunt to come with us for Family and

Friends Day," Devaughn offered.

Sasha's face twisted up. "Hunt ain't hardly going to nobody's church house. He's more spiritual than religious, but I'd love to come. Just keep me posted."

Devaughn nodded in approval, then looked past Sasha as Zion's bright face lit up after laying eyes on him.

"Daddy!" she squealed, racing toward him.

He scooped her up. Immediately, she held out her perfectly painted, red-tinted nails.

"Pretty?" she questioned.

"Yes, pretty, Princess. Ms. Sasha is going to turn you into a diva."

He smiled as his eyes unconsciously landed on Sasha again. Damnit…something was going to have to give. He looked at her and saw his future, but he wasn't sure she noticed him in that type of way.

CHAPTER FIFTEEN

DALLAS'S EYES SHUT tightly as she shook her head. This wasn't happening. Messiah Jr. knew better. As a matter of fact, where did he get a knife from? She let out a deep sigh.

"I agree, Mrs. Stephenson. I'm on my way; his father, too. We understand, and we will handle it."

She was most indeed going to handle it. Dallas had a belt with Messiah's name on it. She planned to tear his little ass up. Threatening some poor little boy with a knife? Who does that?

Pushing herself from her desk, she trudged to her manager's office, explained her emergency, and left for the day, seeing red. Messiah Jr. could have gotten everybody in a world of trouble, including landing himself in a juvenile detention center.

Just as Dallas made it to the car, her cell phone chimed, displaying Messiah Sr.'s cell number.

"Yes, Messiah," she groaned.

"You know this is your fault, right? Instead of running up the next man's ass, you should have been paying attention to our son," he rumbled.

His voice was rough, deep, and filled with arrogance. Dallas had to pull the phone away from her ear and look at it to make sure she had heard correctly.

No this motherfucka didn't, she thought to herself, inhaling a deep breath of air to calm her nerves.

"You have clearly bumped that big-ass watermelon head, Messiah. I'm hanging up. I'll meet you at the day camp."

She did as she said, disconnecting their call. He was such an asshole. Messiah loved the finger-pointing game; nothing was ever his fault. She hated that he never took accountability for his actions.

Pulling up to the children's daycare, Dallas rolled her eyes at Messiah's Ford Explorer sitting in the space next to hers. If she could have flattened his tires and gotten away with it, she would have done it. Ever since he met Trenton, he had become a complete asshole. He acted as if he was too busy to get them every weekend as he had been doing, and every request for financial help was met with an argument unless she was willing to have sex with him. She was starting to wonder how she lasted fifteen years with a man like him.

It was just past twelve-thirty, and the sun was scorching, relentlessly beaming down on the city. As soon as Dallas turned the air conditioner off, the heat smacked her in the face. She wasn't in the mood to deal with Messiah Jr. or his father. At least, not today.

Peeling herself from the car, she walked past the playground and into the building. Kids were running around, laughing, and playing as usual. Meghan spotted her first. She greeted her with the "someone's in trouble face" before nodding her head in the daycare coordinator's direction. Messiah Sr. seemed to be in a heated conversation, and the pout on Jr.'s face told Dallas that he was receiving the brunt of his anger.

"You're acting like my son is some bad-ass kid with parents who don't love him. I know what he did is unacceptable, but he has two parents who are very involved, ma'am," she heard Messiah Sr. fuss.

Dallas knew from the sharpness in his voice that he was seconds from showing out. So, she picked up her pace to the corner where they were talking. Lord knows she couldn't afford for the kids to get kicked out of day camp. They had less than two weeks before school started back up, and finding another sitter would be hell.

"Calm down, Messiah." She touched his arm, stepping forward to control the conversation. "Hello, Mrs. Stephenson.

Can you tell me again what my child did?"

Mrs. Stephenson was an older Caucasian lady. Her teeth were stained from drinking entirely too much coffee, and her hair was a dull white from lack of proper care. She owned the daycare and had been looking after the kids since Meghan was two and Messiah was four.

"Well, Messiah here took the plastic knife and waved it at Austin like he was going to stab him. Of course, I know Messiah Jr. is a good kid, but I can't tolerate that here. I don't want the other kids to fear for their safety."

Dallas kneaded at her temples to release the pressure from the headache brewing.

"So, what are you saying, Mrs. Stephenson?"

"I'm saying that maybe he should stay home for the rest of this break. Austin's mother was very upset. He's welcome to come back next summer when school lets out and during breaks. I just want the situation to die down, ya know?"

Mrs. Stephenson offered a sympathetic smile before focusing on Messiah Jr. Tears trickled down his little face because he knew he was in trouble. He knew he would have a well-whooped ass when his parents were done with him.

"Nah, we're okay. Why the hell did you allow him to get ahold of a knife in the first place? Our kids don't have to come back into this ma'fucka. Ever!" Messiah Sr. boomed.

Dallas sighed. "Messiah, calm down. Don't say that."

He turned to Dallas. "Don't tell me what to say. You already know how I feel. Get Meghan. Me and my son will meet you at the house. I need to see what the hell is going through his head."

Messiah never gave Dallas a chance to respond. He grabbed Jr.'s arm and began to walk them to his truck. Dallas watched them disappear.

"I'm sorry, Mrs. Stephenson. Messiah Sr. gets irrational when it comes to the kids. I'll handle things," Dallas assured her before signing the children out and signaling Meghan to meet her at the door.

Her cell phone chimed as soon as she made it back to the car. It was Trenton, and Dallas needed his voice of reason desperately. She couldn't understand how Messiah Sr. blamed her relationship with Trenton for Jr.'s behavioral issues when the man had been the only reason she smiled lately. Trenton gave her the power to keep pushing. He took her pain away and replaced it with a strength she never knew she had. Hell no, dating Trenton was a blessing.

"Hey, beautiful. Talk to me. I went to pick you up for lunch, and you were gone. Is everything okay?"

Dallas shook her head as if he could see her. Realizing he couldn't, she spoke up.

"No. My child waved a plastic knife at someone, got kicked out of daycare, and his asshole of—"

She paused mid-sentence when she remembered that Meghan was sitting next to her. She refused to bash her child's father in front of the kids.

"I mean, my donor seems to think it's my fault that he's acting out because I'm dating you."

Dallas could hear Trenton kiss his teeth.

"You don't believe that bullshit, do you? He has a whole fiancée, and your relationship is to blame? He's a selfish motherfucker if you ask me. He's mad that you're finally happy."

"I know, Trenton. It just annoys me that all this is happening. I know our separation is affecting the children, and I feel bad about it. I guess I should have given them more time to heal."

"Don't start blaming yourself, Dallas. Come on, man. He's the one who left you and is marrying some random broad. His stupid ass probably realized what he lost, and it's hitting him hard that he'll never get it back. I'm not giving up on us. I'm not losing my peace to nobody."

"I know, Trenton. Listen, we just pulled up to the house. Let me handle things, and I'll call you back later."

"Alright, Dallas. I'm counting on you to remember that you're a grown-ass woman and can stand up for yourself. Say what you mean and mean what you say."

"I will. Thank you, Trenton," she promised before ending the call.

She trudged into the house where Messiah Sr. and Jr. were already having a talk. Dallas had forgotten that her ex still had the key. He never used it. However, since the dynamics of their relationship had changed, she figured she'd better get her key back from him or change the locks.

Messiah Sr.'s gaze landed on Dallas. He took her in, really appreciating her beauty. She was dressed in a form-fitting, classy two-piece black skirt and blazer set. Her heels made her legs firm and curve out into thick hips, and her face was naturally beautiful. *Damn.* He missed her so gotdamn bad. He was ready for his family back. She was supposed to be his. She was supposed to be sitting around waiting for him to decide that he wasn't missing anything in the dating world and his family was the most valuable thing in his life.

Instead of admitting how wrong he was, his facial expression told a complete lie. His brows knitted together tightly, and his lips curved down into a frown.

"Tell her what you told me, Jr.," he coerced his son.

Jr.'s eyes lowered to the ground as he shoved his hands in his pocket. "I don't like Trenton. I hate him. He messed up our family."

Dallas's brows furrowed. Her eyes traveled to Meghan, who was standing next to her with her hands on her hips.

"Meghan, go to your room, baby. Let us talk to your brother."

"Okay, Mom. But before I go, I want to say that I like him. He's funny, and you're not sad anymore. Dad has Tatiana, so you can have Trenton," Meghan expressed, then rolled her eyes at Messiah Jr. before walking off.

Dallas waited for Meghan to disappear before making her way over to Messiah Jr. and kneeling in front of him.

"Why would you say that, son? What has Trent done to you?"

"You cheated, and now Dad is not coming back. He ruined everything," Messiah Jr. said, a tear rolling down his cheek.

Messiah Jr. was always the strong child. He was tough as nails, spoke his mind, and rarely cried. She knew their split affected him, but she didn't understand how much. She felt like shit for forcing Trenton on her children. It didn't matter what Messiah Sr. did; her job as a mother was to protect her babies.

"See, I told you that you needed to tend to our kids rather than running behind some random dude out of spite. Your actions are affecting our son."

Now Dallas was appalled. Instead of correcting their son, he wanted to add fuel to the fire. No matter how much she hated him, she always had his back. She couldn't believe that her forever had turned into such a disaster.

Rolling her eyes at Messiah Sr., she focused on her son. "Baby, I did not cheat on your father. Sometimes, parents just grow apart. He's marrying Tatiana now, and you have to accept that. Mommy has to be happy, too. I explained that to you."

"We don't make you happy? Dad can have you and her. I seen y'all. I wasn't sleep. Now Trenton messed that up. Y'all are never going to get back together."

Dallas was speechless, angry, and hurt all at the same time. She didn't want to set that example for her son and have him thinking it was okay to sleep around while a woman sat crying over him. She hated Messiah Sr. for implanting that into his head and not being man enough to correct it.

"Messiah, it is not okay to have two girlfriends." Dallas sighed, throwing daggers at her ex. "Would you explain to him how a relationship is supposed to go, please?"

Messiah Sr. shrugged. The smug look on his face made Dallas want to slap it off him.

"Son, you can't help who you fall in love with, and if you love her or them, as long as you treat them right and provide for them, you can love who you want."

Dallas's brows crinkled. He completely danced off-topic. Nothing he said made sense or had relevance to their conversation.

"Listen, it doesn't matter what goes on between me and your father. We'll talk about that later. Why would you wave a knife at somebody? Do you want to go to jail, little boy? Do you want to get me and Daddy in trouble?"

"No," Jr. muttered just above a whisper as his eyes traveled to the ground.

"Look at me when I'm talking to you, Messiah. There is no excuse for your behavior. You better hope your grandmother will keep you while I'm at work. Do not pick up that PlayStation, tablet, or TV remote. I want to beat your ass so bad, but you're lucky. Go to your room. Now!" she demanded, pointing to the stairs.

She wasn't in her right mind to check him. Messiah Sr. had her livid.

"And you…" She turned to face Messiah Sr. "Please step into the basement with me. We need to talk," she growled forcefully, walking off before he could respond.

When they made it out of the kids' earshot, Dallas went in for the kill.

"Why the hell did you not have my back like I have yours? There's so much I can say about your low-down, selfish ass, but I don't. This breakup is not my fault. It isn't cool that you didn't explain to your child how having two women is wrong. This is why I feel so stupid over you. I'm setting all the wrong examples for him."

"Yes, you are," he agreed curtly. "You can't just bring random men around the kids. You—"

Slap!

Dallas's hand landed across his face. Another would have followed if he hadn't grabbed her and pinned her against the wall.

"Keep your hands to yourself, Dallas. I respect you. So, you have some respect for me, too, damnit."

His grip was firm, and their bodies were entirely too close. Dallas was a ball of emotions, ready to explode at any moment.

"Now I know you're hurting, and I apologize for hurting you," he whispered. "I'm not marrying Tatiana no more. I know you want to do the family thing. So, I'm with it. I'm going to rock with you. Okay?"

He said those words as if he was a prize and Dallas ought to be lucky to win him. It was too late to try to do the family thing. When she wanted him, he didn't want her. She shed far too many tears over him. He had sucker punched her soul and shot too many bullets through her heart.

Dallas tried to ignore the ache that settled just behind her chest. When Messiah's lips pressed against hers without warning, a neatly buried, deep-down fury tipped the corners of her lips. She pushed him away with so much force that it shocked him.

"No! Don't you dare feed me that bullshit and think you can kiss away all the pain your sorry-ass caused me. Enough, Messiah. I will no longer be your slave. We have kids to co-parent. But as for you and me..." She pointed between the both of them. "We'll never have anything else going on. I have a good man who cares about me. He never makes me fight for his attention. And you know what? He cares about our children's well-being. I'm scared shitless to love because of the way you broke me, but I will not let you do this to me any longer."

Messiah Sr. took a step forward, gripping her hip and gyrating his throbbing bulge against her thigh. "I bet he don't know the right spots to make you squirt like I do."

Dallas reached up and unhooked Messiah's hand from her waist. "No, he's nothing like you. I can agree with that. He makes my body feel way better than you ever could, and he hasn't even smelled the pussy yet."

Messiah's jaw flexed. He was angry, really angry. Dallas could tell he was cooking up something hurtful to say. However, nothing could hurt her worse than what he had already done to her.

Chest out, shoulders back, Dallas confidently closed Messiah's chapter in her life. She found her voice and sang proudly tonight. It felt amazing.

CHAPTER SIXTEEN

"OH MY GOD! You just got paint all over my clothes," Candace said, poking out her bottom lip and folding her arms across her chest.

She was at the studio with Diego; their date consisted of painting, dusting, and watching him fix the walls. It was coming along so wonderfully, and Candace was excited.

In two months, her dreams were going to come true. She wanted the grand opening to be lavish: champagne, hors d'oeuvres, good music, and good vibes. For once in Candace's life, she felt complete. She was happy, and nothing could change that.

"Stop pouting with your prissy ass. I told you we was going to get dirty today. You the one that wanted to come out the house looking like Diamond from *Player's Club*," Diego teased, letting out a hearty laugh as Candace swatted at his arm.

"Whatever. I know you are not trying to say I look like a stripper. Besides, when you said we was getting dirty, I thought you was trying to get nasty." She rolled her eyes. Diego's tongue slid across his lips as he took in the dips and curves of her body. Tight denim shorts molded to her thick hips and thighs, her T-shirt clung to her ample breasts perfectly, and a wealth of thick, silky hair framed her beautiful face. Average wasn't a word that could ever be used to describe her. Candace was simply gorgeous.

"We was going to do that regardless." He chortled, smacking her ass. "But, I guess we can head out because I see you not feeling getting your hands dirty."

"Not with shorts on and these nails. I just got them done. And stop trying to play me like I'm lazy."

"Oh, I know you ain't lazy," Diego responded with a smirk as he removed his safety goggles from his eyes and the gloves from his hands.

He oozed power, authority, and raw confidence. Candace loved that about him.

Diego stepped closer into her personal space and placed his hands on her waist. Candace thought she would drown in his gaze. Exactly one month and four days had made her fall in love with him. She'd known Diego for years, twenty-one, give or take. Yet, thirty-four days had changed everything.

"Your mother is going to freak out when she finds out you decided to be my little boo thang," Candace teased, wrapping her arms around his neck and staring up at him like a lovesick teenager.

"Nah, I told her a few years back that I was going to marry you. She knows what's up. She's ready for a grandbaby now. I told her to chill. I got to trick you into loving me first." He smiled that sexy, contagious grin. "You think you can fall in love with a cat like me?"

"Hmmm..." Candace playfully cocked her head to the side. "I thought marriage came before babies?"

"We can do that, too," Diego said, then shrugged.

The seriousness in his voice caused Candace to blush. He was so unfiltered and open about his feelings for her.

Diego's cell phone chirped, and Candace welcomed the distraction. She started to make her way to the other side of the room to give him a little privacy as he answered his call, but he held on to her waist, keeping her in place.

"Where you going?" he questioned, pressing the phone to his ear. "What's going on, bro?" he added, talking into his cell.

"Stop bullshitting me. Don't tell me no shit like that."

His voice was a deep rasp, and it cracked just as he finished his sentence. Haunted sorrow and murder swirled in the cadence of his tone.

"I'm on my way." Diego ended the call. He blankly stared at the ground for a pregnant second, then released an agonizing breath of air. "Fuck! We have to go, Candy. We got to go now."

He whisked her away before she could blink, locking up the studio and speeding off into the streets of Detroit.

Candy wanted to ask what was wrong. However, the level of intensity in his glare silenced her. She focused on the moving buildings instead, then the road as they zoomed in and out of traffic until they pulled up to Henry Ford Hospital. Diego hopped out of the car at the emergency room entrance, barely throwing it in park.

Security tried stopping him. It was two of them. They told him that he couldn't just park at the entrance. Diego ignored them, pushing past the poor guys as if they were a feather's weight. He reminded Candace of the Incredible Hulk as he bulldozed his way through the revolving doors.

"I'll move it. It's okay. He left the car keys," Candace called out to security, who had begun talking into their walkie-talkies.

The last thing she needed was for Diego to end up in jail. He was a sweetheart to her; however, he had a side to him that could freeze hell and send a chill up the devil's spine.

"Please, is there a public parking area? I'll move it," she added, feeling her heart thump harder. She didn't have a clue as to what was going on, and it scared her.

Candace found the public parking area, paid to park, and released a deep breath of air as she made it through the structure and into the hospital to find Diego, which wasn't hard. He was the only person yelling like a crazed man.

"What'chu mean I can't go back there? That's my motherfuckin' brother in there fighting for his life!" he yelled, pointing to the double doors leading to the Intensive Care Unit.

"Calm down, bro. We can't help him locked up," some guy—no, some thug—tried whispering in Diego's ear.

It wasn't much of a whisper, though. His voice was deep and menacing, his pants nearly falling off his ass, and the tattoos that covered his arms made their way up to his neck, bringing out his street edge. He was a hustler. That was evident. His coal-black eyes screamed, *I'm up to no good.* Candace knew he wasn't someone Diego needed to be hanging with. He had changed his life around, and she didn't want nothing or no one reverting him.

"Diego," Candace called out to him, touching his arm, "are you okay, babe?"

He connected eyes with her and let out a stressed breath of air. "No! My best fucking friend is sitting back there shot up, and this broad trying to tell me I can't see him. Fuck that! He needs me. I knew I shouldn't have left him behind."

"Sir, he's in surgery. We're trying to do all we can to stabilize him," the blonde porcelain-complexioned nurse tried to explain.

"Yeah, Nino. Calm down. Brian, gon' be a'ight. He a soldier!" the friend tried assuring him. "But let me holla at you right quick. I need to put you hip to something." He eyed Candace before gesturing for Diego to follow him to the corner.

Candace knew that whatever the guy was about to *put Diego hip to* wasn't a good thing. She had known Brian, Diego's best friend, since she was a teenager. The boys were inseparable until Diego left the streets, but Brian didn't. So, whatever had gotten him shot up was trouble that Diego didn't need.

She watched them as they moved to a quiet corner. Diego stood with his arms crossed firmly over his chest, a hard frown plastered on his face. The more his friend spoke, the deeper his frown became. It terrified Candace. No matter how much Diego had changed, he was still a man of the streets. He still had a code he lived by, and she knew how it went. Retaliation was a must.

Candace paced the floor. The hospital had a steady flow of traffic in the lobby. Some looked cheerful, some genuinely sick, and others nervous. She focused on a beautiful lemon-skinned woman with blonde streaks and a dainty nose. Her eyes were puffy, and the little girl hanging on to her leg seemed to be crying, too. She recognized her from a few gatherings over the years. It was Brian's girlfriend, Tracy.

Tracy was Brian's rider. She held him down and fought for her position as his wifey. Candace even heard about how she had done six months in Huron Valley Correctional Facility for Brian on a drug charge. Now, she was sitting in a hospital lobby, clueless about whether her man would live or die, and Candace didn't want that. She was starting to remember why she had never really considered dating Diego. He was too rough around the edges. She didn't want to be his ride-or-die. She wanted to be his wife, and they were supposed to hold each other up together.

Candace had become lost in her thoughts until Diego's voice snapped her out of it.

"Did you hear me, Candy?"

She shook her head from side to side. "No, I didn't. Is Brian okay? What's going on?"

"I don't know yet, but I need you to take the car and go home. I have a few runs to make. I'll swing by your house after I'm done."

"Diego," his name came out as a whine, "baby, I know you're about to do something crazy. I'm not doing this. I promise I can't end up like her." Candace discreetly pointed at Brian's girlfriend. "Didn't you say he needs you? Let's wait here together," she begged as the idea of losing Diego to the streets weaved an unsettling path through her conscience.

Diego looked off before focusing on Candace again. They both knew what was about to happen. He had worked hard to change his life around, be a better man, and beat the odds stacked against him. And he was ready to throw it all away in a single night. According to Dino, Brian's right-hand man, a local dealer, had grown jealous of Brian's success and tried to take him out. What kind of friend would just let that slide? He couldn't knowingly allow the person who made an attempt on his best friend's life to continue to breathe. Diego wasn't built like that.

"Go home, Candy. I'll be there," he promised, walking away before Candace could respond.

As much as she wanted to obey him and be that true-rider girlfriend waiting for him to return, it wasn't her. She made up her mind. If Diego did anything stupid to jeopardize his life or freedom, she would be done with him. She couldn't do it.

Candace sat at her home's mini bar with ice clinking inside of a watered-down glass of Crown Royal. With her cell phone pressed to her ear, she dialed Diego for the thousandth time. Her heart couldn't take it. This was the part of dating him that would take her out—worrying about where he was and if he was okay.

"Drop me a line."

She was tired of hearing his voicemail. Every time he didn't answer, she felt that queasy feeling in the pit of her stomach.

"Where the hell are you?" She sighed, aggravated with herself for allowing her heart to be taken by him.

Diego scared her shitless. She didn't want to be that chick. Visiting him at a graveyard or talking to him from the other side of prison glass wasn't in the cards for her.

"I'm not about to do this with this nigga."

She tossed her phone down, dragging her hand through her hair.

He got me fucked up. I told his ass that I wasn't the one. I'm not holding no nigga down because he wants to be stupid.

"Fucking stupid!" Candace yelled as her cell phone chimed with a notification.

She snatched it up, hoping it was Diego texting back. Instead, it was a Facebook tag from Jaxon's *supposed* ex-chick. Candace studied the photo, shaking her head. Why did the world see it fit to play with her tonight?

She studied the picture once more. It was a photo of Jaxon and his whore hugged up at the Kem concert. The caption read: *When the love is real, no bitch can come between it. Stick to those whack-ass dance classes.*

"Oh, this little bitch wants to play. I got time tonight," Candace spoke to the screen as if Arianna could hear her.

She began searching through her pictures on her cell. She found the one with them in Miami, the picture of them holding out her hand showcasing her promise ring, the one in the Bahamas, and the picture she snuck of Jaxon playfully kissing her toes. Candace commented them all on the post. Then she typed a nice, long comment: *I gave him back to you, sweetie. Have fun. Enjoy your man before I stop feeling sorry for you and take him just to fuck with you. Don't tag me anymore. I have real-life issues.*

After going off on Jaxon's whore, it only fired Candace up even more. Where was Diego? She was going crazy. Lord, she prayed he didn't do anything crazy. He had her entire soul in his pocket.

Several hours later, Diego was still nowhere to be found. As Candace sat on the phone with Dallas, she felt as if she would lose her mind.

"Candace! Stop tripping. He is going to be fine," Dallas chuckled, apologizing with her eyes to Trenton for taking up so much of their alone time consoling Candace.

Her friend was hysterical, and it took thirty minutes to calm her down.

Candace sighed. "I don't even smoke, but I need a blunt right now. Thank you for talking to me, Dallas. I love you. Let me try calling Diego back."

After Candace ended the call, Dallas tossed her cell phone back onto the table. The kids were with her mother for the night, allowing them to spend much-needed quality time.

For the past few weeks, Dallas and Trenton spent every second they could sneak alone together. Trenton helped to ease the pain that Messiah Sr. caused. He made her days easier and her smile brighter. He was different. She didn't have to question her position with him. He made it known that he wanted her and treated her like a queen.

"So, am I cooking, or are you trying to go out to eat?" Trenton asked, watching how her meaty ass bounced to its own rhythm as she sauntered over to the stereo system and bent over, flicking through the stations.

She was oblivious to the fact that he was dying to be inside her. She wanted him just as much, but they both were treading lightly.

Dallas looked over her shoulder, skeptically taking him in. "I don't know about your cooking. You look like you don't know how to cook," she teased, giggling as his face screwed up.

"What? Don't play with me. My momma used to have me living in the kitchen. If I didn't cook, I didn't eat."

"Really? You never talk about your mother. How is she?"

Trenton shrugged. "She was cool. She had her issues, but who doesn't? I still loved her."

"Loved?"

"My mom passed away a couple of months before I joined

the army. She overdosed on prescription pain meds."

His voice was calm, but Dallas still heard the pain behind his words.

"We were beefing before she passed. I never got a chance to apologize and tell her I loved her," he added.

"Wow. I'm so sorry, Trenton."

"Hey, it is what it is. She made her decision, and death was the consequence. Maybe she's better off than suffering here on Earth with these devils."

"Don't say that."

Trenton looked into Dallas's eyes. They were still innocent and genuine. He appreciated them.

"See, you haven't seen the world like I seen it. There's some sick individuals on this earth." He ran his hand through his freshly lined beard, thinking about his words. "You know, I thought about ending it all before. I actually tried. I realized how much bullshit the army had me doing, and it was almost too much. They really fucked my head up. Then they called me crazy, threw me some pills, and sent me on my way like I didn't mean shit to them."

Trenton's voice cracked as he reminisced on one of the darkest times in his life. Dallas didn't know that when he met her three months later, she had changed him—giving him something to live for.

"I don't know what to say, Trent. You are not fucked up. And I'm so glad the devil did not succeed in whatever he was trying to accomplish with you because I would have never met you." She smiled, wrapping her arms around his neck. "You're the best thing to happen to me in a long time."

Trenton smiled, too. "Nah, I think you mean more to me than I mean to you, but I'm going to get you there. I love the woman you are. Don't change for nobody."

"I won't. You just make sure you stay the person you are."

Dallas's heart melted as she pecked his lips. She didn't know where he had come from, but she was glad he did.

"Good." Trenton tapped her leg. "When was the last time you went dancing?" he suggested, a smile playing on his lips as he watched her try to debate the thought.

"Like a date-date?" she questioned before shrugging. "It's been a very long time. Messiah stopped doing a lot of things my man was supposed to do as my mate. I should have noticed the signs," she added, her voice trailing off.

Trenton saw the pain in her eyes. The last thing he wanted to do was bring back memories of another man. He didn't even want her ex to affect her still.

"Come on. I know this spot on the Eastside that has a mean band and good food."

"I have no rhythm at all," Dallas chuckled.

There was that smile Trent was growing to love.

"So? I can't dance either." He smiled deviously. "All I'm trying to do is cop a few free feels. I'll stand there, and you just move your hips."

"Is that all you want?" Dallas challenged.

"For now." Trenton pecked her forehead and then stood up as if plans were finalized.

He took in her meaty hips and couldn't help the sinful thoughts that flowed through his head. Dallas was beyond gorgeous. He didn't understand how Messiah could give up on a woman like her. But he was thankful he did because Trenton planned to make her his, and he wasn't letting go.

An hour later, they had made it to the bar. The Green Tavern was a hole-in-the-wall spot located right off Jefferson Avenue. The crowd was older, calm, and intimate. Dallas and Trenton hadn't left the dancefloor since they arrived. She was having the time of her life, messing up dance moves and all. Trent smiled at her.

"You really can't dance, baby."

"I told you that already." Dallas chuckled. "Never could. This place is nice, though. I'm having a good time. I almost forgot what it felt like."

"That's a shame." Trent shook his head, guiding her to an empty booth. "We have to change that."

"I like the sound of that," Dallas replied, her sultry voice massaging his ears.

She had chosen a floral sundress that stuck to her curves, perfectly displaying them. Her skin was glowing, and her natural hair was pulled back in a neat ponytail.

"I love that smile. I got to figure out how to keep it on your face," Trent said, flagging the waitress down.

He ordered them drinks, the house steak and lobster meals, and then focused on Dallas again.

"I love this song," Dallas said while nodding her head and snapping her fingers.

It was a melody by Jhene Aiko, pouring her soul out to a man. She closed her eyes, soaking in Trenton's words while pretending to be enthralled by the song. When she reopened them, he was staring into her soul as if trying to figure her out.

"Be honest with me at all times. I mean, just don't hurt me, Trenton. And know that I'm not perfect. I'm working on me. So, be patient."

"That's all it takes?"

Dallas nodded.

"Well, I think I can handle that and so much more," he stated with a wink.

CHAPTER SEVENTEEN

BETTY WRIGHT'S *"Clean Up Woman"* blared through the speakers as Sasha shook the ice cubes in her glass, creating a clinking sound. She stared off at the wall as fresh tears slid down her face. Hunter didn't come home the night before until the wee hours of the morning, and he was gone by daybreak. He hadn't answered a single call or sent her a single text—nothing. She felt as if she was going insane. Her head was throbbing, chest tight.

"Stop crying, Sasha. Hunt loves you. I know there's a good reason," Dallas tried reasoning.

Sasha shook her head as if Dallas could see her. "No. Hunter never does this. It's another woman. You don't have to lie for him. I'm changing the locks on his ass. I'm not taking this, Dallas. It's starting to mess with my mental."

"Hear him out, please. Don't up and make decisions off your emotions."

Sasha rolled her eyes, releasing a husky breath of air. "Don't tell me I'm acting off emotions, Dallas. You know what? Let me call you back."

"I'm not judging you. You don't have to hang up with me. I'm only telling you this because I love you. You're my sister."

"I love you, too, Dallas, but I still have to call you back."

Sasha blew a kiss into the phone and hung up before Dallas could respond. She had her mind made up. Hunter had to go. Her peace of mind meant more than holding on to the relationship.

Sasha looked around at the plush furnishings of their house—the painting, the expensive gadgets, the memories. She wondered where things had gone left. Hunter was everything a woman could have prayed for in a man. She didn't want their fairytale to end, but what was she supposed to do?

Taking a sip of her drink, consisting of an aged wine with a shot of Tequila for a kick, Sasha tried Hunter's phone again. No answer. Now she was pissed. Banging on her cell phone screen, she searched for a locksmith, found the info she needed, and called to schedule a visit.

Sasha would have accepted almost anything from her man. But cheating? That was out of the equation. She had too much respect for herself. She got so worked up that she ended up crying herself to sleep.

Knock! Bam! Boom!

The taps on the door startled her out of her sleep. It started soft, then gradually grew into a loud thunder. Sasha was sure the door would break down soon. She heard the hinges getting weaker.

She forgot she called the locksmith and had the locks changed earlier that evening. When Hunter never showed up after he promised they could spend quality time together, she came to the conclusion that he didn't care anymore.

"Sasha, if you don't open this gotdamn door, there's going to be serious problems," he hissed, his words coming out with an edge of anger and impatience.

Sasha's body pressed against the door as she squeezed her eyes shut tightly.

"I waited for you," she dragged in an agonized whisper. Then she cleared the fog from her throat, standing upright. "I waited up last night and tonight, too. You never came back. You didn't offer an apology; you didn't offer an explanation, either. You just said fuck me, Hunt. Who is she?"

She'd found her voice. She had finally become fed up with stressing over making Hunter happy when it was obvious someone else had his attention.

"You got me looking stupid out here, Sash. Why would you change the locks on the house I paid for? Huh? You're so busy in your own little world that you don't realize you're pushing me away. And don't insult me. If I wanted to deal with another woman and her mood swings, I would have left you, Sasha. I love your crazy ass and would never hurt you like that."

Sasha let out a small laugh as tears began to cascade down her cheek. "You would never hurt me, yet you're avoiding me like the plague. Don't insult my intelligence, Hunter. I'm tired of crying, and I'm tired of wondering what I'm doing wrong. I'm the only one fighting for this relationship."

"Look, I'm not about to have this conversation with you through a door. Let me in the house, Sasha. Please? It's hot, and I'm tired, I just want to take a shower and figure out how you can possibly think I don't love you to death. Is it him? Is he putting poison in your head, making you think these crazy thoughts?"

"He who?" Sasha frowned, swinging the door open and pressing her hands to her hips. "Devaughn? He's a friend, Hunter. Don't try to flip it on me. Who is she? Let me know now because I don't want to marry you and find out down the line that you have secrets. My heart is so fragile. You're breaking me."

The pain was slowly settling in, the weight of it almost crushing her. They had built their relationship on honesty and integrity, but the past few weeks were causing her to develop serious trust issues.

Hunter stepped closer to Sasha, cupping her chin to make her look at him.

"I love you and only you, Sasha. It kills me to see you so down all the time. I just try to give you your space to mourn and pray that whatever we're going through will pass. I give you access to my emails, social media, phone, everything because I want you to know what I'm doing at all times. I want you to be assured that I love you, and I'm not out here doing nothing stupid to lose you, baby."

"But staying away from me isn't the answer, Hunt. Talk to me. Let's work it out together. Let's pray or something. Devaughn asked us to church. Let's go to church this Sunday. We need a little God in our relationship."

Hunter rubbed his hands through his waved hair. He wanted to decline her offer, but he agreed to appease Sasha. He was willing to do whatever he had to do to get their relationship on track.

"You know church ain't me, Sasha, but I'll try it for you. Let me back in. Tell me what I have to do to make you smile again. Okay?"

"Okay." Sasha nodded as Hunter leaned in and pecked her lips.

"Now, what's up on that Netflix and chilling? You changed the locks on me. Guess I need to do some making up because my baby was serious." He chuckled. "But, for the record, one of the twins had to be rushed to the hospital last night. He swallowed some bleach, and you know Alicia's crazy ass don't got a car, and her sorry-ass baby's father is a deadbeat."

Sasha's heart sank. She felt awful. Here she was thinking Hunter was out doing wrong, and they had a family emergency.

"Goodness. Why didn't you call me, Hunter? Is he okay?"

Hunt shrugged. "Yeah, he's fine. CPS was up at the hospital questioning her. They're talking about opening a case."

"Make sure you let her know that we have her back. If she needs a break, I'm always here for the twins. You know I love them like they're my family."

"That's why I appreciate you." He pecked her lips again.

"Trenton's crazy ass is with her now. He quit the security job already."

Hunter frowned, almost as if mentioning Trenton's name left a bad taste in his mouth.

Sasha eyed him skeptically. "What is it with you two? One minute, everything is good. The next, y'all seem like you hate each other."

"He's jealous of me. Always has been. Plus, that army stuff messed his head up. You know he gets a crazy check, right? He got full disability because he's nuts." Hunter shook his head.

"Well, why would you allow me to hook my best friend up with him? She has kids, Hunter."

"She's okay for now. You need to tell her to leave that crazy nigga alone, though," he warned, loosening his tie and unbuttoning the top three buttons of his shirt. "Enough about them. Pop some popcorn, and I'll start looking for a movie. Then we can make our own movie," he shot deviously, causing Sasha's kitty to purr. Sex with her man sounded so promising.

Sasha eyed Hunt as he trudged to the backroom. She sighed before closing the front door and heading to the kitchen to pop the popcorn.

Her mind was racing. Part of her wondered if the relationship with Devaughn was deeper than she let on, and if so, was it that obvious? He was kind of cute and easy to talk to. They had even found themselves conversing over the phone a few times. *No.* Sasha shook her head. They were strictly friends, nothing more.

Sasha smiled, stuffing the bag of popcorn in the microwave and setting it to three minutes. The aroma of the popcorn quickly began to fill the room. She had smelled it a thousand times, but today, it was too overbearing. Dry-heaving, she hastily made her way to the bathroom and curled over the porcelain toilet. She felt the swish in her insides, making it just in time to release her lunch and afternoon snack.

"Are you okay?" Hunter leaned into the bathroom with a questioning glare.

"No. That popcorn just made me sick. The smell of it."

Pregnancy crossed her mind. What if it finally happened? What if God had answered her prayers? A smile tipped the corners of her lips.

"Babe! I think we did it. God, please let me be pregnant," she squealed, hopping up and turning on the water to rinse her mouth out.

Hunter didn't seem to share the same enthusiasm. In fact, his glare seemed cold.

"Hmph," was all he offered.

"Hmph?" Sasha mimicked him, cocking her head to the side. "Did you not just hear me? We may be pregnant, and all you can say is hmph?"

"I mean, I don't know what else to say, Sash. I don't want to get my hopes up until we know for sure, and the thought bothers me. I don't want you to go through another one of your episodes if you're not."

"An *episode*? Wow, Hunter. You know what? I'm going to go lay down because I suddenly don't feel well. Thank you for the quality time. It was much needed," she said sarcastically.

He had ruined the night. She didn't want to spend it with him, pretending they were okay. Something was off with their relationship, and she prayed it could be fixed before they ruined each other.

Hunter allowed Sasha to leave. He didn't try to stop her and whisper sweet nothings in her ear like he normally would. That alarmed her.

CHAPTER EIGHTEEN

DALLAS COULDN'T BELIEVE she allowed him to talk her into it. She hadn't been skating in years, and with the way Messiah Jr. had been acting, she wasn't sure if he deserved to have fun. However, Trenton insisted they needed time to bond and that he would eventually get Messiah to come around. She hoped so.

Detroit Roller Wheels was located right in the middle of the hood. It was a bright blue building and the spot for teens on a Saturday night. The place was packed, and Migos' "MotorSport" was blaring through the speakers as half the crowd moved around the rink doing their fancy dances on skates, the other half trying not to fall while still looking cool.

"Be careful, Messiah," Dallas called out as he zoomed past them on the rink, nearly knocking over the person ahead of him.

He and Meghan were racing. She was losing terribly. Trenton let out a chuckle as he held Dallas's hand.

"Let that boy be. You're so protective over him. He'll be fine."

"It's too many people in here, and he's going too fast," Dallas fussed, nearly losing her balance, only for Trenton to hold her up. "And stop laughing at me," she pouted, tapping his arm as he burst into laughter.

"You're too old not to know how to skate. Come on. Let me buy you a slice of pizza and a pickle."

Trenton continued to laugh as Dallas tried her best not to fall. She was a clumsy mess, sliding all over the place.

"I don't want pizza or a pickle. I want to take these things off and watch the kids have fun like normal adults. I think I allowed enough people to get their laughs at my expense for tonight."

Trenton's brow raised. "I didn't let you fall one time, did I? Ain't nobody laughing at you. They're all wondering how you got so fine." He winked.

Dallas couldn't deny his charm. Staring at him always caused her to blush. She wondered where he'd come from. He was perfect...almost too perfect. She was starting to worry that Sasha claiming he was crazy had some truth to it. Like, there had to be something wrong with him.

They played the Pac-Man machine and a shooting game. By the time they sat down, Messiah and Meghan were racing to the table.

"Ma, can I have five dollars to get something from the counter?" Messiah Jr. giggled, blocking Meghan from sitting in the booth next to Dallas.

Trenton smiled at him, pulling out a twenty-dollar bill. "Here, little man. Go get you and your sister something." He held the bill out for Messiah to take it.

As if Trenton wasn't talking to him, Messiah's eyes stayed trained on Dallas.

"Ma, can we get some money, please?" he impatiently prodded.

The corners of Dallas's mouth tugged downward. She was almost in disbelief that her baby boy would be so disrespectful. They joked around, but she raised him with manners.

"Little boy, you're going to make me hurt you. Didn't you hear him talking to you?"

"I don't want his money. I'm okay. I'll eat when I get home."

Messiah Jr. pushed off the table to skate away, but Dallas grabbed his arm, stopping him.

"Messiah Jr., if you don't check yourself and apologize to this man, there's going to be some serious problems," Dallas growled through gritted teeth.

"Chill," Trenton warned, softly touching her arm to release

Messiah. "Don't embarrass him in public. If he doesn't want my money, it's cool. I can respect it," he added calmly, as strong eyes lifted and set on Messiah Jr.

He wasn't a bad kid. Trenton could tell it. He was hurting. His life was normal, and then it wasn't. Trenton got that. He was Messiah Jr. at one point in his life, but ten times worse. It took him going to the army and becoming a man to understand how the world worked.

"But what we're not going to do is disrespect each other, Messiah. I'm not going to hurt you or your mother. I'm not here to take your father's place, either."

"I don't have to talk to you. My daddy said I don't have to. I'm ready to go home, Momma. I'm just ready to go."

Messiah Jr. pouted as he skated to the other side of the cafeteria and plopped down on a bench. Dallas gave Trenton a sympathetic glance.

"I'm sorry, Trenton. We can just go. I think we need to give him a little more time to get over things. Otherwise, I will end up in jail for murdering a ten-year-old." She turned to Meghan. "Go turn your skates in so we can go," she ordered, watching the pout form on her baby's face.

Why couldn't Messiah Jr. be easy-going like her? Meghan stayed in a child's place and learned to just *go with the flow*.

The next day…

"Are you sure you know what you're doing?" Dallas's mother asked, letting out a labored sigh as her eyes traveled to her grandchildren and back to her only baby.

Dallas was her heart. Maria didn't play about her baby, and that's why she despised Messiah Sr.'s guts. He robbed Dallas of her innocence, tricked her with his lies to use and abuse her, and then when he got tired of milking the cow, he threw her to the side like a dilapidated ragdoll.

Dallas trusted too easily and loved too hard. Maria hated it because she was the one left picking up the pieces of her daughter's shattered heart and helping her to move on. No mother wanted to see their child hurting.

Dallas's nose crinkled as she blankly stared at her mother. "Sure about what, Mom? Trenton? We're just friends."

"Friends? Hmph! Seems like more than that to me. All I'm saying is that it's a little too soon to jump out of one relationship and right into another. You were with Messiah since you were a little girl. Be free. Learn how to make Dallas happy. I'm not saying be a hoe, but enjoy life before you settle back into a relationship."

"Ma, I'm fine." Dallas rolled her eyes.

Everyone seemed to be against Trenton, and it was becoming frustrating. She was tired of living for someone else's happiness. Trenton made her feel good, and she wished the universe would allow her to be happy for once.

Maria fastened her hand on her hips. She was fifty-six years young and didn't look a day over forty. She had an old soul, went to church every Sunday, and smiled even when the world didn't see it fit to do so. Her motto was, *"If you're breathing, you're blessed. So, waking up to life is a reason to smile."*

"Well, I pray that you do. And, for the record, my grandson is going through his own issues. You may not think the breakup is a big deal, but in his head, his whole world is destroyed. Give him time to cope, too. Go have your fun, but don't force it on the kids."

"Okay, Ma. I have to go. Thanks for keeping the kids for me. You can drop Meghan off at daycare tomorrow, and I'll pick her up."

"No, I got them. Well, at least until school starts up on the eighth. I was planning to take them to Georgia with me to visit their folks. Enjoy yourself, Dallas. I want to give you a break to discover you. Okay?"

Dallas couldn't help the smile of relief that formed on her face. She hugged her mother and all but ran out of her house. She had a lunch date planned with the ladies, and she seriously needed her girls' time to sip a few drinks and talk. Then she planned to end the night in Trenton's arms. They both agreed to take it slow with involving the kids. Instead, they would spend time together when Dallas was kid-free, and now she had nearly two weeks.

On the way to Beans and Cornbread, Dallas decided to call Messiah. They seriously needed to talk. She didn't appreciate him poisoning their son's head with foolishness. He was inconsiderate, immature, and selfish. He really needed to grow up.

"What's up, Dallas?" Messiah answered in his cheerful tone. "You must have felt me thinking about you," he chuckled, and Dallas rolled her eyes.

"Shouldn't you be thinking about your fiancée?" Dallas scoffed. "Furthermore, why would you tell your son that it's okay to disrespect Trenton? What is your problem?"

"Because he doesn't have to like that man if he doesn't want to. Just because I have Tatiana doesn't mean you have to force him on our kids. I understand you're bitter about me and Tati's situation, but we don't have to play tit for tat. Shit, if you had just given me a little time, I would have come back home."

Bitter? Tit for tat? He is so full of himself. Dallas frowned.

"How could you possibly think I would want you to come back? Have you bumped your big-ass head?"

Messiah let out a small laugh. "You're not fooling nobody. You still love me, Dallas. I know you do, and I still love you. I think I made a mistake," he said, continuing to laugh, "I ain't marrying her."

"Are you drunk? Your wedding is in a few weeks." Dallas's brows furrowed.

"Yep, drunk off missing yo' loving. Can I come over tonight and poke your stomach meat?"

Dallas tried her best not to giggle. "Bye, Messiah."

"Don't hang up. I'm tired of hearing 'Bye, Messiah.' You don't miss me?"

Dallas sighed. "I miss what used to be. I could never miss what we've become. I'm genuinely happy. Let me be happy. As much as I hated to see you and her happy, I allowed you to be until she showed up at my house."

"Because you were too scared to stand up for what you wanted. You didn't fight for me, Dallas. I'm about to get my family back. Watch."

"If you say so. I have to go, Messiah. And for the record, my mother is taking the kids to Georgia until the seventh. So, you don't have to worry about them or an excuse to drop by my house. I mean it. We are done, Messiah."

He started to say something, but Dallas pressed *end* on their conversation. There wasn't anything else to talk about, although the thought of Messiah begging and groveling to get her back caused her to smile.

Beans and Cornbread was an upbeat soul food restaurant in Southfield, Michigan. It had a grown and sexy feel, music, and a bar area. Sasha had picked it for their lunch date, saying she was craving the catfish and macaroni and cheese.

When Dallas made it inside, Candace and Sasha were already seated at the back of the restaurant.

"Y'all started without me." Dallas frowned.

"Girl, please. You always take forever. I needed a drink, and Ms. Piggy here was acting like she was starving. She's getting a little thick. She may be with child." Candace rolled her eyes.

"I'm praying I am," Sasha confirmed as Dallas took a seat next to her. "I haven't been feeling good lately, but I'm scared to take a test. I know it's going to kill me if I'm not. Not to mention, Hunt has been a complete asshole ever since the other day. It's almost as if he has an attitude that I might be pregnant when we've been fighting for this for two years." She sighed, frustrated.

"Attitude, how?" Dallas questioned.

"Like, he won't touch me and acts like I'm spitting on him whenever I bring up pregnancy. Then, the other day, he accused me of sleeping with Devaughn. It took everything in me not to slap Hunt. He has lost his mind, and he'd better find it before there be some problems," Sasha spat, taking a sip from her strawberry lemonade. She needed a strong shot of Hennessey, but the lemonade would do.

"Maybe he's scared, Sash. Give Hunt a little time. Now, let's talk about your brother. I'm done with him. I know he went out there and did something stupid the other day. I know he did. I can't do it." Candace shook her head from side to side.

"How would you know if you don't talk to him? I knew this was going to happen—y'all was going to fall out and worry me to death about it. Diego almost lost his best friend, and you're being childish. Support my brother; be there for him. You know he loves you."

"Love?" Candace crinkled her nose.

"Stop playing. Diego has been in love with your funny-looking ass since the beginning of time. You make him happy. And I know he makes you happy. Talk to that negro before I have to slap him in the head."

Candace giggled. "I wasn't going to be able to stay away from him too much longer anyway. I miss him. I just wanted him to sweat. He needs to know I will not put up with him falling back into his old ways."

"As you shouldn't," Sasha agreed, focusing on Dallas. "And why are you sitting over here all quiet? What's been going on with you and Trenton?"

Dallas shrugged. "Nothing. We're happy. I'm finally happy. Messiah Jr. is still adjusting, and asshole decided to want to come back home now that I've moved on."

"Asshole who? I know Messiah's tired ass doesn't think he has a chance," Sasha shrieked.

"Girl, yes. He says he's not marrying that girl and misses his family. She's probably giving him hell since she caught him at my house. I don't understand how he can play with my heart and think it's cool. Shit, I don't understand how I lasted fifteen years with him. I look at him and almost throw up in my mouth now."

Candace giggled. "Because Trenton introduced you to what it's like to be with a real man. Messiah's a little boy in a grown man's body. Messiah realizes what he's missing, and it's going to kill him to see you move on. Death to the grown little boys and shout out to the real men," Candace chanted, taking a sip from her drink.

"Yes, indeed. If I had a drink, I would toast to that. So, what's going on with Jaxon?" Dallas questioned as the waiter returned to take their orders.

Sasha ordered the catfish dinner with macaroni and cheese and yams, Dallas ordered the rib tip dinner and fries, while Candace ordered the turkey and dressing dinner with red beans and rice. After the waiter left, they picked up their conversation where it ended.

"Jaxon is a different kind of headache. He's been calling and threatening me. I feel bad about the way things played out and understand that he's hurt, but I'm starting to get worried. I haven't said anything to Diego because his crazy ass will end up locked up over nothing, but it's getting creepy." Candace sighed.

"Threatening you how, Candy? You just said that like women don't go missing every day over jealous exes. Have you watched *Snapped*? You need to take it a little more seriously," Dallas fussed.

"Girl, Jaxon isn't stupid. He just keeps saying he invested too much money in me, and he's not going to allow me to play him. I—"

"Chile, he can't be that gotdamn petty," Sasha cut her off. "I was actually rooting for him. Invested too much money? He did what he was supposed to do as your man. He got all the free coochie he wanted, right? You cooked for him and listened to him complain about his day. Tell him to pay you for your time and the miles he ran up on your kitty." Sasha frowned.

Both Candace and Dallas giggled.

"Exactly. I'm not worried about Jaxon. He needs to worry about Arianna. I heard he lives with the heffa. After the fight with Diego, the little girl tagged me in some Facebook mess. I ignored her, but I did scroll through her page. There were several pictures of them together…recent pictures."

Sasha cocked her head to the side in disbelief. "The same girl you got into it with that he swore was an ex? And you want to have my brother blowing up my phone over pettiness? At least Diego would never intentionally hurt you. He's a real one. If he cares, he's going to hold you down, and he isn't afraid to show it."

"I know, Sash. I told you. The other day bothered me. You didn't see the pain on Brian's girlfriend's face. I don't want to be her. I don't want to have to worry if my man will come home at night because he's in the streets making stupid decisions," Candace complained.

"He doesn't have to make stupid decisions for something to happen to him. He's a black man in America, and that's reason enough. You can lose him coming home from the gas station. He could be doing everything right, and something could still happen to him. You better pray over him every day that he leaves the house and love on your man before someone else does." Sasha frowned.

Candace smiled. "Listen to you, Iyanla Vanzant. I hear you preaching, girl," she teased. "I'm going to make things right with your big-head brother."

"I know you are. Diego wasn't going to have it any other way. Now, enough about him. I want to have a little get-together at They Say. Nothing major. Hunt and I have been so stressed. We need to get out and surround ourselves with love." Sasha sighed.

"Are you sure about that? You know Trenton's crazy ass will be by my side, and the last time they were in the same room, it didn't go well," Dallas commented.

Sasha waved her off. "He'll be fine. I think Hunt was just having a moment. And about the crazy thing. If he makes you happy, so long as he continues to do that, I'm going to mind my business."

"I agree." Dallas nodded as the waiter came back with their food.

They ate, laughed a little, and enjoyed the dynamics of their sisterhood. Blood couldn't make them closer.

CHAPTER NINETEEN

A SHOCK OF PLEASURE stole what breath remained in Candace's lungs as Diego crashed into her love canal, finding his way to her spot. His stroke was rough yet gentle at the same time. Candace felt as if the intensity of their lovemaking would drive her insane.

"Don't you ever keep this away from me." Diego's deep rasp caused the hairs on Candace's neck to stand at attention. "This is me. All me. You understand that, Candy?" he growled, pushing deeper inside her, filling her to capacity, forcing her to take all of him.

It hurt so good. Candace could hear, see, smell, feel, and taste him within her. He'd awakened all of her senses.

"Answer me, Candy. Tell me you understand that this shit's forever," Diego urged, lifting her body in the air and sandwiching her between the wall and his hard chest.

Her legs wrapped around his waist, and her arms draped his neck. Sweat glazed both of their bodies as an electric current heated them up.

"Yesss," she croaked in an inaudible moan.

He had taken sole ownership of her mind, body, and soul.

"You better act like you know what's up then," he growled, taking her to new heights.

They fucked against the wall as he devoured her like it would be his last meal. Moving to the bed, they ended their session with him snatching the soul out of her body and giving her his own. It felt so good that tears escaped her lids and traveled down her cheeks.

Candace's eyes felt heavy. She allowed them to slide closed as Diego grabbed her body and snuggled next to her. She felt small and vulnerable in his arms. The intensity of their kinetic energy was almost frightening.

"You scare me, Diego," Candace admitted out loud.

She turned to face him. She had to look him in the eyes.

He smiled, pecking her forehead. "Wha'chu scared of, Candy? I should be the least of your fears. When you think of me, you should automatically know you're good because you got me by your side."

"I know, but it's the whole Brian thing. I watched his girlfriend nearly break down, shaken with fear that she was going to lose her man. I don't want that. I want a normal, secure life. I want to be confident that we're working toward a solid future, building an empire we can pass down to our kids. I want to know that you put your family first in everything you do. We can't benefit with you behind bars or dead."

Diego let out a sigh as he swiped the sticky sweat from his forehead. "Honestly, I *was* about to do something stupid. I even went to the crib and grabbed my nine. But I'm better than that, Candy. I realized that I walked away from that bullshit for a reason. That battle ain't mine no more. I want more. I'm thirty-four years old. What I look like still being out here gangbanging in the streets?"

"Right. And just so you know, it was hell ignoring you, but I will walk away. Because—"

"You ain't going nowhere," Diego said, cutting her off. He pressed his lips against her mouth, kissing her deep and hard. "I'm addicted to you already. You can't just take a fiend away from his fix."

Candace smiled. "Well, don't make me send you to rehab."

Candace awakened to an empty bed the next morning, and a pout immediately formed on her lips. Her eyes squinted as she searched for Diego. The faint hint of light from the sun brightened up the room just a bit, and the birds sitting on the tree outside of her window sang a song that she didn't understand. She wasn't a morning person, but she was still disappointed that Diego didn't wake her up before he left.

Reaching over, Candace grabbed her cell phone from the nightstand and began scanning through it. She had two missed calls from Sasha, a missed call from a private number, and several texts from Jaxon. She rolled her eyes, tossed her cell phone next to her, and peeled herself from the bed to handle her morning hygiene.

She didn't have any classes scheduled for the day. However, she did plan to do a little window shopping at Art Van and Pier 1 for decorations for the studio. Her mouth tipped into a lazy grin at the thought of her grand opening. It was less than two months away, and for once in her life, she was in a place where she was truly at peace.

Candace had done heavy social media marketing, and Diego had gotten her a slot on the radio with DJBJ and a scheduled news interview with FOX 2. It meant everything that he put his life on hold to bring her dreams to fruition. He invested in her with more than words and encouraged her success every day. He confidently stepped up to be everything she needed, and sometimes she found herself questioning if he was too good to be true. However, deep down in her heart, she knew he was the keeper of her soul, and she needed to get used to the love of a real man.

As if on cue, her cell phone chimed as she made it back into the bedroom. Her face lit up at the sight of Diego's phone number dancing across the screen, and his voice massaged her ears as soon as she said hello.

"I just knew you wasn't gon' be up yet. I was about to leave you a voicemail and tell you how much I missed hearing you snore already. Did you wipe that crust from your lips?" he teased, causing Candace to roll her eyes playfully.

"Whatever. I do not snore, and there's no crusties on my lips, thank you very much. Why did you leave without saying anything?"

"You miss me?"

"I didn't ask you that," Candace told him, tightening the towel around her waist.

"Well, I asked you. I'm at the studio. The electrician called me early as hell to meet him here."

"I always miss you," Candace admitted. "But I guess I'll make a few runs and get my day started. I want Chili's for dinner. Is it a date?"

"You can have whatever you want. Let me know, and it's yours, baby?"

Candace blushed. Her cheeks turned a rosy red as her smile brightened. "With your smooth, Rico Suave ass. Don't be making me feel all fuzzy inside like you love me or something."

"It's my job to make you feel good. If you don't know I love you by now, I need to step up my game. I shouldn't have to say it for you to feel it."

Candace grew quiet for a second. She did feel his love. She knew he cared, but for him to say he loved her felt…*different*. She wondered if they were moving too fast. They'd known each other practically all their lives, but the whole couple thing was new to her. It scared her even more that she loved him, too. Like, she saw a whole future with him—kids, marriage, and a house on the hills.

"I guess I love you, too. I have to go. I'll ca—"

"No. Don't hang up this phone, Candy. Say that shit again," Diego drawled, his voice sending vibrations deep into the core of her body.

"Say what?" Candace feigned ignorance.

"Don't play with me."

Candace let out a sigh. "I said I love you, too, Diego Riley. Happy?"

"Nope. You got to say that shit with a little emotion. Make me feel all warm and fuzzy inside," he teased, causing Candace to chuckle at the cadence of his voice.

"You're an asshole, but I do love you. I love the way you make me feel. I love you because I feel like I can accomplish anything as long as I'm standing next to you. I love you because I trust your lead and know you got my best interest at heart. I just pray you don't awaken all these feelings and set me up for failure," Candace admitted.

"I'm not here to play with you, Candy. I'm not a little ass boy, and I ain't into saying nothing that I don't mean. I need communication. I want you to always express how you feel like you just did. Thank you for trusting me with your heart, though. I'm gon' guard that ma'fucka with my life."

"You better." Candace smiled. She couldn't erase the grin if she tried. "Now, hurry up over there so you can get back here to me."

"I got you, babe. I'll see you in a minute." Diego ended the call.

Before Candace could place her phone down, it vibrated again with an incoming text from Jaxon. She already knew what it would say, along with the other two he had sent. It would read somewhere along the lines of, *You're a no-good slut, and I should beat your ass for playing with me.* Or, *I bought you. I'm not letting you just walk away.*

Candace rolled her eyes, deciding to humor herself with his messages. As expected, the first two read exactly how she figured they would. However, the last message caused her to stare at the phone screen for a few seconds longer.

I know you didn't think I was going to allow you to just ride off into the sunset with him. You need to meet up with me ASAP. I got something you need to see.

"Something is wrong with this boy."

Candace shook her head as she erased all of his messages. As far as she was concerned, they didn't have anything left to say to one another. He was a lying, cheating, disrespectful devil with a halo spinning around his head. If Jaxon didn't leave her alone, she was going to tell Diego. She didn't want to go that route, but she knew her man would definitely handle things.

CHAPTER TWENTY

"GOOD MORNING TO you, too," Sasha whispered under her breath as Hunter walked past her and out the front door.

He had been distant for the past week, and she was sick of it. It was just after nine o'clock in the morning, and she was wide awake with nothing to do.

Devaughn called and told her that he was taking the day off. So, her date with Zion was canceled, which meant her babysitting gig was officially over. School started the following Monday, and it sort of saddened Sasha.

She couldn't stand to sit in the house all day and stare at the walls, so she decided to treat herself to breakfast and catch the matinee showing of *Beauty and the Beast*. She was supposed to watch it with Zion. The thought of inviting Devaughn and Zion to see the movie crossed her mind, but she quickly dismissed it. Hunter would have a complete heart attack if he found out.

"What am I doing?" Sasha sighed, trying to shake the inappropriate thoughts of Devaughn that were flowing through her head.

She knew he was attracted to her, and the reality was she was attracted to him, too. Sasha had grown accustomed to their daily interactions. She almost felt as if she needed the attention he gave her. Lord knows Hunter didn't bother giving her any these days.

Biting down on her bottom lip, she decided to throw caution out the window and call him. With each ring, her heart beat a little faster. Sasha honestly didn't know what she was doing. She just knew she needed his companionship.

"Hey, Sash. Is everything okay?" Devaughn answered, sounding as if he was juggling several tasks. "One second... Go get Zion, please," he muttered, then returned to the phone. "My bad. Is everything okay?"

Sasha's brows furrowed. "You sound busy. I didn't want anything. I was just about to go to the movies and was trying to see if you and Zion wanted to tag along."

Devaughn paused, which made Sasha nervous.

"I mean, it was just a suggestion. I had promised Zion we were going today. I know you have plans and don't want to deal with me, and—"

"Sasha!" Devaughn chuckled, stopping her from rambling. "I would have loved to steal a little of your time. I'm never too busy for you. We were just heading out in a few. I'll take a raincheck for the movie date, though."

Date? Sasha thought to herself. The way he said it sounded so intimate.

"Playdate with Zion," he corrected himself. "Are you still stopping by church Sunday? Maybe we can go afterward."

Sasha smiled. "Yes, Hunt and I are coming. It's fine. I don't know what I was thinking. I got so used to Zion being here I started missing her. I won't bug you guys. Have fun and tell Zion she owes me a movie date."

"You could never bug me, Sash. As I've told you a thousand times already, I'm here whenever you need me. You have been a blessing for Zion and me."

There was another awkward pause before Sasha decided to end the conversation. The feelings flowing through the phone were disrespectful. He was her neighbor...her fine, charming, and totally available neighbor.

After realizing she was stuck facing the day alone, Sasha

decided to throw on her clothes and head out. It was going on ten o'clock, and the show started at noon. It was perfect timing to grab breakfast and snacks.

Thirty minutes later, Sasha was dressed casually in a pair of PINK leggings, a tee, and Nike running shoes. She checked the bun neatly sitting atop her head and smudged on a coat of lip gloss. Then she grabbed her purse and headed out. She didn't feel like getting all made up to hide in the darkness of a movie theater.

"Sashyyyyy," a tiny voice shouted from the front porch steps. It was her nickname that Zion only used.

She smiled as the toddler ran to her and wrapped her little arms around her legs.

"Hey, Zion," she cooed, scooping her up. A crease of confusion wrinkled Sasha's forehead as she stared at a beautiful Latina woman standing a few feet away, staring cumbersomely at them.

"Hey," the lady said, offering a half-wave. "Come on, Zi. We're about to go get ice cream."

Zion shook her head. "No. I stay with her," she demanded, pointing at Sasha's chest.

The lady poked her pink lips out and plastered a puppy dog pout on her face.

"Mommy hasn't seen you in months. Don't you want to come with me?" she whined.

She was gorgeous, and Sasha hated it. She had a petite, tight frame with just enough curves to make you notice them. Her hair was set in curls that fell to the middle of her back, and her light brown eyes went well against her vanilla skin.

So this is Zion's mother, Sasha thought to herself as Devaughn's shadow appeared.

He offered her an uneasy glance. Sasha could tell he was uncomfortable. For some reason, she imagined the woman ashy, fat, or maybe strung out on drugs—not perfect. Then again,

Devaughn was almost perfect, so she shouldn't have expected anything less.

"Hey, Sash. This is Zion's mother, Christina. Chris, this is my friend Sasha. She's been holding Zion down for us."

For us? Sasha had to stop herself from rolling her eyes. However, Ms. Perfect beamed with the widest smile. Sasha hated that, too.

"Omg, thanks so much for all that you do, chica. Zion talks my ears off about you. Devaughn appreciates you, too. Ain't that right, babe?"

Babe? Why the hell was Sasha so bothered? For the life of her, she couldn't understand why. She was in a relationship, and Devaughn didn't belong to her. As tempting as it was to embarrass herself and stake her claim on her neighbor, she decided to bow out of the awkward moment gracefully.

"It was no problem at all. Zion is a good kid, and Devaughn is amazing, as well. You picked an amazing family," she offered, then placed Zion back onto her feet. "I guess I need to get going. See you later, munchkin." She smiled at Zion.

"I go with you!" Zion whined.

"No, baby. You have to stay with Mommy. She misses you, okay?" Sasha tried explaining, but Zion wasn't having it.

She fell out, crying to go with Sasha. Her bond with another woman obviously didn't sit well with Christina because she scooped Zion up and marched off with an attitude.

"We'll be in the car, Vaughn. Hurry, I'm hungry," Christina fussed without saying goodbye to Sasha.

Devaughn watched his child's mother as she walked off. He couldn't necessarily say he felt butterflies by her presence or that the sight of her made his heart race like it did a few years back when they were foolishly in love. In fact, he didn't feel a thing when he looked at her. He even wondered if he was making the right decision by allowing her back into Zion's life.

"So, that's Zion's mother…your girlfriend?" Sasha asked, snapping him from his thoughts.

Devaughn shrugged. "Her mother? Yes. Girlfriend? Hell no. Christina and I could never be together again."

"Hmph," Sasha snorted, looking off at the ants crawling on the concrete. "Well, I need to get going."

She turned to leave, but Devaughn grabbed her arm.

"Sasha, wait. She missed Zion, and I couldn't keep her from her daughter. She's only here for a week."

He felt the need to explain. Their chemistry was crazy. He sensed her disappointment, even if she didn't want to express it. In a way, he felt like he was cheating on her, even though she wasn't his woman.

A smile creased Sasha's lips. It wasn't a genuine smile but a *"I-don't-know-what-else-to-say-and-this-is-really-awkward"* smile.

"It's fine, Devaughn. You don't owe me any explanations. That's your business."

"Yet, I feel like I do for some reason, and it's driving me crazy." He took in Sasha's sparkling brown eyes, released a sigh of frustration, then looked off. "I'd better get going. See you Sunday, right?"

Sasha nodded. "Right," she confirmed before turning to make her way to her car.

She felt Devaughn staring; she even felt the connection between them. But she forced herself to keep walking before forbidden boundaries were crossed.

Needless to say, Sasha's day was ruined. Breakfast, a movie, and even a little shopping couldn't take her mind off Devaughn. Her feelings were hurt, but they had no good reason to be. She needed to shake her feelings.

"Take it," Hunter's voice rumbled as he let out a deeply aggravated sigh.

It was past ten o'clock. He'd been gone all day; no phone call, no text, nothing.

Sasha's eyes landed on the white box with the pregnancy test inside, then back up at Hunter. Her full lips thinned in anger. She didn't know if she wanted to curse him out or cry.

"I need you to ease my mind, Sash. This shit has been fucking with my head." Hunter licked his lips, then nodded his head toward the test. "Take it. Put me out of my misery."

Sasha's heart began to thump faster. She didn't know why taking a stupid test terrified her so much. All the signs were there. She was more tired than usual, had picked up a seafood craving, and let's not forget the popcorn smell thing. She had to be pregnant. She had psyched her mind to believe she was, and it would crush her to find out she wasn't.

Sasha exhaled a nervous breath of air. "I'm scared."

"Either way it goes, we're going to get through this together, Sash. But, for my sanity, I need to know if you're pregnant."

Sasha picked up the package and took a deep breath. Hunter gave her a reassuring glare, and she forced herself to face the moment of truth. Her hands shook as she peed on that little stick. Her nerves were so shot that as soon as she placed the test on the bathroom counter, she stormed out to the kitchen for a glass of juice. She wanted wine, but juice would have to do.

"So, what's the word?" Hunter's deep rasp tickled her eardrums as he walked up behind her and wrapped his arms around her waist.

Sasha shrugged. "I don't know. I didn't wait to see."

Hunter kissed her cheek before releasing her. "I'll check," he told her.

She never turned around to watch him walk away, and when he returned, her eyes squeezed together tightly. Nervous energy flowed through her entire being.

"Look at me, Sash." Hunter sighed, gripping her arm to turn her to face him. "Seriously, look up."

He nudged her chin. When their eyes connected, he gave her a reassuring smile.

"You know everything happens for a reason, babe. I don't know our reason, but we got this. We can go down to the agency Tuesday and look into adoption, and—"

"I'm not pregnant?" Sasha cut him off, her voice a low whisper.

She could feel the hurricane of emotions stirring inside her— hurt, disappointment, anger, pain. She was starting to feel that God loved seeing her suffer.

"Stop it. Don't cry, Sash. He's testing our faith. We're going to church Sunday, right? We're going to pray our way through this," Hunter told her, taking her in and holding her close.

He wasn't the religious type, but if praying would help them weather the storm, he was down.

He felt her caving. Her body shrank and began to shake violently as she wept. This was what he was hoping to avoid. He couldn't go through another one of her phases of depression. He was scared it may completely push them apart.

CHAPTER TWENTY-ONE

"GOOD MORNING, BEAUTIFUL." Trenton smiled as Dallas began to stir. "You were taking too long to wake up, so I had to wake you up."

Trenton's deep rasp sent a chill up Dallas's spine. She was in heaven—no kids, no drama, and waking up to *him* every morning. Three days in a row, Dallas had awakened to his soft kisses all over her face. She loved that he didn't pressure her to be physically intimate with him, but being in his presence was satisfying all the same.

A smile tipped the corners of her lips as she peeled her eyes open and caught sight of the most beautiful creature she had seen in a long time. Trenton was simply gorgeous. Sitting next to her, his bare chest was exposed, showcasing the single tattoo right above his heart. It was a picture of a burning American flag. She studied it, wondering what it meant to him. She eventually gave way to her curiosity and asked.

"You served fifteen years for this country. What made you get that tattoo?"

Trenton's hand ran across his chest as his eyes traveled to the tattoo and then back to Dallas.

"Fuck this country," he shot calmly. "I'm trying to figure out if my stroke game was proper. With the way you were calling out my name, my little man had to be doing me some justice in that dream."

He let out a small laugh as he watched Dallas's cheeks stain red. It took everything in him not to push her panties to the side and make her dreams a reality. That's why he chose to wake her up instead.

Dallas covered her eyes in embarrassment. She did have a dream about him, and the sex was amazing. She would never let him know that, though.

"Oh my God. I did not scream your name."

"Yes, you did. I bet your next-door neighbors know my name now. It was sexy, though. You lucky I know you're not ready for what I have to give. I'm not trying to mess your little head up," he teased, leaning over and pecking her lips.

"You are so cocky, and I'm embarrassed."

"Embarrassed for what? I told you that shit was sexy. I'm just trying to figure out what I'm going to do when the fairytale is over. You're spoiling me, allowing me to wake up to that pretty face every morning. I'm not going to know what to do with myself when the kids come back," Trenton told her.

Wrapping his arms around Dallas, Trenton pulled her close to him. He needed to feel her closeness and bask in the heat of their bodies touching.

"I know. These last three days have been everything. I keep thinking I'm going to wake up, and it's all going to be a dream. Like, this is too good to be true."

Trenton chuckled. "Stop thinking so much. Just ride this wave. I know I'm going to ride the hell out of it," he whispered, dusting his lips across her neck and inhaling her scent.

"I'm trying so hard to, Trenton. I've been down this road before, and it scares me. One day, Messiah was my everything; then, the next day, I didn't even recognize him."

"Good thing I'm not him, though." Trenton smiled, tapping her thigh. "Get up. I'm about to starve. Let's hit Big Boys. Then I want to go to Somerset to pick up a few things."

Dallas smiled. "Shopping on you?"

"Yep. I'll buy you the world, but you got to give me a little time to get my money up."

Dallas blushed again. "You're just too cool for school, I see."

"It's the truth, though. If you let me in and stop comparing me to that other lame, I'm going to make sure you want for nothing. That's my job as your man."

Dallas didn't respond. She felt her emotions kick into overload. It scared her to think about falling in love with another man only to end up being used and abused. But Trenton made it hard not to fall for him. He said all the right things, and his actions spoke volumes. He was all about her, and it felt good to have someone in her corner who cared just as much as she did.

"Repeat that one more time."

Trenton's voice was sharp as his eyes narrowed on the ignorant, inconsiderate asshole standing in front of them. He was out of line, and as much as Dallas felt he needed to be checked, now wasn't the time. She didn't expect such a wonderful day to end in complete chaos. They went to breakfast, shopped at Somerset Mall, caught a movie, and now they were out to eat. They were just about to leave before they were rudely interrupted.

"I said I'm tired of you niggers thinking you can do what you want and expect the government to solve ya problems. Get out of my face, boy."

If Dallas didn't hear it with her own two ears, she wouldn't have believed the man said it. She was speechless. All that confusion over her bumping into the asshole was uncalled for, especially since she hadn't meant to. She had looked down at her ringing cell phone to see who was calling, and he appeared out of nowhere—the two colliding.

Dallas saw how Trenton's eyes twitched and his fists balled, then flexed.

"Trenton, let's just go. He's not even worth a response. Please, let's go," she begged, grabbing his arm.

Trenton ran his hands through his beard to try to calm his anger. The man didn't know he was seconds from getting his ass whooped. He definitely didn't know Trenton had murdered close to forty-five people, all in the name of serving his country. Murdering had become as easy as breathing to him, and he didn't give a fuck about doing it again. However, Trenton had already weighed his options. The army made it legal to kill innocent citizens. If he killed this lily-white asshole, he'd get railroaded through the prison system and thrown under the cell, even though he'd given his country fifteen years. Hypocrites.

"What, you can't hear, boy? I said—"

"I heard what you said," Trenton spoke calmly. "But I don't think you understand what you said. Because if you did, you would know that you bleed the same red blood that I bleed, and you're fucking with a man that ain't got 'em all, *boy*," he shot back sarcastically. "You know what I would have done back in Iraq to a bitch like you? Nah, I don't think you know." He let out a small laugh. "That's why I'm going to give you a pass. Apologize to my lady, though."

The man's cheeks turned red with anger. Trenton could tell he was spitting fire.

"You don't scare me, nigger," he said, charging toward Trenton and swinging a wild left hook that barely connected with Trenton's shoulder.

Before he could regain his balance, Trenton had knocked him in his face so hard that he saw stars. He then proceeded to thoroughly whip his ass. Trenton's hits were vicious, and each one was precisely executed.

It was horrible. Dallas watched as a woman grabbed her two children and scurried to the other side of the restaurant. Some screamed; some watched on in horror. Finally, two male patrons and a male staff member were able to pull Trenton off the poor man and hold him down.

"Let me the fuck go!" Trent snatched away, shaking the Good Samaritans off him as if they were trash. "Y'all need to be handling that ignorant bastard. I bet he'll think twice before coming at a nigga like me again," Trenton growled.

His anger was blinding him. Flashbacks of his time in Iraq surged through his mind, which only pissed him off further. He wanted to get one more hit in, maybe a kick to the face, so he could knock some sense into the bastard. However, he had to practice control. He had to attempt the breathing methods that his therapist had taught him. He had to calm down.

"Trenton, baby, let's go," Dallas pleaded, cupping her slender fingers around his beefy arms.

She was scared. His eyes. He had gone to another place.

"I think it's best you leave," the yellow-haired, pale-faced female manager said with a frown, staring sternly at Trent. "I've called the police. We will not allow this in our restaurant," she snarled, handing the asshole a napkin to help nurse his wounds.

Trenton frowned. "Called the police on who? This ma'fucka assaulted me and my lady. I'll sit my black ass right here until the police come. I don't give two fucks," he added, folding his arms over his chest.

"Let him go. I'm fine." The prick let out a groan, spitting blood onto the floor. "Get 'em away from me 'fore I kill 'em."

Trenton had broken his face up pretty badly. His nose had blood gushing from it, his lip was cut, and the bruising under his right eye was most definitely going to be pretty nasty.

Trenton let out a small laugh. He started to respond but

thought better of it. The man was lucky Dallas was by his side…
really lucky. The demonic thoughts going through his head weren't
good for society. They actually scared him. After a brief mental
tussle between his half-angel, half-devil conscience, Trenton
decided it was time for him to leave.

"Let's go, Dallas," he growled, continuing his breathing
exercise.

Dallas gladly followed Trenton out of the restaurant. She
didn't know what to think. For a second, Trenton had lost it, and it
didn't sit well with her.

"What happened back there, Trent?" she asked, letting out a
breath along with a ball of nerves. "You can't just go hitting people
because you don't like what they say," she added as he merged onto
Interstate 75 South.

Trenton's forehead knitted together as he glanced over at
Dallas to see if she was serious. A hard frown pressed his lips
together.

"Are you for real right now? Did you not see that man attack
me after he disrespected me and my woman? What type of man
do you take me for, Dallas?"

"It's not about being a man. It's about self-control. Learn
how to walk away from certain situations."

Trenton let out a small laugh. "You know what? Stop talking
to me before I say something we both regret."

He turned up the volume on the radio, allowing an old Mary
J. Blige song to fill the air.

"Nah, fuck this." Trenton slammed his colossal hand against
the dashboard, shutting off the radio. "Do you know what the fuck
I've been through, Dallas? As a black man? Hell no, you don't. Try
being told you ain't shit all your life just because of your skin color.
Try giving fifteen years of your life just to be reminded you're still
just another nigger they manipulated to carry out their corrupted-

ass plot."

Trenton let out a flustered breath of air, pulling at the hairs on his chin.

"I've done a lot of fucked up shit, Dallas. I lost my soul along the way. I killed a little boy in front of his daddy because his father wouldn't tell us what we needed to know. I killed a pregnant mother in front of her husband and kids, all in the name of protecting the American Dream. Bullshit! They fooled me into believing I was some hero. I wasn't no fucking hero. So, don't tell me how to control myself, Dallas. I thought I was very much controlled." Anger narrowed his eyes and stiffened his jaw.

Dallas's slender fingers reached over, snaking between Trent's.

"I'm sorry," she whispered.

Trenton's eyes traveled down to her hand holding his. A peace offering, he was sure, because feeling her touch calmed his whole world. Dallas was his peace.

CHAPTER TWENTY-TWO

"WHY DO YOU keep calling me, Jaxon? Leave me alone."

Candace sighed as her eyes slanted toward the bedroom door where Diego was still sleeping peacefully. It was just past nine in the morning, and Jaxon had already rung her phone three times. He was becoming a bit stalkerish, and it almost frightened Candace.

"After all the thousands you took me for, did you think I was just going to allow you to get away with playing with my heart while you and that man ride off into the sunset? It don't work like that, Candace," Jaxon growled.

"I didn't take you for nothing. You gave it to me, and you sure wasn't complaining when you were getting all the free coochie you wanted while going back home to another woman. The same woman you swore was an ex. So, I think we're even. Take your loss and leave me alone."

Candace was trying her best to whisper. Lord knows she didn't want to involve Diego's crazy ass in her drama.

"Nah, don't bullshit me, Candace. How long was you fucking him while we were together, slut? Did he trick on you, too? Meet me. We need to talk."

Fury pounded and rippled in time to the beating of her heart. It took everything in her to fight down the anger nearly choking her. If Jaxon were sitting in her face, she would have slapped the taste out of his mouth.

"First of all, I never slept with anyone the whole time we were together. Second, don't you ever disrespect me like that again, Jaxon. I'm hanging up, and if you keep calling me, I will go down to the police station and report your ass. Try me."

Jaxon let out a small laugh. "Want me to meet you at the station? I bet your boyfriend ends up behind bars before I do. We can do this the easy way or the hard way. Now, are you going to meet up with me?"

"Meet you where and for what, Jaxon?"

At one point in her life, Candace swore she loved him. She was going to spend the rest of her life with this man and give him babies. Now, the thought of him made her sick to her stomach. She hated him.

"Your choice. I have something you need to see, and we can move on from there," Jaxon smugly told her, knowing he now had the upper hand.

Candace rolled her eyes. "I'm not going anywhere that doesn't have a lot of people, and after today, I want you to stop calling me."

"We'll see. Meet me at Kuzzo's on Seven Mile in an hour."

"Bye, Jaxon." Candace hung up, cursing herself for even answering his call.

She wondered what he could possibly have to show her. The twist in her gut caused a whisper of unease to tease her senses.

"Who you in here talking to?"

Diego's deep rasp almost caused Candace to jump out of her skin. Her hand shot to her chest in an attempt to slow the racing of her heart. She watched as he stretched his long torso. The bulge of his morning wood bounced, and a shiver tickled Candace's spine. He walked over, wrapping his arms around her tiny waist, and nibbled at the nape of her neck.

They were more than lovers by now. Diego had possession of her mind, body, and soul. Everyone before him didn't matter anymore, and she couldn't see another man coming after him.

Lying to Diego wasn't something she wanted to make a habit of doing. Still, in her defense, she was protecting their peace.

"A nobody that's getting on my last nerve," she muttered. "I didn't know I was that loud. I didn't mean to wake you."

"You didn't. My Bird called." He shrugged. "Wanting a whole bunch of nothing as usual."

Candace chuckled. "Don't be making that face when you talk about your mother. I love Ms. Riley."

"I love her, too, but she be bugging. She said she gon' kick yo' ass for not coming to kick it with her. Then you know she got to sweating me about grandbabies. I told her to chill out for a couple of months."

"A couple of months?" Candace's brows raised.

"Damn, that's too long, huh? Want to start making 'em now?" he teased, pressing his hardness into her stomach.

Candace giggled. "Boy, stop playing with me." She swatted at his arm. "Seriously, what are your plans for today? I need to make a few runs, but then I wanted you to meet me at Pier 1 for furniture."

"We can do that. I just got to drop some money off to my mom, then stop by the studio to make sure everything is good to go. We should be done next week. You ready to be my famous little ballerina?"

"I was born ready. I'm still in disbelief that you're giving me my own studio. I don't want to fully believe it. Like, I'm scared it's going to get taken away."

Candace had been through so much when it came to the men she dealt with. Each of them used and abused her for their own selfish reasons. She loved to be in love. She loved the security it gave her. So, she accepted certain behaviors that she shouldn't have. Now, here Diego was, ready to give her the world, and she didn't know how to receive it.

"I don't know what kind of cats you're used to dealing with, but I ain't them, Candy. You got my word, and if I don't stand for nothing else, I stand on my word. Remember that. If I say it, you can take that shit to the bank."

How could she not fall in love with a man like Diego? That's why she wanted to close Jaxon's chapter in her life and move on to a future with Diego.

Mist kept the sky company as Candace rode up Seven Mile on her way to Kuzzo's. The gloomy vapor had her deep in thought. Occasionally, she'd look through the rearview mirror to make sure Diego hadn't followed her. She couldn't wait to curse Jaxon out and tell him to go straight to hell. She actually practiced how she would tell him.

Go to hell, you ignorant, no-good, ugly-ass bastard. No, that wasn't hype enough. Fuck you, bitch. Go burn in hell, she coached herself, then giggled at the realization that she was playing it out in her head.

Checking her rearview mirror one last time, Candace released a breath of air as she pulled into a parking space and grabbed her umbrella. She spotted Jaxon's truck parked a few spaces ahead and rolled her eyes.

"Bitch," she muttered, flicking his truck off before entering the restaurant.

Kuzzo's was small, and the place was always packed to capacity. The lines to be seated were long, but the food made it worth the wait. They had the best breakfast in the city of Detroit.

"My Candy Girl. You're so beautiful."

Jaxon's voice caused her to cringe. He was so close that she felt the warmth of his body against her skin. Extending a hand, Candace pushed space between them.

"Back up. Do not be that close to me because I won't be responsible for my reaction," she snarled.

"You were begging me to stay up under you just a while ago. Funny how time changes things," Jaxon retorted, extending his hand. "The table is back in the corner. I ordered for you already."

Maybe she exaggerated a little in the car. Jaxon was far from ugly, but he was indeed an ignorant, no-good bastard. Clad in a pair of denim jeans, a button-up, and a fresh haircut, Candace took in the way his smooth peanut butter skin glowed. He possessed a hot sexuality that used to have her swooning. Now, not so much.

"I didn't plan on eating. I just want to know what you want so we can get this over with, Jaxon," she told him, sliding into the booth across from him.

"You need to answer a few questions first. I'm not getting how you went from promising to marry me to not wanting to talk to me. I mean, how long was you fucking him, Candace? Tell me the truth."

"Jaxon, Diego and I didn't have anything going on until I broke it off with you. Furthermore, stop questioning me about Diego. When were you going to tell me that you lived with Arianna? You had me in that house. You slept with me on the same bed y'all probably fucked on. You were having sex with me raw, Jaxon. You could have given me something."

"I never loved her. I told you, it was circumstantial. Arianna and I are not together. It's complicated. Is that why you left me?"

"No, I left because our time was up. I would have never thought you would be the man that you turned out to be. I'm so glad I dodged the bullet. You are so disrespectful."

Jaxon pursed his lips, staring into Candace's eyes. "I needed to get your attention. I would never put my hands on you, Candy. You hurt me. I feel like a little sissy saying that, but you did. I know you're not a slut. I didn't mean it."

Candace frowned. "You shouldn't say things you don't mean. Furthermore, you definitely don't get my attention like that. Now, what was so important that we had to meet up?"

Jaxon pulled out his cell phone, tapping the screen. After a few seconds of tapping, he slid it across the table.

"So, this is the kind of man you want to associate with? I thought about a few things I could do with these pictures."

Candace stared at the phone's screen in disbelief. It was a picture of Diego beating on some man. He had a gun pressed to the man's temple. Her heart sank. She tossed Jaxon his phone back.

"How did you get those? Why did you take them?"

A vein near her left eye bulged as anger filled her heart. Just the thought of the chaos those pictures could cause had her ready to kill Jaxon herself.

"Well, after he called himself trying to attack me, I started following him. I know he didn't think he was going to attack me, take my woman, and I would just let that slide. Then this fell into my lap. I'm still trying to figure out what I want to do with it. You can help determine that."

"Boy, please. All it shows is a picture of a man getting beaten. It can be self-defense for all anybody knows," Candace argued.

"A felon is not supposed to have a gun, period. Don't play stupid. Besides, I'm sure if the body shows up, murder is another charge. So, where do we go from here? If I can't have you, I'm not going to allow you to be happy with him." Jaxon shrugged as a smug grin formed on his face.

Now was when she was supposed to call him a bitch and tell him to burn in hell. But she was stuck. She was mad at Jaxon for trying to blackmail her. However, she was more disappointed in Diego for lying to her. He promised he wouldn't do anything to jeopardize their future, and he lied to her. He sat in her face and lied.

"And action," Jaxon chuckled, snapping Candace from her thoughts.

She looked up to see Diego heading toward them. A violent light sat in his dark eyes as he locked in on Candace.

"So, this is the run you had to make, huh? I heard you making plans to meet up with this fuck nigga," Diego spat. "I told you I wasn't the one, Candace. I've been trying to do everything I could to show you I was for real, and you sneaking around with this nigga? You ain't even got enough respect to carry this shit somewhere out the hood?"

Candace looked around at the people staring at them.

"Calm down, Diego. You're causing a scene."

"Fuck causing a scene. This shit is whack as hell. He can have you." Diego waved her off, turning to walk away.

"Wait, Diego." Candace peeled herself from the booth, following behind him. "Diego," she called out to him as they made it outside. "It's not even what you think."

He whipped around, letting out a small laugh. "Ain't that what they all say? Then why the fuck was you whispering, Candace? Why the fuck you ain't tell me you was on the phone with him this morning?"

"Why didn't you just tell me that you heard me? You didn't have to follow me," Candace protested. It was natural for her to become defensive.

"I didn't follow you, dummy. Yo' reckless ass decided to cheat two blocks up from the fucking studio. Like I wouldn't see your car parked on the street. I don't have time for this shit, Candy. I'm too good of a man."

"First of all, I wasn't cheating. Why did you lie to me? You said you wouldn't do anything to jeopardize your freedom, but ma'fuckas got pictures of you beating on people and putting guns to their heads."

"Man, whatever, Candace. I'm not doing this with you. Bye. Have that nigga."

"Whatever to you, too. That's right, go out there and be a little wanna-be thug all your life. Stupid self gon' end up in jail just like everybody said," Candace shot.

She knew it was a low blow, but it was the first thing that came to mind.

Diego chuckled. "Bet. Fuck you," he tossed over his shoulder, walking off.

Candace wanted to call after him. She wanted to scream that she didn't mean it. Instead, she allowed him to walk away, and it nearly killed her.

CHAPTER TWENTY-THREE

"FAITH IS HEARING, believing, and acting on the Word of God. It's trusting God in spite of your circumstances. The Bible says, 'Faith comes by hearing and hearing by the word of God.' The Bible also says we are to walk by faith and not by sight."

The preacher stood at the pulpit, his voice projecting, and Sasha felt her chest begin to loosen. She couldn't remember the last time she had stepped foot into a church. It meant the world that Hunter was sitting next to her, especially after the pandemonium their life had become.

Sasha felt tiny hands tap on her knee. She smiled down at Zion, who reached out for her to pick her up. Devaughn and Christina were sitting a row ahead of them. Hunter didn't want to sit next to them, saying they weren't one big happy family.

"Shouldn't she be sitting with her momma and daddy?" Hunter leaned over and whispered into Sasha's ear as she pulled Zion onto her lap.

"She's not hurting anything, Hunter. Are you even listening to the word?"

"Yeah, I'm listening," Hunter snarled, leaning back into the pew.

Candace knew church wasn't his thing. He didn't believe in the whole Bible and God theory. According to him, the Bible was just a bunch of stories told by man, converted a thousand times.

"Now, what we're doing in this series of sermons is simply walking and working our way down through these mighty men and wonderful women of faith. If you want to grow in your faith,

174

walk with the faithful. We're going to worship with Abel, walk with Enoch, work with Noah, and witness in all of these other folks just what kind of faith it takes to get from Earth to heaven. Or maybe just as important as that, what kind of faith it takes to experience a little bit of heaven here on Earth," the preacher spoke.

As the preacher continued, Sasha heard Hunter let out an impatient breath of air. She tried her best to ignore him. Between Zion and staring at the back of Devaughn's head, it worked. She couldn't even focus on the word. How was his head so perfect? A part of her wished she was sitting right next to Devaughn. His baby's mother didn't deserve to be. *And why the hell is she still in town?* Sasha wondered, finding herself rolling her eyes.

As the sermon continued, occasionally Devaughn would look back at Zion and smile, but Sasha swore he was staring into her soul. Her attraction to him came out of nowhere. One minute, they were each other's shoulder; the next, she wanted more.

"Now, can I have every able body stand to their feet and grab your neighbor's hand in prayer."

The whole church stood; Hunter didn't. Sasha couldn't believe it. He had fallen asleep.

She nudged him, causing him to pop his eyes open and pull himself from the bench. Sasha tried not to be mad. Hunter said he wanted to make an honest effort, but the whole situation was uncomfortable.

The preacher ended service shortly after, and Hunter almost ran out of the church, claiming he was getting the car for her. Devaughn asked Sasha to stay behind to meet the preacher. Hunter didn't see a reason for him to stay since he didn't plan on returning.

"I take it he wasn't feeling it today." Devaughn let out a small laugh.

Gosh, he smells good and looks good. Sasha felt horrible lusting after another man in the house of the Lord.

She shrugged. "He'll be okay. Thanks for inviting me out. I needed this."

"Me, too, chica. Devaughn's so amazing. I'm proud of the change in my baby's daddy," Christina gushed, wrapping her arm around Devaughn's waist—a little extra, in Sasha's opinion.

It was a woman thing. Sasha knew Christina was silently marking her territory.

Devaughn stepped out of Christina's embrace, clearing his throat. "Take Zion to the car, Chrissy. I'll be out in a second. I want to introduce Pastor Bolden to Sasha," he ordered, then watched as she snatched Zion up and marched off.

"You didn't have to do that. I don't want her hating me because she thinks there is something between us."

Devaughn frowned. "I don't care what she thinks. Christina and I are not together. I could never be with her again, and she knows it."

There was an unspoken silence between them. Sasha wondered if they were thinking the same thing and if he felt the same way she was beginning to feel. Something was going to have to give.

Several hours later, Sasha and Hunter had unwound. Their disagreement at church was the furthest thing from their minds. They actually had been getting along well.

"So, you're really not coming to my get-together, Diego?" Sasha whined into the phone like she always did to get her way with her brother.

The get-together was in full swing, and drinks were in heavy rotation. Even Trenton and Hunter were getting along. The only thing missing was her big brother.

"Nope. Not if Candace is there. I'm not fucking with her,

Sash." He sighed into the phone.

It was nearly killing him not to be able to feel her touch and see that smile he fell in love with. But he wasn't about to allow her to play on his feelings for her.

"What? But y'all was just all lovey-dovey. What happened?"

"Nothing. She's not ready for me. I don't have time to play cat and mouse with her. If she still wants that nigga, she can have him."

"Wait a minute." Sasha frowned. "What nigga? Candace wouldn't cheat on you. She really loves you," she defended.

It was the truth. It was almost sickening the way Candace would go on and on about Diego.

"Yeah, okay. I guess I didn't find her at the restaurant with that nigga Jaxon. Look, I know that's your homegirl, but I'm not fucking with her. I got to handle something. Let me call you back, Sash."

Diego ended the call, and Sasha's eyes narrowed toward Candace.

"So, you cheated on my brother? You knew why he wasn't coming. Why would you have me call him?" she snarled.

"I didn't cheat on your brother, Sasha. I told you that Jaxon kept calling me and acting stupid. He begged me to meet up with him, and I did," Candace explained.

She hoped Sasha could at least get him face-to-face with her. He had been firm in not answering her phone calls and avoiding her. It was hell without him.

"Girl, you had no business meeting up with him in the first place. I also find it mighty shady that you held that piece of information from me. I thought we was sisters. We don't keep secrets."

"Sasha, stay out their business. Let them work it out." Hunter frowned as Alicia made her way to the empty seat next to him. "Ain't that right, cuz? Keep other folks out of your relationship," he added, staring at Trenton.

Trenton let out a small laugh, wondering if that was supposed to be a shot at him.

"Yeah, but you sound like a hypocrite, *cuz*. Wasn't you the same one going around telling people I'm crazy and not to fuck with me?" Trenton muttered, pushing up from the table. "I'm getting tired of yo' ignorant ass."

Hunter stood, too. "Then why do you keep coming around? We never dealt with each other before you went to the army, and we're not cool now. I would appreciate it if you stay where you're at, and I'll gladly stay over here."

Things seemed to go left out of nowhere. Sasha couldn't understand how the conversation went from Candace cheating to Hunter and Trenton not liking each other.

"Can y'all stop? It's not even that serious. Y'all are family." Sasha sighed. "Deal the cards. Let's get back to the game. Dallas, can you go grab the men some drinks?"

"Nah," Trenton smiled. "I've been trying to keep it cordial for the sake of my cousin and because I'm with your best friend. But, honestly, I don't give a fuck about this man. I never have to step foot in this house again. Let's go, Dallas," he snarled, heading for the door. Stopping just short of reaching it, he added, "By the way, Sash, I'm no kin to this bitch-ass nigga. I'm Alicia's cousin, which is his wife. This hoe-ass nigga didn't tell you that he married her to avoid statutory rape charges for fucking a baby. You've been a step-momma all this time and didn't even know it," he growled.

The whole room went silent. Even Hunter stood there in disbelief.

Blood pounded in Sasha's temple as she absorbed the news. She couldn't believe it. Why would Trenton tell her such a horrible lie?

"You jealous bastard!" Hunter lunged at Trenton, only for Candace and Dallas to step in the way.

Trenton laughed. "Nah, let him through so he can get knocked the fuck out. Oh, wait, while I'm on a roll...tell this woman how you had a vasectomy after the twins. Got this woman stressing over nothing with your hoe-ass knowing you can't have kids."

Hunter was spitting fire. He saw the pain in Sasha's eyes, and for the first time since their relationship began, the thought of losing her scared him. He loved Sasha. He really did. Things had just gotten out of hand, and he did his best to manage them.

"Sasha, baby..." He stopped charging toward Trenton and focused on his fiancée. "Baby—"

"Don't baby me, Hunter. Tell me he's lying. Please, tell me that you didn't have me smiling in this bitch's face, allowing her and her kids into my house, and you were fucking her. Wait a minute. The twins are four, and we've been together..."

Her voice trailed off as she did the math in her head. He cheated. She thought the family had strong genes because the twins looked like him. But they were *his*?

"Everybody leave. Please, get out!" she roared, pointing toward the door. "And you, bitch..." Sasha grabbed Alicia's hair, yanking her back as she tried to walk past her. "You better tell me he's lying. Tell me!"

A dry sob burned her throat, but she refused to let it out. Bone-deep betrayal nearly knocked the wind out of Sasha.

"I'm sorry," Alicia whimpered, covering her face as Sasha hovered over her.

Sasha officially lost it. A tiny spark whispered in her ear to whip Alicia's ass, and she listened. Her eyes clouded with pain, and her fists became thirsty for revenge. The first hit knocked Alicia upside her head so hard that she stumbled to the ground. Everything else was a blur. Sasha saw murder, and the only thing that kept her from it was the set of arms that pulled her away.

"Baby, stop. Calm down," Hunter whispered in her ear, wrapping his arms around her entire chest cavity and restraining her arms.

"Let me go, Hunter! Now! I swear, if I get to that bitch again, I'm going to flatten her face with my foot." She struggled to get loose while Candace helped Alicia out of the house.

Once they were alone, Hunter finally released Sasha.

"Sash, I didn't mean for everything to come out like this. Baby—"

Slap!

Sasha slapped the cowboy piss out of Hunter. It was so loud that the hit echoed throughout the house.

"I don't care what you meant. Get out. I want you to leave this house now. You have hurt me so bad that I feel numb. You watched me struggle and go through depression. You cried with me. You fooled me into believing you wanted us just as much as I did. What kind of monster are you, Hunter?"

Tears streamed down her cheeks as her mouth crumpled into a wail of pain and anger. She bit back the bile as the hurt lacing through her head made her nauseous.

"Get out!" she roared, grabbing the picture off the mantle next to her and lobbing it at Hunter's head. "Leave!" she shouted, grabbing another picture and flinging it. It grazed his ear and shattered against the wall.

Hunter took off, running toward the door. He saw the devil when he looked into Sasha's eyes. He fucked up badly, and he knew it.

CHAPTER TWENTY-FOUR

"DID YOU NEED me to bring you anything, Sash? I get off in an hour." Dallas closed her eyes, biting back the urge to say all the things she wanted to say.

Her opinion didn't matter at the moment, even though she was hurting just as much as Sasha. They were more like sisters than best friends. When one hurt, the other hurt, as well.

"No, I'm fine, Dallas. I'm hurting, but I will be fine. I just can't believe he would do me like that. His wife? I practically raised those fucking kids." The pain was distinct in her voice as she choked those words out. "I loved him, Dallas. Why?"

"Everything happens for a reason, Sash. I don't know why, but you know I'm going to be right next to you helping you get through it. I'm so mad at the way Trenton handled that."

"I know. I just need time. That's all I need. I love you, Dallas. And tell Trent thank you for finally telling the truth. I'm not mad at him, and you shouldn't be, either."

"I guess," Dallas sighed, biting down on her bottom lip.

Things had been awkward with Trenton since the party. The night before, he brought Haagen-Dazs ice cream and a movie as a peace offering. She really enjoyed him.

"Alright, stop worrying about me. I'll be fine. Maybe we can drive up to Chicago this weekend and go to that Kendall concert. You know that's Candace's secret boo. I don't like her ass right now, but we all need a getaway."

Dallas chuckled. "You have to separate the brother thing

from the friendship thing. Plus, I believe Candace. I don't think she would backtrack to Jaxon, of all people. That's not even her style. Both Candace and Diego are being childish."

"Yeah, because Diego is about to drive me crazy asking about that girl. I told him not to say nothing else to me about Candace. If he wants to know how she's doing, he'd better call her himself. Can you believe his ignorant ass planned a grand opening for her next month, and his stubborn ass wants me to say I did it because he doesn't want her to know he still cares?"

"Awww," Dallas cooed. "That's your stubborn brother for you. They'll be back together. But let me get back to work so I can finish this last application of the day. Love you, Sash. Go fuck that sexy-ass neighbor of yours. You'll feel ten times better," Dallas teased, hanging up before Sasha could respond.

He couldn't be serious. No, Messiah had to be playing a joke on her. Dallas's eyes warily slanted toward Messiah as he marched his drunk ass into her house, plopping down on her couch like he belonged there.

"I know you did not just march your happy ass into my house without knocking. You are way out of line, Messiah." She frowned, standing over him with her arms firmly crossed over her chest. "Do you hear me talking to you?"

"I heard you, Dally. Shhhh! My head hurts," he slurred, closing his eyelids and allowing the cool sensation of the leather to relax his body.

It felt like home. He missed that couch, the smell of apple and cinnamon from Dallas's signature candles, and her. He even missed her yelling at him like she was doing at the moment.

"Don't shush me, Messiah. You can't just walk up in here

whenever you please. What if my man was here?"

"So?"

"So?" Dallas hissed. "You have lost your mind."

"I did," he chuckled, reaching out, catching Dallas off guard. He pulled her onto his lap and wrapped his arms around her. "I lost my mind the day I left you. I'm sorry, Dally."

"Ewww!" Dallas hopped up out of his lap like he had a disease. "Don't touch me, Messiah. I know you have to be drunk as hell to come here with this bullshit. Where's your fiancée?"

"Fuck her," he muttered. "Don't you miss me? Don't you miss what I used to do to you?" He wound his hips while biting his bottom lip, pretending to do it to Dallas. "I used to tear that shit up. Didn't I?"

Dallas tried her hardest not to laugh but seeing Messiah cut up was pretty funny. She hated what he had done to them. In the beginning, they were best friends. Sometimes she found herself missing the friendship, and other times, she wanted to thank him for hurting her because she would have never known how to appreciate Trenton.

"Boy, you need to stop it. You better stop playing with me before I put your drunk ass out of this house."

Messiah frowned. "You would put me out, baby momma? All drunk and vulnerable?"

"Apparently, you're not that drunk, Messiah. Sleep it off. As soon as you sober up, you have to go."

"Whatever you say, baby momma. You sure you don't want to see what this deep stroke hitting for?"

Messiah," Dallas groaned. "Go to sleep."

She shook her head, making her way to her room. She had to call Trenton to tell him what was going on. She didn't want any surprise pop-ups and end up falling out like Candace and Diego.

Trenton answered the phone on the second ring. "What's up,

babe? You miss me?"

"I always miss you, but I called because my ignorant baby's father just showed up drunk and passed out on my couch."

"What?"

Dallas heard the anger in his voice.

"Yeah, I forgot he still had the key. He just walked his happy ass into my house and passed out. He's drunk as hell."

"Dallas," Trenton sighed, "you're telling me this like it's cool. Like you having your ex laying his crusty ass on your couch ain't a problem. I'm trying not to spaz out right now."

Dallas closed her eyes and took a deep breath. "Spaz out for what, Trenton? I called you so you wouldn't think anything of it. You can come over here with us if you want. I couldn't just send the father of my children out into the streets for him to get into an accident."

When Trenton hung up in her face, she started to question if she had made the right decision by telling him. She felt he should have trusted her decisions. She didn't want Messiah. They were past done. He'd hurt her so badly that she could never be with him again.

Dallas tried calling back a total of seven times. She even sent him text messages, to no avail. Her doorbell rang, followed by several hard knocks on the door. Suddenly, she knew exactly why he wasn't answering.

"Damn, he got here fast as hell," she whispered to herself, trudging to the door to answer it.

Instead of allowing him inside to go off, she pulled him onto the porch and closed the front door.

"Do not come over here acting a fool, Trenton. If I was on some bullshit, I wouldn't have called you. As I stated before, he's the father of my two children."

Trenton's eyes flickered with rage. "So, you couldn't call the nigga an Uber or put him on the bus? Anywhere but laying up on your fucking couch. That's disrespectful as fuck, Dallas!" he boomed, not even trying to hide his annoyance.

"What, you don't trust me or something?" Dallas frowned.

"Oh, I trust you. I don't trust *that* nigga."

The door creaked open, and before Dallas could respond, Messiah appeared with an alley-cat grin plastered on his face.

"Nah, you shouldn't trust me. That's baby momma right there. You may have her right now, but that heart gon' always belong to me." Messiah chuckled.

If Dallas could have evaporated into thin air and reappeared in a different state, she would have.

"Messiah, do not start that." She released a breath of air, knowing the situation could turn dangerous at any moment. Despite what Messiah thought, Trenton wasn't to be played with, and she'd seen him in action as proof.

"Let him talk, Dallas," Trenton smirked, cocking his head to the side. "But he's drunk, though?" he bore into Dallas.

"We got a family. It's forever." Messiah shrugged arrogantly.

"That's cool. You can be here forever. Y'all are a family," Trenton confirmed. "But, here's where you got the game fucked up. Whatever y'all had is dead. It was dead the minute I spoke to her. See, you don't know me. And that's cool. I know you got to be feeling fucked up losing such a beautiful queen. But if you keep coming at me sideways, I swear we gon' have some problems. I never in my life gave a nigga this many passes. However, I'm respecting you because of Dallas and them kids. I really don't give two fucks about you, so remember that the next time you fix your mouth to come at me out the side of your neck."

"Fuck you," Messiah growled.

"Dallas already handled that," Trenton laughed, stretching the truth, then turned to face Dallas. "I'm leaving before I do something stupid. I expect you to handle that. And I mean, handle that *now*."

His deep rasp was cold as he pecked her forehead and walked off. Dallas watched him leave. Shoulders back, head high, brooding with confidence despite knowing he was pissed.

"You didn't—"

"No, Messiah. Just no. You are such an asshole. I'm so damn sick of you. No more! I can't allow you to keep ruining me. Get your shit together, or stay the hell away from me. I don't want us anymore. I choose me, Messiah. I choose my happiness for once. And until you realize it, we will be going through your mom to drop the kids off. You seem sober enough. Go home, Messiah."

She didn't want to hear his response. Instead, Dallas made her way into her room for her phone. She called Trenton several times before he finally answered.

"What, Dallas?"

"He's gone," she told him just above a whisper.

"Look, I don't have time for dumb shit like that. I'm not competing with your kids' father our whole relationship. It took everything in me not to knock his punk ass out. I don't want to disrespect you or the kids. Respect me, Dallas. If you want a relationship, respect my boundaries."

"I respect you, Trenton," she pleaded.

"We'll see. Let me call you back. I need a little space to calm down. I'll call you later."

For the second time in one day, he hung up on her. She didn't know how things had spiraled so far out of control. However, Dallas did know she wasn't about to allow Messiah to mess up her relationship with Trenton.

CHAPTER TWENTY-FIVE

"Love left me picking up the pieces to a broken heart..."

THE DARKNESS OF the room felt good. Light gave her a headache, food made her nauseous, and being around people only made her realize how stupid Hunter made her look. So, Sasha barricaded herself in her room.

Hunter had ripped her entire soul out of her body. He had broken her down lower than she thought was humanly possible. He had sat in her face discussing marriage plans, knowing he couldn't marry her. He prayed with her about having a child. He gave her his shoulder and cried with her their inability to conceive. He made her feel like less of a woman and broke her down to nothing.

The truth caused her heart to ache something terrible. She had cried so much in the past week that her tear ducts were dry.

"Why me?" she groaned as her eyes rolled to the ceiling.

She trundled over to her side, grabbing her ringing cell phone. It was Hunter. He just didn't get that she wanted nothing to do with him. What could he possibly have to say? Sending his call to voicemail, she scrolled her call log, stopping at Devaughn's number.

She wanted him to comfort her. She needed him to tell her that everything would be okay. Tucking her bottom lip and biting down, she connected the call and pressed the phone to her ear. It was just after eight o'clock. The sun had begun to disappear, and the moon was peeking out onto the sky.

"I need you. I swear I tried to think of someone else to call, but all I could come up with was you."

Sasha didn't recognize her own voice as she poured her heart out to Devaughn, but it was the truth. She did need him.

"It's okay, Sash. I told you I was here for you. What's wrong? Is everything okay?"

"No," Sasha whispered. "Can you meet me somewhere, anywhere?"

"Of course. Zion just went to bed, and Christina's in the room. Where do you need me to meet you?"

Sasha heard him scrambling through the phone.

"I don't know. I just need to get away."

"Is Hunt there? Did he do something to you?" Devaughn asked.

"No...and yes."

"Okay, I'm going to come over. Come out to the porch, Sasha. I need to know you're fine before I meet you anywhere."

"Okay," Sasha sighed.

She gathered enough strength to peel herself from the bed and attempted to brush her long hair into a ponytail. She didn't bother with makeup. She didn't feel pretty.

Devaughn must have run of out the house. What seemed like a minute later, Sasha was swinging the door open and falling into his arms. It felt good there—almost too good for the both of them.

He held her, squeezing her close, and Sasha broke down in tears. Her body shook, chest heaving.

"Talk to me, Sash. What's going on?"

"He's married. He had babies on me. He had a vasectomy. He betrayed me."

Her voice was barely audible as she shook with tears. Sasha didn't even know where they came from. She thought she was all cried out.

He held her tighter, as if that was even possible.

"Wow, I don't know what to say, Sash. Have you eaten today?"

"I'm not hungry."

"Well, you have to eat something. I know this quiet little restaurant with good food. Let me feed you, and we can talk. I'm here for you, Sasha."

He would never let her know he had been secretly hoping Hunter would miraculously mess up, but now that it happened, he didn't feel right getting his chance by default.

Sasha was perfect to Devaughn. It was like the minute he laid eyes on her, she stole a tiny piece of his heart, and the piece seemed to get bigger the longer he was around her. She was beautiful... stunning. However, her aura was what got him. She was the most genuine person Devaughn had met in a long time.

"I really don't want to be out in public, Devaughn. I look horrible. I feel horrible."

"You're beautiful to me." Devaughn smiled. "Snotty nose and all."

Sasha giggled. "My nose is not snotty."

"I got you to smile, so I'll excuse the snot."

Devaughn laughed, then paused for a second as he stared into Sasha's puffy hazel eyes. Her hair was pulled into a taut bun, and her face was bare, exalting all of her natural beauty. He liked it. Actually, he preferred her like that.

"I'll tell you what. I can get a room. We can order Chinese and talk."

Sasha's brows raised as she stared at him. He laughed.

"Not like that. You said you don't want to go out. I'm not sitting in that man's house, and obviously, we both need company."

She did need his company, and unbeknownst to him, being alone in a hotel room was the least of her worries. A good revenge fuck was what she needed.

Several hours later...

"Are you serious? You never told me you could sing." Sasha giggled, tapping Devaughn's arm.

They had gotten a room at the Sheraton out in Novi. They had eaten the Chinese food hours ago, and the bottle of wine was nearly empty. Sasha hadn't smiled as much as she was doing in a long time.

"What? I had a record on the local radio station and everything." Devaughn shrugged, looking off. "I had a deal—a good one. But Christina got pregnant with Zion, and she needed me more than I needed to sing."

His voice dropped as he spoke. Sasha could tell his missed opportunity bothered him.

"It's never too late, you know?" She smiled. "Sing to me. Let me hear your vocals."

Of all songs, he had to sing Maxwell's "This Woman's Work." His voice just had to be beautiful. The passion was intense as she leaned against his chest and he stared down at her. Sasha's heart skipped several beats. She hung on to his every word.

"Oh my God, that was so beautiful. Boy, I was about to take my panties off and throw 'em at you." Sasha giggled, clapping for his performance.

He didn't smile. His head went straight to the gutter, and his dick began to ache for her. It nearly killed him to be so close and not slip inside her walls. She was oblivious to his inner turmoil, and Devaughn figured it was better that way.

"Seriously, if I was your girl, you would have to sing me to sleep every night. Oh, and we would have to lay up and cuddle and talk just like this," she added, beaming.

"That would be something, huh?" Devaughn's voice trailed off.

"Yeah, that would. I shouldn't be enjoying you this much, Devaughn."

"I know. It's all bad," he teased.

"Oh, whatever!" Sasha mushed his arm, spinning around to face him with a smirk. "You are so full of it." The wine was giving her a smooth buzz. "So, you've never thought about us? I tried hard not to, but it's like you give me every reason to."

Devaughn smiled. "Every reason to what?"

"You know. Like, *think about you, think about you.* I had to check myself. So, have you?"

"Of course. More than I want to admit. And if I was your man, these kinds of nights would mean the world to me. Well, you know it would be a little different because Zion swears you belong to her."

Sasha giggled. "I know. That's my lil' best friend."

"I can't do this." Devaughn sighed, confusing Sasha. "I don't think we should be this close or alone. It feels too good, and this conversation is too much. You even got me to sing for you. That's like some top-notch super-secret stuff." He chuckled.

He was deflecting. Lord knows he needed a distraction from the aching in his manhood.

"Well, why can't we say fuck morals and fuck what's right? Why can't we just live in the moment and allow ourselves to feel good for once?"

Her lips were sensual, firm, and had curved into a hint of a smile. She caught Devaughn completely off guard as their mouths touched. A crackle of energy passed between them, hot and raw, carnal.

Her kiss ignited a bone-melting fire that spread through his blood. Devaughn had to pull away before he lost himself. Didn't Sasha know he was trying his damnedest to respect their boundaries? She definitely didn't know that he would take possession of her entire being with just one stroke. She couldn't toy with a man like him. He was a grown-ass man, prepared to do grown-ass things to her body.

"I'm so sorry." Sasha covered her mouth.

She felt the wonder of him in every pore, every nerve, and every pulse. His gaze had become too penetrating, his expression way too unreadable.

"I didn't mean to kiss you. I don't—"

"Sasha," Devaughn cut her off.

"I know we have to respect each other's situations, and it just—"

"Sasha, if you don't shut up." Devaughn exhaled a laugh. Heat curled inside him, threatening his control. "The kiss wasn't a problem. I actually wish I could do more, but I don't want it like this. You're hurting. You're vulnerable. When I get you, I don't want you to give me rebound pussy. I want you to give it to me with a free and clear head."

They were riding the fine edge of not enough and too much. He wanted too much, but she needed not enough.

"It wouldn't be a rebound thing. I'm genuinely attracted to you." She paused. "I guess you're right. We do need to slow down."

"Yeah, we do. So, stop being thirsty and tell me something." He chuckled, watching the way her face screwed up. "You're trying to jump my bones, and I don't even know your last name, your favorite color, your favorite food, what makes you smile, what pisses you off so I know not to do it. I want to know everything."

Sasha couldn't hold back the smile that forced its way onto her face. How did he become so perfect? Where did he come from?

CHAPTER TWENTY-SIX

CHICAGO WAS FUN. The buildings downtown were big, the streets were packed, and a day of shopping and eating turned into drinks and dancing at the Rec Room. The girls had taken several Instagram selfies and received so many offers from guys to buy their drinks that they should have been drunk out of their minds. However, their rules had always been to stay together as a group and buy their own drinks. So, in the moment, they were enjoying each other.

Dallas nudged Candace, nodding her head over to the VIP section. "Is that Kendall?"

Candace squinted as he and his entourage came walking... no, gliding into the building like they owned the place. Kendall was sexy. His hair was freshly cut and lined up, his outfit was crispy and fit perfectly, and his jewelry was shiny enough to light up the dance floor. He had a Trey Songz sex appeal and Tank's looks. Dallas saw that; all of the ladies saw that.

They were supposed to make it to his concert, but tickets were sold out. When the radio announced that the after-party would be at the Rec Room, Candace didn't believe he would actually show.

A smile creased Candace's lips. "Yes! That is him with his fine self. Diego better quit playing with me before I replace him. Let's go over there." Candace said, tugging on Sasha's and Dallas's arms.

"Uh-uh, Trenton ain't gon' kill me. Besides, look at all those girls flocking to him. They're not about to treat me like just another groupie," Dallas complained.

"Would y'all stop being party-poopers and come on?"

Candace sighed, smoothing out her dress.

Her hair was pressed straight with a part down the middle, and she was confident that the little black dress she chose accented her curves perfectly. She was looking good and feeling even better. There was no way she wasn't at least speaking to him.

"Diego's going to kick your ass," Sasha whispered into her ear as they made their way to the VIP section.

Candace rolled her eyes. "Diego won't even talk to me, so I doubt he kicks anybody's ass," she stated confidently.

It was all a charade. She missed her man like hell. He was so stubborn, and she hated it.

Candace thought it would be hard to get through the velvet red ropes, but as soon as Kendall saw her, he pulled the girls into his section, allowing them to sit with him.

"Candace, right?" Kendall leaned over and said in her ear. He smelled as good as he looked. "I told management about you. They were supposed to hit you up."

His eyes lazily studied her curves. He made no attempt to hide his appreciation. She was a beautiful girl, and he happened to be an admirer of beauty.

Candace smacked her lips. "Yeah, right. I gave you my card months ago, and you haven't used my number yet. I bet you don't even have the card anymore."

Kendall smiled. His teeth were perfect, too.

"I do." He pulled out his wallet and flashed the pretty pink business card, causing Candace to blush. "What was that you were saying?" He put a hand to his ear as if he was trying to hear her better. "Now you have to have a drink with me for doubting me."

He waved his hand, and the waiter came rushing to him as if he was the King of Zamunda.

"I need a bottle of Ace of Spades and whatever these ladies are drinking." He leaned over toward Sasha and Dallas. "Order what you want, ladies. It's on me tonight," he added. "What are y'all doing after the party? We were planning to hit the strip club and enjoy Chicago. My flight leaves first thing in the morning, so there's no point in going to sleep."

Candace cocked her head to the side. "I definitely don't think it's appropriate to hang out after the club. You are not about to have me on the news because Diego's ignorant ass sliced me up and put me in a trunk." She frowned.

Kendall chuckled. It was worth a try. She was tempting, but if she was still involved with Diego, it wasn't worth the headache. Kendall had grown up in Detroit and ran in the same circle as Diego. Kendall knew firsthand how much of a menace the man was. Diego had come a long way and changed a lot.

"So, y'all are together?" He pretended to pout. "I thought I had my chance to shoot my shot. Why he let you out looking so good?"

Candace blushed. "Because he's stubborn and calls himself being mad at me. I told him he better stop playing before I make you my baby daddy," Candace teased, laughing out loud at the intrigued expression on Kendall's face.

"I'm not about to play with you, girl." He chuckled, taking in the crowd. "Look, I'm about to hit the stage and do a song in a minute. I'll have my manager call you for real this time. Where's your phone?" he asked, watching as Candace pulled it out of her clutch. "Take a selfie for the 'Gram with me. Make that big nigga real mad," he teased, leaning over and draping his arm over her shoulder, posing for the picture.

"Alright, stay beautiful." Kendall stood up. "You know how it goes. I'm a squirrel looking for a nut, and one of these chicks gon' get blessed tonight." He winked, signaling for his security to usher him out of the section.

Candace knew she could have easily been the one being *blessed*, but even Kendall wasn't worth losing Diego. He needed to get his life together. She missed him like crazy.

Thank goodness for Uber. The ladies had partied until three o'clock in the morning and were drunk. It was going on four o'clock when they stumbled back into the hotel. It had been a long time since they took a minute to just enjoy life. In their early twenties, they traveled everywhere: Vegas, Miami, New York, Atlanta. And the trip to Jamaica was one for the books. Life had consumed them, stressed them out, and forced them to be grownups.

"Why would you post that picture with Kendall? You know Diego is going to be spitting fire." Sasha giggled as they made their way through the lobby of the Sheraton Hotel.

After pressing the *up* button for the elevator, Sasha leaned against the wall to keep her balance. The elevator opened immediately, whisking them to the fourth floor. She had partied the hardest. After everything she'd been through, she needed the release the most.

"Girl, you said that like I'm scared of your brother." Candace rolled her eyes. "Maybe it will get him to talk to me. He's lucky all I did was take a picture. Kendall was trying to jump my bones."

"Alright, Billy Bad Ass. We'll see when you're face to face with my brother." Sasha gave her a knowing look as she used the key card to open the room door.

"Like I said, ain't nobody think—"

Candace nearly jumped out of her skin upon seeing Diego sitting snugly on the recliner chair next to the window. His dark eyes were intense, and the frown on his face had her ready to run out of the room and reappear as if he would just disappear.

"Oh shit, somebody's in trouble." Sasha covered her mouth, then grabbed Dallas's arm, pulling her into the next room of the two-bedroom suite connected by a living room area.

"How did you get here?" Candace asked, frowning as she

pulled off her heels that were wreaking havoc on her feet.

Ignoring her question, he stood to his feet. "Come holla at me."

Damn, he missed her. He didn't realize how much being without his woman affected him until he saw her face-to-face.

"You ignored me all this time over nothing, and you think I want to come holla at you now? Nope."

He was closing in on her, sending an aching straight to her kitty. She began to purr for him. She knew who her owner was and was going crazy for his presence.

"Don't come over here, Diego," Candace weakly protested as his cologne invaded her nostrils and the heat from his body sent a chill up her spine.

"Don't tell me what to do. Are you going to walk over to my room, or do I have to carry your ass?"

Carrying her didn't sound too bad, but she chose to walk. She didn't plan to end the night alone with him. She didn't plan to feel him inside of her like she had been craving for the past two weeks while he called himself being mad at her. However, Candace was sure both would be rewarding.

Diego had rented the next room over. The walk was short, and he was on her as soon as they got inside, invading her personal space.

"Why was you all up in that nigga's face?" he growled, devouring her with his glare.

After he checked her, he planned to thoroughly make love to her body. He planned to take all his frustration out on her center and kiss it until she exploded from the pleasure.

Candace sucked her teeth. "I know you did not come all the way to Chicago to check me about that bullshit. You hurt me, Diego. You left me alone to miss you and cry over you. I play tough, but that shit hurt my feelings. And since we're questioning each other, why do ma'fuckas have pictures of you putting guns to folks' heads? You promised me that you wouldn't do anything to jeopardize your freedom. You lied to me. That night Brian was shot, what did you do?"

"Nothing," Diego shrugged.

Candace shook her head. "Uh-uh. Don't 'nothing' me. Jaxon showed me the pictures. His ugly ass tried to blackmail me. He threatened to have you locked up, and I almost hate you for giving him fuel for his sick-ass fire."

"Jaxon is a bitch. I'm not worried about him. I think we got an understanding. And, for the last time, I didn't do nothing. I could have. I was about to, but something wouldn't let me pull the trigger. I got too much to lose now."

He stared into her eyes, showcasing his sincerity. He wanted Candace to know he wasn't trying to lose her. She was his world.

"So, you just let him walk away? I highly doubt that."

Diego smirked. "I didn't say that, either. I didn't do nothing he won't get over. Bones heal."

"I hate you," Candace whispered, biting down on her bottom lip. She didn't mean it. Diego knew she didn't mean it, also.

"No, you don't. And don't keep saying that out your mouth. Hate is a strong word and should never be used with me in the same sentence."

"You left me."

"I know. And I apologize. It's a respect thing, Candy. Don't lie to me. Keep it one hundred with me, and I'll always keep it one hundred with you."

"I didn't know how to tell you," Candace moaned, lifting her neck a bit so he could have full access to it. "He was trying to blackmail me, and I didn't want to get you involved. I was scared you would do something stupid. Jaxon was following you. He has the pictures."

"I'm not worried about him, and you shouldn't be either. What you should be worried about is figuring out how to make up with my lil' man. He's mad at you. It's going to take some extra nasty shit, too."

He smiled, and Candace's body throbbed in places she didn't know were capable of throbbing. Fresh urgency plowed through her as he pressed his hard body deeper against her. Making up was going to be fun...really fun.

CHAPTER TWENTY-SEVEN

DALLAS FLICKED THE light switch several times, hoping the outcome would be different. She scratched her head, trying to figure out the last time she had paid the light bill. She knew DTE Energy gave grace periods. She could skip a month and still be okay. However, she couldn't remember if she had missed one month or two.

"Residential customers, press one. Commercial customers, press two."

Dallas tapped the one button on her cell phone, pressing it to her ear. She followed the prompts, and when the automated system told her that her service had been interrupted for nonpayment, she cursed her luck. The heifer told her it would take six hundred and thirty-two dollars to restore services. She didn't have that kind of money in her account and wouldn't get paid for another week.

"I knew I should have stayed my ass at home," she mumbled, rumbling through the kitchen cabinets for the candles she stashed away after the last power outage.

Messiah Sr. was due to drop the kids off at any moment, and she instantly grew frustrated with embarrassment. He was going to have a field day about her not paying the light bill. It was as if he found pleasure in making her miserable.

It was an honest mistake on her part. She was pretty good at managing her bills. Her children never went without, even though she barely made ends meet and never asked Messiah for a dime or child support.

Dallas rolled her eyes. "He's going to have to step up," she concluded.

She had close to four hundred dollars in her account, so she didn't need much. There was food in the refrigerator that she hoped wouldn't spoil before she could get the lights on. And her gas tank was full. They'd manage until Friday.

The doorbell rang as Dallas came to the decision to put her pride to the side and ask Messiah for the money to get the lights cut back on. It was just past eight o'clock. The night sky was dark, offering not a single hint of light into the house. As soon as Dallas swung the door open, Messiah Jr.'s lips turned up. He stepped into the house, flicking the light switch.

"Why you got it all dark in here, Ma? You trying to be a vampire?" He giggled. However, when the lights never turned on, his smile vanished. "The lights don't work, Ma? Aww, man. Don't tell me we don't got no power. Dad got me 2k18, and I was about to play Jamal on the game," he whined.

"Just take your sister and go into the living room for a second. We'll probably go to Granny's tonight. Let me talk to your dad right quick," Dallas instructed, pointing to the front room where she had two candles glowing.

Messiah Sr. smirked as his tall outline leaned against the door frame.

"What's going on here?" He pointed into the darkness. "Don't tell me you was shaking your ass in Chicago all weekend and didn't pay your bills."

Dallas held up her hand, warning him that she wasn't in the mood for his jokes.

"Messiah, that is irrelevant. You know I'm not that irresponsible where I would put a trip before my household needs. I forgot to pay the light bill and don't get paid until Friday. I have four hundred and only need the other three to pay it."

"What?" Messiah sent her an amused, raised brow.

"You heard me. I need you to help with the light bill. I barely ask you for anything when it comes to our kids, and we need help."

Messiah let out a small laugh. "You got a whole boyfriend, won't give me no pussy, and have been on some funny shit lately. What I look like helping you pay a bill so you can sit up and play house with the next nigga? If he can't help you keep your bills paid, it looks like you need to step your game up, Dallas."

"Are you serious? What does me having sex with you or dating Trenton have to do with helping to keep your kids with lights? It's not his job to help pay my bills. It's yours."

"No, I do my part to help. It ain't my job to pay your bills either. I don't ask you for nothing when they come to my house every weekend."

"Messiah, you barely hold up your end with getting them every weekend, and that is beside the point. What about after-school activities, school clothes, doctor's appointments, and eating during the week? Feeding them on the weekends doesn't hold a candle to what I have to take care of, and I rarely ask for a thing. You should gladly give me a measly three hundred dollars to make sure your kids aren't in the dark."

Messiah smirked. He found it hilarious that Dallas couldn't pay her bills.

"Well, if it's just a measly three hundred, then pull it out your ass and get these lights on. Or ask that nigga you're fucking."

"You know what? Me and my babies will be alright. I promise we will. I hate the day that I met you."

"And I hate you, too," he snarled, pressing the door open and leaving.

If Dallas had something close by to clock him upside the head, she would have knocked him clean out.

"It's okay, Ma. When I get rich, I'm going to buy you a castle," Messiah Jr. said. "I don't like him no more. I hate him."

Dallas's heart broke. She didn't mean for her son to hear them arguing. The look of hatred in his eyes tore at her soul.

"No, you don't hate him, Messiah Jr. It's okay. I'm going to handle it. Go in the front room with Meghan. I need to get us some clothes so we can go to your grandmother's house."

Messiah trudged off, his chest poked out. He loved his daddy for the most part. However, as time passed, he was growing to see his father wasn't the hero his mother painted him to be. Dallas did a good job of covering his flaws. But Messiah Jr. was getting older, and it was impossible to cover them all.

As soon as Dallas was alone in her room, she broke down. It had been a long time since she cried one of those heart-aching, gut-wrenching cries. But she needed to get it out. She was so tired of Messiah Sr. hurting her. She was tired of even allowing him to hurt her.

"Ma?" Messiah Jr. knocked on the door. "Trenton's on the phone. Talk to him so you won't be sad no more. He makes you smile," he called through the door, pushing it open. "Here, I already told him you was crying."

Messiah Jr. shoved the phone in her face and kissed her forehead after she took it. Then he left out, closing the door behind him. He was a momma's boy to the core. He heard her sobs and didn't know what to do to make her stop. So, he called Trenton.

"Hello," Dallas sniffled.

"First, I'm going to need you to give me your DTE info so I can pay the bill. Second, I'm going to need you to tell me why you're sitting in your room crying with the lights off instead of calling me," he growled into the phone.

"But—"

"But nothing, Dallas," he cut her off. "Give me your DTE information first so I can pay the bill online. I'm pissed. Messiah Jr. had to call me? Really?"

After Dallas read off her account information, Trenton used

his debit card to pay the entire bill.

He sighed into the phone. "Dallas, why wouldn't you tell me you needed help?"

"Because it's not your job to help me. I never ask him for anything, ever. The one time I do, he laughs in my face. I hate him so much. I've been trying to stay strong, but I hate him!" she cried.

"You're going to stop playing me like some peon. Fuck him. You don't need him for nothing as long as I'm your man. It's my job to make sure you're good at all times."

"I have his kids. I shouldn't have to ask you."

"And you have my heart, so you can ask me for anything. If I got it, it's yours, Dallas. We're moving, but you're still not fully letting me in. I'm not him. I don't know what you're used to, but I'm going to need you to open your heart and let me mend it."

His voice was a sincere low vibration that shivered through her soul.

"I know you're not him, but how does my heart distinguish between the two? How can I forget what someone I loved with my entire soul did to me and trust that it won't happen again?"

Trenton sighed. "That's the funny thing. Life is about taking chances. You have to trust me with your heart even though you're not sure. I'm not asking you to forget what you've been through. You just have to forgive enough to make room for me."

Dallas nodded, biting down on her bottom lip. It was funny to her how even Messiah Jr. knew that Trenton was her happiness. She knew it took a lot for her son to build up the courage to call Trenton, and for that reason alone, she decided to try to let go and allow him in fully.

CHAPTER TWENTY-EIGHT

IT WAS FUNNY how life seemed to have its way of playing out. You could be in control one minute, and the next, things could spiral so far out of control that it looked impossible to restore order. Sasha felt as if she was at the point of no return.

"Yes, Mr. Barksdale removed you from the account this morning. I'm sorry," the almond-tinted bank teller told Sasha. She offered a sympathetic smile, then began typing on her computer. "Did you want to do another transaction?"

Sasha nodded, snatching up another withdrawal slip and scribbling down her other account number.

"Yes, you can take the money from my personal checking. Instead of two thousand, make it fifteen hundred, please."

It was taking everything in her to remain calm. She couldn't believe Hunter would take her name off their joint account. They both contributed to it. She had a portion of the earnings from the boutique deposited into the account, and he matched her deposits. Thank God she wasn't crazy enough to keep all her eggs in one basket.

Fortunately for Sasha, she had a separate savings account that she swore not to touch. She didn't have to bother it because Hunter made decent money and met all her needs. But he had turned into such an asshole that she couldn't wait to free herself from him completely.

The night before, they had a two-hour-long conversation, discussing their problems. It resolved nothing because it turned into a screaming match. Sasha told him that she was moving out, and he went ballistic. She never thought he'd go so far as to remove her from the account. He was turning into a demon that she didn't even recognize.

It broke Sasha's heart. Hunter was perfect in every way. She had placed him on the highest pedestal. Then, he betrayed her in the worst way, only for him to act as if he didn't care about hurting her. Sasha regretted giving so much of herself to a man. She didn't want to experience the pain she was feeling again, ever.

After leaving the bank, she headed to her appointment at the apartment complex in Novi. She had already gone through the application process and just needed to sign her lease and receive her keys. It was a two-bedroom loft-style apartment in a decent neighborhood. The rent was only seven hundred a month—perfect for her to restart her life. With her savings and the revenue from the boutique, she would be fine.

"Be careful in there, Sasha. Call me if you need me," Devaughn told her, staring up the driveway of Sasha's house before focusing on her sparkling hazels.

The possessive glare in his eyes caused Sasha's heart to warm. She waved him off. Hunter wasn't a threat. She only wanted to get her things and free herself from the nightmare their life had become.

"I'm fine. I'm not worried about Hunt. I just need to grab a bag. I have an air mattress to sleep on at the apartment until Gardner White delivers my furniture. I refuse to stay another night under the same roof as him."

"Well, hurry up. I'll feel better when I know you're safe. I need to check on Zion. Chrissy's been acting strange lately. Her flight leaves for Chicago Friday, and she's mad I won't let her stay." Devaughn shook his head. "She accused me of sleeping with you.

She's crazy."

Sasha smiled. "The people we chose to share our lives with. What were we thinking? They need to be thrown on an island together somewhere."

"Nah, I wouldn't wish that headache on no one," Devaughn murmured.

Sasha pushed a stray strand of hair behind her ear. "Hmph, I bet the headache she gets from Hunt won't be nearly as bad as what she gives him."

Devaughn's shoulders shook with laughter. "You're right. He may have her beat. Well, go ahead in. Call me when you leave."

"Will do."

Sasha's need to press her lips against his and taste his mouth was so urgent that she had to focus her attention elsewhere, forcing herself to walk away. She didn't know how long she'd be able to keep things in the friend zone. She wanted more from him. No, she needed more.

Actually, she needed a gun. If she had one, she would have shot Hunter's trifling, dirty-dick, grimy, despicable, low-life ass right in the forehead. Her stomach twisted so tight that she thought she would vomit. The wind had been knocked from her chest.

"Baby, wait. Shit." Hunter pushed Christina from between his legs and stumbled over his pants, trying to make it to Sasha. When they locked eyes, his heart sank. He didn't hear her walk into the house or expect her to be home so early. "Fuck. Sash, I didn't mean for this to happen."

"Fuck you, Hunter," she cried, cursing the tears that fell from her eyes.

He didn't deserve the satisfaction of seeing her cry, of knowing he had just thrown salt on an already open wound.

"Wait." Hunter grabbed her arm, attempting to stop her.

Sasha's fist swung so fast that he never had the chance to

duck. It landed on his forehead, and if he weren't so shocked that she decked him in the face, it would have stung. She began to swing wildly. He tried restraining her, but somehow, they ended up against the wall with her hands pinned.

"Calm down!" he growled. "That hoe pushed herself on me. I never—"

"Who you calling a hoe?" Christina said, cutting him off.

The smug look on her face only infuriated Sasha more. It was like she meant for her to catch them.

"Obviously, you're the trifling hoe. If you don't get the fuck out of my house, I will stomp a mud-hole in your taco-eating ass," Sasha yelled, trying her best to free herself.

She wanted to beat the girl's ass so badly.

"You're a joke," Chrissy laughed, taunting Sasha as she slowly made her way toward the door.

She was so lucky, Sasha swore.

"Just get the fuck out of my house," Hunter growled, then focused on Sasha. "I'm sorry, Sash. I know we're beefing, but I wouldn't intentionally do no selfish stuff like that. I don't want you to leave. Why would I try to jeopardize our relationship? I filed for divorce from Alicia."

He was a real class act.

Sasha frowned. "Whoopty fucking do! Want a cookie? Let me go, Hunter. What type of monster would be so cruel?"

"No, I don't want a cookie, Sash. I want you to listen to me. I fucked up, but I never meant for things to go this far. You said you didn't want kids, so I thought I was safe with getting myself fixed."

Sasha's eyes narrowed on him. "Wow, you fucking lied to me. You were married, Hunter. What, so that was your way of getting all the pussy you wanted without having consequences? I swear, I hate you. You had kids on me. You had that bitch in my house. You had me babysitting and playing house with those little motherfuckers."

"Yo, watch your mouth, Sash. The kids don't have anything to do with this."

"Fuck the kids," she spat angrily. She didn't really mean it. She loved the twins and Tasia. She couldn't believe he had three whole babies.

Slap!

It was Sasha's turn to be shocked. He really slapped her. Her heart stopped, and slowly, she lifted her gaze to meet his. The breath whooshed out of her like she had been sucker-punched. A shimmering wave of pulsing fury clouded her vision.

"Now, you can disrespect me all you want, but I told you to keep the kids out of this, Sasha. I know what I did was fucked up, but let's not pretend that everything has been peachy between us. You get into your little moods and forget that anything other than yourself exists. You know what? I still loved you through it all. I still loved you like the queen you are."

"You don't love me, Hunter. Love isn't supposed to hurt this badly. Love would have never ripped my soul out of my chest and stomped on it." She let out a small laugh, shaking her head. "And love wouldn't have me coming home to find the neighbor's baby's mother sucking your dick."

Hunter smirked. "Says the woman who spent the night out with that same woman's baby's father. She told me, Sasha. How long were you and him fucking?" he probed.

Christina caught Hunter coming into the house, claiming she only wanted to talk. She broke down, hurt that Devaughn was having an affair with Sasha. One thing led to another; the next thing Hunter knew, she was sucking him off. It felt too good to stop her.

"Devaughn and I have nothing going on at all. Unlike you, I respect boundaries. He was just a shoulder to cry on when you abandoned me," Sasha retorted.

Dark shadows filled her once-happy eyes. Her failed relationship was finally starting to sink in. She loved Hunter Barksdale with every fiber in her being. She had trusted him.

Hunter released a wary breath of air. "So, where do we go from here? How do we move forward?"

"There is no moving forward. You showed me who you are, and I'll be damned if I don't take the warning. By the way, removing my name from the account won't make or break me," she told him defiantly.

"If you leave today, I'm taking everything from you. I'll give the boutique to Alicia and sell your car. You have nothing without me, Sasha," he threatened.

Sasha could only laugh to keep from crying.

"That's where you're wrong. I'll have peace of mind and my self-respect. I am no longer your fool, Hunter Barksdale. No more."

She didn't need a response. She didn't need to hear his rebuttals, either. She left the house with her dignity and got in the car he *thought* she was going to let him take from her.

CHAPTER TWENTY-NINE

JITTERS OF NERVES ate at Candace's stomach as she took in the studio's décor. Paintings of different dancers graced the walls. The furniture consisted of a plush lavender couch and throw rug, a desk with a register, and a vending machine with drinks and snacks in the lobby area. Tall mirrors and open space made up the actual studio. It was gorgeous. Diego had turned it into everything she imagined it to be.

"It's almost show time," he whispered in her ear. "You look so good I almost want to say fuck this party," Diego added as his hands roamed her curves, landing on her ass.

She was aching for him to be inside of her. Just his touch set Candace off.

"You are not about to mess up my hair or makeup, Diego. The guests will be here in an hour. Stop being a horn ball," Candace giggled, wrapping her hands around his neck and popping a kiss on his lips.

"Fuck them guests. Just let me stick the tip in, Candy. I'm gon' be quick."

Candace rolled her eyes. "Stop lying. Nothing is ever quick with you. Yo' ass thinks you're the Energizer bunny or some shit." She gave him a knowing grin.

"So, you'd rather me last two minutes?"

"I'm not complaining. I said the guests will be here in an hour and the catering crew in the next thirty minutes. Sasha's always-on-time ass is probably on her way—"

"You saying a lot, but you not saying nothing. Can I get some pussy?" Diego cut her off. "I at least deserve to stick the tip in."

"Why are you so nasty?" Candace whined, even though her eyes were already scanning the room to peep the most secluded area they could get their freak on in without being caught. "I promise, if you take all day to cum, you will be stuck with blue balls all night," she warned, pointing an accusing finger.

Diego's sexual appetite was almost as insatiable as hers, and she loved it.

Diego chuckled. "Stop fronting like you don't want it," he growled as his fingers traced the outline of her breasts through her dress. "Come to the bathroom so you can bend over the sink. Let me hit it from the back. You know I can't last long watching your ass bounce."

It didn't take much. As soon as they hit the bathroom, Candace's dress was hiked up, and Diego's hardness was deep inside her, exploring every dip and curve of her walls. He filled her to capacity, and Candace found herself nearly delirious from the pleasure.

Candace closed her eyes. She could feel her juices stirring, building to the point where they started overflowing. She swore Diego was some top-flight dick pusher because he was knocking the lining out of her poor little coochie.

Before him, she thought orgasms from penetration were a myth. Of course, she had faked a few. But there was no faking the funk when it came to him. Her pussy was like a leaky faucet. Her juices flowed every time he found himself inside of her.

"Damn, I love you, girl."

Diego leaned over, never missing a beat. Electricity sizzled from his balls, up his spine, and centered in his brain. He began to nibble at her neck as he thumbed her clit while stroking her spot.

"What are you doing to me?"

No, the question was, what was *he* doing to *her*? Sensations curled through her like a tidal wave and pushed her into the rapture. She could have floated on the whisper-thin cloud of pleasure forever, but she knew they needed to hurry up.

"Cum with me, baby," Candace groaned, throwing her ass back.

Her body moved in a creative rhythm, matching his stroke. Several pumps later, the explosion that detonated inside them sent them over the edge.

"You so nasty," Candace giggled once she regained her composure.

"And you love it."

Music was thumping, guests were dancing, champagne was flowing, and Candace was in her element. The studio was packed with friends, clients, and family—all there to celebrate her. If she weren't trying so hard to protect her makeup, she would have allowed the tears of joy to overflow.

She prayed that everything would be perfect, stressed over it even. And it was. God must have heard her prayers because the grand opening of Candy Girl's Dance Studio was amazing.

"Girl, this place is everything!" Sasha squealed, grabbing her best friend up for a hug. "You and Diego are goals"

Candace blushed. "Whatever! Your brother is something else. I'm still tripping off the fact that we ended up together. I never saw it coming."

"I did," Sasha said, rolling her eyes. "Diego used to always talk my head off about you. That boy has been in love with you for years."

"But, why me?"

"Why not you, Candace? You are dope, girl."

"I am pretty dope, ain't I?" Candace teased, nudging Sasha as her eyes landed on Devaughn. "I think you and your friend have been a little too close lately. What's going on with that?"

"Girl, not enough. This whole taking it slow thing is about to drive me crazy. I'm starting to think he has a little dick or is on the down low. He's got to be hiding something. I've been practically throwing it at him, but he's been dodging me like he's in the Olympics. I think I'm going to just rape him. I'm ready to catch my first rape charge."

Sasha exhaled as her eyes joined Candace's, landing on her *friend*. As if he felt her looking at him, they caught eyes, and he winked. Devaughn knew he was a sexy piece of man.

"Girl, you are not going to have to rape him. I think it's cute that he's getting to know you first. Try it. Stop being such a horn ball. I see it must run in y'all family because Diego stay trying to—"

"Too much info." Sasha covered her ears, cutting Candace off. "I love my brother, but I do not want to hear about y'all sexcapades."

They both giggled as Candace felt those familiar arms wrap around her waist. His lips grazed her ear, and his scent invaded her nostrils.

"Come dance with me," Diego whispered.

"I was talking to your sister."

"Man, you and Sash talk all day, every day. Forget her. Come dance with your man."

He tugged at her arm, pulling her into the middle of the floor, and nodded toward the deejay. Jessie Powell's "You" blared through the speakers as he held her close and rocked with her to the beat. As he whispered the lyrics to the song in her ear, Candace swore she would burst with emotions. The powerful rush of pure adoration had her heart full with love. She loved Diego Riley more than he could ever imagine.

"Don't be singing in my ear like that," she teased. "Stop being so perfect. It's scaring me."

"You ain't got nothing to be scared of, girl. It's all love this way until I can't love you no more."

Candace smiled. "Well, even when I can't love you no more, I'm going to find a way. You better step your game up, boy."

Diego chuckled. "That's no doubt. It's forever. That's why I'm trying to make you my wife."

"Don't play with me." Candace scrunched her face up.

"So, you don't want to marry me?"

"Get me a ring, and then we can talk."

Diego smirked as a small laugh escaped his mouth. He stopped dancing, digging into his pocket to pull out a black velvet box.

"You ain't said nothing but a word, Candy. Like I said, you trying to be my wife?" he challenged, pulling his pants leg up and dropping to one knee.

The crowd erupted into a fit of oohs and ahhs. Candace's heart stopped. It was really happening. Of course, she'd marry Diego. She would go to the moon and back with him.

All of her efforts not to cry went out the window. She began to sob like a baby as her fiancé pushed the rock on her finger. She jumped into his arms and held him so tight that he thought he'd suffocate.

"Today is the first day of our forever, Candy. We got an empire to build. You ready for the ride, Mrs. Riley?"

"I was born ready, Mr. Riley," she confirmed.

Time had stopped. They were in their own little world. The room was packed, but all they saw was each other. They were so caught up in the fantasy that they never heard the music stop or the whispers of the crowd. When the officer tapped Diego's shoulder, he was thrown entirely off guard.

"Diego Riley, you are under arrest for the possession of a felony firearm and felonious assault. You have the right to remain silent. Anything you say or do can be held against you…"

Candace heard the officer talking, but it all became a blur.

"Noooo," she cried as they pulled her forever away abruptly.

Her voice was nothing more than a broken whisper. The happiest day of her life couldn't be ending in such a nightmare.

"You can't take him away from me."

She finally found her voice…a little too late. They were already whisking him away, and all she could do was cry. They just couldn't take him away from her.

CHAPTER THIRTY

BETWEEN DEALING WITH Hunter's ignorance, working, and going to trial for Diego, Sasha's free time for peace was few and far between. Dallas had gotten her a teller job at the credit union, which wasn't as bad as she thought it would be. Hunter had spoiled her. She never had to work, and it felt good to be standing on her own two feet.

He thought she'd crumble and come crawling back to him. Sasha would never give Hunter the satisfaction. After he had taken the money out of the account, taken away the boutique, and tried to take her car, there was no way she could continue to be with him. Though he had a messed up way of showing it, deep down, Sasha knew Hunter loved her and was only being an asshole because he was hurt. Hurt people, hurt people.

Sasha's phone rang, interrupting her train of thought. It was Diego calling from prison, and she hurriedly connected the call. She missed her brother like crazy and hated his circumstances. He had been doing so good.

"What's up, ugly?" he spoke into the phone as soon as she answered. "Candy told me you out there on your grown woman shit. I'm proud of you, Sasha."

She smiled. "Thank you, Diego. It'll be so much better when they let you out. Mom has been sick about it. She's not doing too good."

"She don't care. She always said I was gon' end up dead or in jail. This probably what she wanted. I love her, but I resent her for not forcing me to be a better man and make better decisions."

"Don't fault her, Diego. She never knew how to be a mother

and was trying the best she could. It was Curtis poisoning her head. He was taking care of her, so she lived off his every word."

Sasha chewed on her lip. The realization that she had repeated the cycle with Hunter had her thankful she'd broken it. She allowed a man to consume her entire life. She lived and breathed for Hunter. She gave him the power. She would never give another man complete control over her happiness again.

"Nah, that's no excuse. I know I was a bad-ass lil' nigga, but she should have still done her job instead of chasing a man." There was a short pause. "Look, I don't want to talk about that. Check on my baby. Make sure she good. Take her out to get her hair and nails done and buy her a little outfit. Get her cute for me."

"I've been checking on her for you. I'll take her out. That girl loves you so much. She feels like it's her fault you're locked up. She's mad at herself about what Jaxon did."

"I keep telling that girl it ain't her fault. I made the choice. I'll be good. The most they can get me on is a weapons charge, but I got the lawyer on it. It will be over soon."

"I know it will."

Sasha smiled as Devaughn came walking into the door with Zion running in front of him. She crashed into Sasha's legs, wrapping her arms around them.

"Sassshy," she squealed.

Diego laughed. "I hear your stepdaughter. That's my cue to get off the phone. I love you. Tell Devaughn I said what's up," Diego told her before hanging up.

Sasha smiled as Devaughn sauntered his handsome, massive frame over to her and popped a kiss on her forehead.

"Diego said what's up."

"Oh, yeah? How is he holding up? It'll all be over with in due time."

"I hope so. These past two months have been hell. I'm just ready for the nightmare to end so things can return to normal."

"Things will never be back to normal. It can only get better from here, especially since Zion brought *Frozen* with her." Devaughn smirked as his eyes slanted over to his daughter, who was already pulling the DVD out of her book bag.

Sasha giggled. "OMG, shouldn't she be tired of that movie? We've watched it a thousand times already. I'm going to turn into Elsa if we watch it again."

"Elsa is kind of cute." Devaughn pressed his lips together to stifle a laugh.

"Whatever. Get the movie started, and I'll go make us a snack tray. Zion is lucky I love her little self. She's going to be a problem. Both of us will be wrapped around her little finger."

"Tell me about it," Devaughn said, then bent down, scooped his baby up, and carried her to the living room to start the movie.

He was such a good father. She couldn't wait for them to move to the next level and have kids of their own. Sasha loved Zion to pieces; another baby would only mean more blessings.

Minutes later, the movie was going, snacks were on the table, and Zion was stretched out, sitting in Sasha's lap with her feet propped on Devaughn. The bond they were forming was priceless. Sasha was the closest thing to a mother that Zion had ever had.

She looked up at Sasha's face, rubbing her cheek with her tiny lemon-tinted hand.

"I love you infinity, Sashy," she said, her sweet voice melting Sasha's heart.

"Aww, and I love you infinity and beyond, Zion."

Zion's smile deepened as her feet wiggled on Devaughn's lap. Moments like the current meant everything to him. The relationship she had with Zion was more valuable than anything in the world. He just couldn't understand how a total stranger could love his daughter more than her own mother did.

After the stunt Christina pulled, Devaughn put her out of his house, but he had never put her out of their child's life. She chose to walk away, and the letter he received the night before offended him. She only wanted to be in Zion's life if she could have him. She called their daughter a mistake. What type of mother could carry a child in their womb for nine months, go through eleven hours of labor, and still not feel a single morsel of obligation to that child? He tolerated a lot of shit from Christina, but when it came to his daughter, he didn't play.

"Wait a minute, Zion. What about Daddy? You don't love me, too?" He poked his lip out, pretending to be hurt.

Zion nodded. "I love you, Da," she said as if it was an afterthought.

"Don't be jealous. This is a me and Zion thing. Daddies aren't allowed." Sasha smirked.

"Ain't that 'bout a…" Devaughn chuckled. "I feed her little self every day, but she wants to love you infinity?"

"Shhh. I watchin' the movie."

Zion shushed Devaughn, causing Sasha to burst into laughter. Zion was too much.

They enjoyed the movie, and when Zion finally fell asleep, Devaughn carried her to the spare bedroom and found his place next to Sasha again.

"She's out for the night," he told her, pulling Sasha into his chest.

Sasha's head snuggled against him, and his arms fit perfectly around her. Ending the night cuddling had become their favorite pastime.

"Zion is such a sweetheart. She makes it impossible not to love her."

"Tell me about it. That's why I'm not understanding how Chrissy can be like that toward her. She can hate me all she wants, but she doesn't have to take it out on my daughter."

Devaughn absently traced his thumb across her cheek.

"What happened between you two anyway? Why did you guys break up?"

Devaughn shrugged, looking off. He worked his ass off to

take care of his family. He'd given up his dreams…major dreams. And she shattered his heart.

"Chrissy had another daughter…" His voice trailed off. "After Zion, we had Vanessa. She only lived three weeks—heart complications. But I loved her all the same. Come to find out, she wasn't even my child. Chrissy had slept with my father. She left me for him and thought I was fool enough to take her back when he broke her heart. I gave up everything for that girl. It hurt so bad that I had to get away and start fresh. I won't let her fuck with Zion or me any longer."

Sasha heard the pain in his voice and saw the regret etched on his forehead. She glided her hand across his back, comforting him.

"I won't allow her to hurt you anymore, either. You're mine now. She signed over her parental rights, and I'll gladly accept Zion as my own. She already acts like it."

"I love the way you love her. It makes me love you even more, Sasha. You're rare."

"No, I'm not. I'm just plain old Sasha. Zion makes it easy to love her. And you, mister, you make it easy to love you, too. I've been hurt so badly, but you're right here mending my heart. You didn't even give me a chance to hurt behind what Hunt did to me because it doesn't even matter as long as you're by my side. I'm finally free for once in my life. I'm not inviting any unnecessary negativity into my space, and you shouldn't, either."

Devaughn leaned in and softly pressed his lips onto her forehead. When she looked up into his eyes, he found her lips, kissing her deeply.

"I've been waiting to do that all day."

"I've been waiting for you to do it. It scares me that I love you already. And despite what you think, it's not a rebound type of thing. I genuinely care about you, and I'm praying you don't hurt me."

"Picture that." Devaughn gently brushed dark curls back from her forehead. "That should be the least of your worries. I'd never hurt you, Sasha. I'm not a kid. I want a wife and a family with you. I need to make love to your mind before I fall in love with your body. That's why I'm taking it slow."

Sasha rolled her eyes. "I wish you wouldn't."

Devaughn laughed at her little pout, but Sasha didn't find it funny. It was nearly killing her not to feel him inside of her, to express her love in the most intimate way possible, for him to accept her body and take ownership of what was already his.

"You're so thirsty," he teased.

"Apparently, you're not thirsty enough," Sasha muttered, trying to ignore the aching in her center.

In a way, she respected him for not pressuring her about sex. They were both healing from their past, and when the time came to get nasty finally, Sasha planned to fuck him so good he would lose his entire mind——a punishment for making her wait her whole life to find him.

Devaughn woke in the middle of the night, adjusting his eyes to the room's darkness. The air was stuffy, and those silky legs tangled between his definitely wasn't familiar territory. A smile tipped the corners of his lips upon realizing his peace was lying right next to him. He felt the smooth easiness like back in the day when he had no worries—before Christina came and ruined his life. He'd taken a lot of shit from her. She almost destroyed him.

Sasha's grip tightened around Devaughn as he tried to slip out of bed to go and check on Zion, who was in the next room. It had become a habit...waking up to check on her. She was his prized possession. He often worried about her safety when he had nothing to worry about.

"Where you going?" Sasha's groggy voice whispered, never opening her eyes.

"Zion," Devaughn answered. "I wanted to go check on her."

"She's fine, you know?" Sasha told him, sitting up. "You check on her a lot. Like you're scared of something."

"I am…" His voice trailed off as he answered.

Sasha's slender frame touched him, her arms wrapping around those broad shoulders. They could feel and hear one another's breathing.

"Talk to me." Sasha kissed his back.

"I lost her." His hand found Sasha's, and he caressed her knuckles. "I hated myself for a long time. I thought I was the better parent. I took her away from Chrissy, and I lost her."

Sasha felt him inhale and exhale. A silence fell between them, and she didn't know if she should probe any further. She could hear the pain in his voice, but she needed clarity. She wanted him to open up completely to her.

Sasha frowned. "Lost her how?"

"I took her to the park. I turned my head for two seconds, and she was gone. That was the worst forty-eight hours of my life."

"How?"

"I ask myself that all the time, Sasha. I don't know what they did to her. I still don't know what my daughter went through for forty-eight fucking hours. That's why I hold her close. My daughter is my everything, and for you to love her just as much as I do means everything to me. I just don't want to mess it up by rushing things. Don't think I'm not attracted to you and that not having sex is easy for me. It's harder than you'd ever know."

Sasha held him tighter. "I love you already, and we barely know each other." She chuckled. "And I'll always protect her as if she's my own. I appreciate you trusting me with her. But if you don't give me some dick already, you're going to mess everything up."

Devaughn chuckled. Did she know how much restraint it took not to bend her over and fuck the cowboy shit out of her? It took everything in him, but he put his selfishness aside, wanting to be there for her in her time of need. He wanted to build with her first.

"It's not funny, Devaughn. We're both grown. Grown-ups have sex."

Devaughn caught a glimpse of the soft features of her face through the sparkle of light from the moon. She was beautiful—so fucking beautiful.

"You're hot in the ass," he teased, cracking up with laughter as Sasha popped him in his bare chest.

"I'm here to stay. So, it's okay to be hot in the ass for you," she told him.

Her hands left his chest and traveled downward, exploring his entire body until she reached his erect manhood.

"See? He wants me. Are you really going to deny him good sex?"

"Is that all it is to you?" Devaughn moaned as her fingers massaged his little head. His breathing accelerated. "You better stop, Sasha. There's no turning back if we go there."

"Boy, I've been trying to go there since forever. Stop talking so much and fuck me."

Devaughn's soldier extended into a full salute. Damn, her aggressiveness was sexy. Sasha didn't even see it coming when he flipped her over and pressed his body on top of hers.

"I tried to play nice, Sash. But, believe me, you're about to lose your mind," he growled.

His length was pulsating against her thigh. Lord, she felt it. She was soaking wet for him.

"Stop talking so much."

Sasha didn't have to tell him twice. He practically ripped her clothes off, and his two fingers found her pink pearl as his lips caressed her neck, preparing her for his entrance. Sasha's head fell back. Electricity flowed from her body and resonated inside of him. The pure urgency possessed them both. She was juicy and hot.

"Sssss." Devaughn's body jerked as he replaced his hand with his dick and plunged inside her tight cave. Her pussy muscles squeezed and clamped around his dick perfectly.

"Damnit, Devaughn," Sasha whispered, her breath caught

with each thrust.

He filled her to capacity, and she had to adjust to his rhythm. But damn, did it hurt so good. They both released long-awaited groans of satisfaction.

"Throw it back, Sash," Devaughn growled, gripping her thigh as he slid in and out of her. "A-fucking-mazing. That's it, baby. Take daddy's dick," he whispered into the crook of her neck.

"Oh God," she moaned.

It had been a long time since Sasha had felt so euphoric. Of course, Hunter fucked her good, but Devaughn was going in for the kill. He was so gotdamn passionate with his loving. He was finding secret spots that she didn't even know she had.

"Right there, Devaughn. Shit. Please don't make me scream. I don't want to wake Zion."

"Well, be quiet and take this dick. This is what you wanted, right?"

Sasha couldn't answer him. She could feel her pussy muscles contracting and an orgasm building.

"I asked you a question," Devaughn growled, drilling harder into her spot. "This is what you wanted, right, Sasha?"

"Yesssssss," she howled.

She lost control. She saw the sun, the moon, and the stars as she rode ecstasy's wave. She was officially addicted.

"What you looking all exhausted for?" Devaughn chuckled, nibbling on her neck.

He allowed her to regain her composure after her first nut, but he wasn't done with her and had no problem letting her know.

"You woke up the sleeping giant. So, you're going to take all of me. Ain't no quitting, baby."

Sasha didn't want him to quit. How could they turn back now? Having him inside of her erased her tears. It kissed the pain away, and if he could make a home inside of her, she would have lived in the feeling forever.

CHAPTER THIRTY-ONE

"TRENTON, DO YOU have any fears? Like, what scares you?" Dallas asked, looking up into his coal-black eyes and admiring the masculinity of his face.

His bone structure was perfect, and his juicy lips were kissable.

Trenton's brows knitted together. "Of course, I have fears, Dallas. Everybody has something they're scared of."

"So, what are you afraid of?" she probed.

He shrugged. "I'm scared of God not forgiving me for all the pain I caused while I was in the Army. I knew what I was doing was wrong, but I still did it. In a sick way, I let them make me believe I was saving the country. That was bullshit. Those folks didn't deserve to die. I have to deal with that burden every day."

"You know it's not your fault, right?"

"I guess, but I don't want to talk about that. Why you ask me that? What's your fears?"

Dallas smiled. "I'm scared that being with you is too good to be true and that I'll mess it up one day because, as much as I try to let the past go, I can't. I hate Messiah for what he did to me and is currently doing. I try not to have so much hatred in my blood, but I can't help it. Sometimes, it has me thinking certain things about you that I know aren't true."

Trenton's brows creased. "Certain things like what? You know I'm here for you and those kids, Dallas. Nothing can pull me away from y'all. You need to let that hatred go."

"It's easier said than done. As strong as I try to be, fifteen years just doesn't go away. He shattered me, Trenton, and I was foolish enough to keep allowing him to break me down further than I even knew I could go. It scares me because I don't think I can build myself up fast enough to let you in completely. I don't want to push you away."

"Heal, Dallas. What's the rush? I'm going to be here. We got forever to live."

Before Dallas could respond, Meghan and Messiah came bursting through the door and jumping on the bed with them.

"Y'all doing too much. How long y'all gon' be in here? You was supposed to take me to get a haircut and stuff before we go to wrestling, man," Messiah Jr. whined, attempting to push Trenton out the bed.

Trenton laughed. "Man, you always rushing somebody. Did y'all finish the breakfast I cooked? I thought me and your momma had a little alone time to spare."

"Nah, man." Messiah shook his head. "We got to get our hair cut, and they need to go do girly stuff. WrestleMania starts at five, and I don't want to be late. I can't believe you got me tickets for wrestling, Trent. I'm gon' make a big sign, and when John Cena comes out, he gon' see it and shake my hand. Watch."

Dallas chuckled. "Boy, if y'all don't get out my room. We have a whole six hours before that thing starts. You just go make sure you get your things on so y'all can leave out. You, too, Meghan. We'll be downstairs in a second."

"Okay," Messiah Jr. said, hopping up. "I'm about to go call my dad and tell him Trenton taking me to wrestling."

"Are you sure you need to do that, Messiah? You know how your father is. Maybe you should hold off on telling him," Dallas suggested.

The last thing she needed was for Messiah Sr. to start his bullshit. He swore that Dallas was trying to turn his kids against him. He didn't understand that he was doing it on his own. They weren't babies anymore, especially Jr. He understood what was going on and was old enough to make his own decisions.

Messiah Jr. sighed. "You're right, Ma. Dad's a hater. I'll call him when we get back."

Dallas didn't mean to, but she couldn't stifle the giggle that escaped.

"Don't say that, MJ. Your daddy is not a hater."

"Yes, he is, Ma. Do you even know what a hater is?"

"Yes, I do, lil' boy. Why wouldn't I?"

Messiah Jr. shrugged. "Because you're old. You like thirty or something."

Trenton burst into laughter as Dallas swatted Messiah away.

"Boy, get your little ass out my face. I am not old. Get to thirty, then come holler at me."

Messiah Jr. let out a playful laugh as he ran out of the room. "That's like in twenty more years...oldddd," he called over his shoulders.

Trenton thought it was so funny, and Dallas had to roll her eyes.

"What are you laughing at? You're older than me, so that makes you ancient."

He shrugged. "But we're not talking about me. He didn't say I was old. He said you was."

"Fuck you," Dallas shot back, pretending to pout.

Trenton wrapped his arms around Dallas and began to nibble at her ear. "I'm trying to tonight. Are you going to let me?"

"Hmph! I'm not trying to give you worms since I'm old and all."

"Shit, the older the berry, the sweeter the juice. I'm trying to see what that juice tastes like."

Dallas's center tingled. It had been a long time since her body had been touched by a man, almost too long. She needed to feel him inside her.

"That's not the way the saying goes, but I'll think about it. You hurt my feelings when you laughed at me." She continued to pout.

"Stop acting like a baby. You know what's up." He tapped her leg for her to stand. "Let's go before we be stuck in this room. My shit so hard it's about to break, and we can't do nothing to take care of it."

"You'll be okay. How long has it been that you've been keeping the dick from me? I've never had to wait nearly six months to get a sample. Now I'm scared you might have a malfunction or something."

Trenton cocked his head to the side. "Stop it. I definitely don't have those issues."

"Well, have you been having sex with someone else? I never asked, although I should have."

"Stop playing with me, Dallas. Sex ain't everything to me. I mean, it is, but I wasn't trying to go there until I knew for sure you was over Messiah. I'm possessive, man. If you give me that pussy, you better make sure you're ready for the commitment."

Dallas smiled. "I've been ready. You should have said that sooner. It would have saved us both frustration."

"We'll see." Trenton planted a kiss on her lips before calling out to Messiah Jr. "MJ, get your jacket! Let's roll, lil' man!"

As she watched him walk out of the room, the butterflies in her stomach began to stir. It meant everything in the world for the two most important men in her life to come to an understanding.

"Look, there goes Dad, Tatiana, and Corey." Messiah Jr. excitedly pointed, standing and waving as they made it up the arena's stairs.

Dallas blew out a breath of air. She so wasn't in the mood for his drama.

"Dad!" Jr. called out.

Messiah lifted his head and smiled in his son's direction...

until he saw Trenton sitting next to Dallas. His face instantly turned into a snarl as he walked past them and found his seat. It was so childish and petty to Dallas.

"I'm about to go show him my sign we made, Ma. I'll be right back."

Messiah Jr. raced off before she could protest. As a mother, she wanted to protect her son's peace. If he knew the monster his father was, he'd be crushed.

Trenton nudged her. "Breathe, Dallas. It's going to be okay."

She shook her head. "No, it's not okay. He waltzes his ass up in here with that bitch and another man's child. He knows how much Messiah loves wrestling, but he didn't have the decency to pick up his son and bring him? That's so wrong."

"But MJ is here. That's all that matters."

"No, it's not. Messiah Jr. worships the ground that man walks on. He says little shit to try to make me happy, but I know how much he loves his father. He can't keep treating my son like this."

Trenton grabbed her hand and gave it a squeeze. "MJ will see for himself what he's dealing with. Stop stressing yourself out about things you can't change."

Dallas tried hard not to stress, but she couldn't help it. She couldn't even focus on the show because she was so in her feelings. She couldn't wait for it to be over so she could get the hell away from her sperm donor.

Unfortunately for her, Messiah had parked two spaces over, and they just happened to leave at the same time.

"Dallas," he called out to her. "Let me talk to you right quick."

Trenton squeezed her arm, seeing her discomfort. "Calm down. I'm going to take the kids and go to the car. It's okay, Dallas."

"I'm fine." She nodded, then turned to face the man she had given far too much power. She couldn't even see how she ever loved a devil like him. "What, Messiah?"

His jaw flexed as he watched Trenton help the kids into the car. "I don't appreciate you parading around the city with my son like y'all the Brady Bunch and shit. I haven't even took my son to wrestling, but you let this nigga do it before me?" he growled, visibly upset.

Dallas's eyes narrowed into little slits. "Do you know how dumb you sound? If you wanted to bring him to a wrestling match, he would have been here with you today. Instead, you're here with her and her son."

"That's not her son. That's her little brother. That's my wife. She bought tickets, so I had to come."

"Your wife?" Dallas frowned.

"Yeah, I married her. What you acting all surprised for? You knew I was going to do it."

She shook her head. "No, when you came to my house trying to destroy what I was building because you're selfish, you said you wasn't marrying her. I hate you so much sometimes."

She felt the tears welling in her eyes.

"I hate you, too, and I'm not about to let you play house with my kids. You already trying to turn my son against me. I never pegged you to be bitter."

"Bitter?"

"Yes, bitter. You keep throwing that nigga in my face like I'm supposed to care. I married who I wanted to marry. I'm not tripping off your little relationship. Just keep my kids out of it."

Hurt, Dallas lost it. She completely went off, shouting all types of obscenities. Blind rage consumed her as tears fell from her eyes. She didn't notice she was shaking until Trenton's arms wrapped around her.

"Why you always making my momma cry?" Messiah Jr. yelled.

He came out of nowhere, and the mug on his face hurt Dallas even more. She saw pure hatred in his eyes.

"Why you don't want to see my momma happy? She let you be happy. I hate you sometimes, Dad. I hate what you be doing to my momma."

"Go in the car, Messiah Jr. I'm fine," Dallas sniffled, cursing herself for losing her temper.

"Nah, stay yo' little ass right here." Messiah Sr. gripped him up by his arm. "Who are you talking to? I'll whip your little ass if you disrespect me again," he growled.

Messiah Jr. snatched away, his fists clenched tight as his chest heaved.

"You disrespectin' my momma, so I don't care about no whooping. I'll take a whooping for her," he muttered.

His teeth were clenched so tight and his frown so hard that the words barely left his mouth. He was so mad tears were streaming down his face.

"Hey, lil' man, it's okay," Trenton told him, squatting as he touched his shoulder. "Your mother is going to be okay. Go to the car and check on Meghan for us. Can you do that for me, man?"

Messiah Jr. nodded. He triedhard to be tough, but the tears wouldn't stop flowing. He loved his father but hated how he treated his mother.

"Ain't that about a bitch! That's that lil' nigga's problem. That's my son. I don't need you saying shit to him," Messiah Sr. roared as Trenton stood back up.

"Look, man," Trenton sighed, "if you not about to beat my ass, all that yelling ain't even called for. I'm not with the back and forth. Swing or calm yo' ass down." His glare was deadly, silencing Messiah like the punk he was. "Now, I ain't trying to take your place. He knows who his daddy is. You need to get out your feelings and realize what you doing to that boy."

"I ain't doing shit to him."

"You're hurting his mother. That's enough. And as her man,

I don't like that shit. We about to have some real problems. It's my job to protect her, and I'll be damned if I keep allowing you to interrupt our peace."

"Fuck y'all peace. You want to be me so bad. Take care of them. I'm done. I ain't got no more kids."

Messiah Sr. walked off, and Dallas let him leave. He was never going to change. If she kept allowing him to get under her skin, the wounds would never heal. She needed to free herself. It was a necessity. That's why she allowed him to leave without saying a word. Eventually, he'd calm down and find his way back into his children's lives. She would even allow him in, but his power ended at that very moment.

CHAPTER THIRTY-TWO

"ALRIGHT. SEE Y'ALL next week!" Candace yelled as the ladies began to file out of the dance studio.

Her eyes traveled to the door. If Diego were home, he'd be right there, walking the girls to their cars. Then they'd lock up and go home to make love all night and cuddle.

She missed him. She missed seeing that crooked grin and hearing him nag her about not keeping her doors locked. She had a bad habit of not locking doors.

"Don't be in here too long, Candy. You know how these crazy negros are on Seven Mile." Tangie twisted her lips as she stared into the night, then back at Candace. "I tried to wait for you, but I have to pick up Jermaine's badass from daycare and cook my husband's greedy ass dinner." She bit the folds of her cheek, studying Candace. "It's going to be okay, boo. Diego will be home before you know it," she added.

Candace sighed. "I know. Thank you, Tangie. Diego's friend should be pulling up any minute. I'll be fine. You know his crazy ass treats me like a baby, even behind bars."

Tangie chuckled. "Because he loves you. Be safe and come lock this door," she called over her shoulder before making her exit.

Candace took a second to finish sending off the JPay email to Diego before making her way to the door to lock up. As soon as she reached it, it swung open, nearly hitting her face.

A frown instantly found its way onto Candace's lips. Jaxon was the last person she wanted to see. She hated him and was liable to punch his crazy ass in the throat without warning.

"You have some nerve waltzing your happy ass in here. What do you want, Jaxon? We have nothing to talk about."

Her hands defiantly fastened on her hips as she shifted her weight to one leg. She didn't trust him as far as she could throw him. That's why her eyes discreetly traveled the room for something she could clock him over the head with if he wanted to act stupid.

"So, I can't check up on my ex-fiancée?"

"Boy, please." Candace waved him off. "You was never my fiancé. That was a punk-ass promise ring, remember?"

"Same thing." Jaxon shrugged, stepping closer into Candace's personal space.

She was still beautiful. He hated how much he was still attracted to what could have been. Despite what she thought, he was eventually going to leave Arianna alone so he and Candy could start their future, but she had to fuck it up by being a hoe.

"I loved you," Jaxon confessed, grabbing her by the waist and pulling Candace into him.

Candace frowned. "Get your hands off of me, nigga. Ain't no love this way. You don't even know what love is. Leave before I call the police on your crazy ass."

She pushed his hands off of her. Her heart began to race. Jaxon could take full advantage of her, and there would be nothing she could do. His massive frame was almost two times the size of hers.

"Didn't you just hear me say I love you, though? That means nothing to you, huh? Your gold-digging ass never loved me." He used his pointer finger to mush Candace in the forehead.

She tried pushing space between them, but Jaxon grabbed her up by her arms.

"Do not touch me! Let me go!" she yelled.

Jaxon let out a cynical chuckle.

"And what you gon' do if I don't? Beat my ass? We both know

you can't do that. Who's going to protect you now, Candace? Your boyfriend is too busy trying not to drop the soap. Is that what type of niggas you like?"

"I fucking hate you," Candace muttered, feeling the tears of hatred drop down her cheek. "You already ruined my life. Why can't you just leave me alone?"

"Because you need to be taught a lesson. I'm not somebody you can use and toss to the side."

He pushed her, slamming her back into the wall. He slapped her so hard that the sound echoed throughout the studio. Her cheek instantly began to sting.

"Jaxon, please don't do this," she begged, holding her face.

"Don't beg now. You made me look like a fool bringing that nigga in my face, all while fucking him behind my back."

He lunged at her, grabbing her by her throat and squeezing so tight she thought her windpipe would burst. Candace clawed at his hands, but nothing worked. Just when she had given in to the fact that she was about to die, Jaxon released her, sending her crashing to the floor. She tried crawling away, gasping for air. It was taking all the fight in her. She was not about to die in that dance studio.

"Where do you think you're going, bitch?"

He grabbed her by her hair, yanking her back. Candace felt as if he was pulling her brains out. She let out an agonizing groan, praying he would stop and the pain would go away.

Luckily for Candace, God always heard her cries. The front door swung open, and Diego's friend, Chino, waltzed into the studio. Jaxon darted around him and out of the door like his life depended on it. It actually did. Chino's reactions weren't usually so delayed, but he was shocked to find Candace lying on the ground half beaten.

"Damn, Candy," he groaned, fighting between going after Jaxon to put two bullets in his head and helping Candace off the ground.

He chose to help Candace for now and handle Jaxon later. He knew if the roles were reversed, Diego would do the same for him. After assisting Candace to her feet, he grabbed her keys and purse, then helped her out of the studio after locking it.

"Fuck. Diego is going to kick my ass," he cursed himself.

He was only twenty minutes late. Things had gotten out of hand between him and his girl. The sex was too good to pull out and had cost Candace an ass whooping.

Candace still hadn't said a word. She couldn't. She was in shock. All she wanted was Diego, but he was gone. He couldn't protect her behind bars.

"Candy, you have to get it together. It's been a whole week. They arrested Jaxon last night. You don't have to hide in this room all day," Sasha said, pulling the curtains open to allow the sun to light up the room.

"Go away," Candace whined. "I'm going to sit in here until they free my man. I need him."

She felt her emotions stirring. She was so tired of crying.

"I hate Jaxon. I hope he dies in that cell," she grumbled.

"Don't be wishing death on nobody. He's getting his." Sasha sat on the bed next to Candace, rubbing her back. "Luckily, he didn't do any real damage, Candace. You're breathing. Forgive that man. You're still giving him the power by holding hatred in your heart." She pulled the covers off of Candace. "Come on. Let's get yo' funky ass out of this bed and in a tub. We have a hair appointment with Atlantis. You smell horrible, Candy." Sasha playfully covered her nose.

"Fuck you." Candace cracked the first smile in days. "Why

can't you just let me mourn in peace?"

"Because that's not what friends do. Get your ass up, Candace."

Candace groaned, peeling herself up from the bed. "Ugh! I can't stand you."

"Yeah, I love you more."

Candace made her way to the bathroom and hopped in the shower, then brushed her teeth and pulled her hair into a bun. It felt good to get herself together. Tightening the towel around her body, she headed back to her bedroom to get dressed.

"Sasha. You are so lucky I love you," she called out to her best friend. "You better not be in my closet, or I'm gonna—"

Her words caught in her throat. She thought her eyes were playing tricks on her. Diego couldn't be sitting on her bed with that same crooked grin she had missed like hell. Her hands shot to her mouth.

"You missed me?" He smirked, waiting for her to come to him, but she didn't. She stood there crying like a baby. "Girl, if you don't stop all that crying and come give me some lovin', it's going to be some problems." He smiled, curling his index finger to call her to him.

Candace ran and jumped into his arms. She didn't care about her towel falling or that she was supposed to be mad at him for leaving her. All that mattered was her man was home.

"I missed you so much," Candace sobbed.

"I know, baby. I missed you, too."

"You left me. You weren't here to protect me," she whispered in his ear while squeezing him tight. If she let go, she was afraid he'd disappear.

"I'm sorry, baby. Never again. I promise."

Candace shook her head, staring into his face. "Don't make me no promises you can't keep, Diego. How did you get out?"

Diego shrugged. "I broke out. I had to come make sure my

baby was straight."

He frowned, then burst into laughter at how Candace's face twisted up.

"I'm fucking with you, girl. They told me my case was dismissed this morning and sent me home. I didn't ask no questions. I ran up out of there before they changed their minds."

Candace popped him upside the head. Now that the shock had worn off, she wanted him to know she was mad.

"That's for leaving me. It was hell without you."

"Tell me about it. I got you. But, for now, let's not talk. I need to feel my body next to yours. I love you, Candace."

"I love you more, Diego Riley," she told him and meant it.

Candace took in her man's smell, drowned in his feel, and thanked God for creating him. She was no longer love's fool. She was love's survivor, because she planned never to let him go.

EPILOGUE

Six months later...

DALLAS WATCHED AS Messiah made his way through the restaurant and sat at a booth in the back. A sour taste churned in the pit of her stomach, and she checked herself for even having feelings. He wasn't her headache anymore. She had a real man—a man who loved her unselfishly, flaws and all.

Trenton wasn't perfect. He had his quirks. However, one thing was for certain. He made sure she and the kids were always together. She didn't want for a thing.

"That nigga will never change. Look at his cheating ass," Candace snarled as her head tilted in the direction Dallas was trying to avoid.

"That's why I gave him the boot. His wife can have all the headaches she wants. I accept my loss with pride." Dallas shook her head as she sipped on her margarita. "Besides, we have wedding plans to discuss. I can't believe you and Diego are getting married in a month!" she squealed excitedly.

"Shit, I can. They've been on some top-flight secret shit since we were kids. You're the only woman I'll ever approve of dating my brother, though," Sasha said, beaming as she rubbed on her protruding belly.

She had finally done it. Well, Devaughn had. It was unexpected, but she welcomed her pregnancy with open arms. Four months in, she couldn't wait to meet her child.

"Here you go." Candace rolled her eyes with a blush. Diego

was her knight, her king, her everything. "Anyways, back to you, Dallas. I know you've been all happy and in love or whatnot, but you're better than me. I would have snapped a picture of him and that bitch with the quickness. I would rub it all in that wife's face."

"I could, but that's giving him too much power. That would mean I still care, and I don't. He'll get his karma when the judge awards me my child support. I'm so over going through the motions with Messiah. He was such a good father until I stopped fucking him and got a man. Fifteen years? That's nearly half my life, only to find out he's a monster disguised in a man's body." Dallas sighed.

"Nah, you had to go through that. How else would you have been able to appreciate the love of a real man? I mean, Hunt hurt me to the depths of my soul. He cried with me, prayed with me, and promised me the world. In a sick way, I know he still loves me, always have. But we needed to go through that, too. I would have never appreciated Devaughn the way I do. There's happiness after the storm, and I'm living it."

Sasha was glowing. Dallas took note.

"We have been through a lot, huh?" Dallas's eyes slanted back toward Messiah.

She cursed her luck when they locked eyes. He smiled. She looked away.

"Lord, please don't let him bring his soul over here. I'm having a good day."

"You didn't pray hard enough, boo. He's on his way," Candace muttered, her face twisted. She hated Messiah's guts. "Ummm, can I help you?" Candace said with a roll of her eyes as soon as he was within ear's reach. "This table is for positive vibes only. We don't need your bad energy," she added, studying her freshly painted nails.

Messiah never acknowledged her. Instead, he focused his attention on Dallas.

"Can I talk to you right quick, Dally?"

"Dallas," she corrected him sarcastically. "My name is Dallas. We haven't been talking, so we don't need to start now. Your secret is safe with me. I wouldn't want to hurt your young hoe as much as she hurt me."

"I'm sorry."

Dallas's eyes shot up to the man she had dedicated half her life to, and her brows knitted together. She thanked God she didn't feel the tightness in her chest anymore. The butterflies didn't flutter, and the pulse of her heart no longer raised for him. She was free. Finally, Dallas had released herself from his shackles.

"Sorry for what exactly, Messiah? Never mind all the heartache you put me through. You hurt our kids. You took what we were going through out on my babies. I would never have taken you to be that guy."

Messiah licked his lips as he searched the room, hating the show they were giving. Of course, he knew he had fucked up. No one compared to Dallas. She was the real deal, and he missed her. Somehow, he thought she would always be there…waiting. Didn't she know he was hurting, too? Watching her ride off into the sunset with another man nearly killed him.

"Look, can you please just give me a couple of minutes? Not in front of your hype man," he snarled, glancing over at Candace.

"Boy, bye. Ain't no—"

Dallas touched Candace's arm, stopping her. "It's okay. We need to talk. At the end of the day, we have kids."

"Don't let this nigga talk you out of that child support order. Get your money, boo. Niggas switch up every day, B."

Dallas had to laugh at her best friend as she followed her ex out of the restaurant. She didn't know what she was doing or why she was even giving him her time. He made his choice. He hadn't seen the kids more than three times since running into him at the wrestling match.

"What do you want to talk about, Messiah?" Dallas folded her arms across her chest as soon as they made it outside. The sun was blazing as the cool fall breeze hit her arms.

"I miss y'all. I apologize for what I put you through. I've been wanting to tell you that for a long time but was too stupid to do it."

Dallas shook her head. "Don't do that. You created this storm and ran as soon as it got too big. You left me for another woman, and I had to accept it. But the minute I moved on and actually accepted it, you couldn't take it. The kids didn't deserve that."

Messiah frowned. "So, I'm supposed to accept another man taking my forever? That's the thing. I was always coming back, Dallas. I had to get my head together. I was coming back, but you didn't wait for me."

Dallas had to cock her head a bit. She figured it would help her understand better. It didn't. She concluded that he had lost his rabid-ass mind. She shook her head.

"Bye, Messiah. I'm not doing this with you. Go back to the little hoe that's not your wife and continue to cheat like you always do. I thought we were going to come to an understanding for the kids, but you're still stupid."

She began to walk off, but Messiah cupped her elbow.

"Wait." He ignored her frown. "I want to see my kids and for us to get back to normal. You got to get rid of that nigga, though. We can't get right with him in the picture. I heard he crazy, too. He takes medication, and I don't want my kids around that."

Dallas could only shake her head at his audacity.

"You will never get it. Bye. We'll settle everything in court. You're welcome to get your kids, but my personal life isn't open for discussion. I've been done the minute you stepped out on me. It just took a little time for me to comprehend it." She snatched away from Messiah's touch. "Now, if you'll excuse me, I was having lunch with my girls."

Dallas sang along to DVSN's *The Line* as she sat in front of her vanity mirror, cleaning the makeup off her face. She couldn't help the warm feeling that washed over her. Just months ago, her run-in with Messiah would have ruined her whole day. Not tonight, though. The kids were gone, and her man was on his way home. She couldn't wait to show Trenton how much she loved and appreciated him. Lord knows he had to be heaven-sent.

A smile creased the corners of her lips as the front door opened. She heard her man. His footsteps clinking against the floor sent butterflies through her entire being. Trenton was her everything.

"You home, bae?" Trenton's deep rasp called out. "Where you at?"

"In the room. Here I come."

Tightening her robe, Dallas stood and took a deep breath. It was just Trenton, right? The same man who had proven he could love every part of her. The same man who kissed her mind, body, and soul. Shit. Jitters of bliss caused her smile to widen as she laid eyes on her man.

Dressed in a black suit, he was giving *Men in Black* vibes, but he was way sexier than Will Smith. His hair was freshly cut, and his goatee was lined up to perfection. Dallas's center began to thump, pounding with anxiety, begging to be stroked.

"What you in—"

Trenton's words caught in his throat as Dallas dropped the robe, revealing her perfectly-shaped caramel body. Even the maze that pregnancy left on her stomach was sexy to him. Her pussy was freshly lined, and her hips curved out just right.

"Why you playing with me like that, girl?" he growled hungrily.

She smiled, stepping into her man's personal space. His arms wasted no time swallowing her in his embrace. Trenton's hands were like an octopus, exploring every dip and curve of her being. He leaned down and licked her neck, stopping at the pulse point before capturing her ear lobe.

"I'm about to fuck you like you've never been fucked, and I need you to take this dick. I don't want to hear nothing but you calling my name."

Dallas pulsated with anticipation. There was nothing she needed more than to be intimate with him. She wanted to express her love and appreciation through touch. She felt his body grind into hers, his pubic bone pressing into her clit. Her heart began to pound in her chest as she pushed his body toward the bed, using her slender fingers to slide his blazer off. His hands were all over her, and hers were all over him, stripping him, begging him to hurry and fuck her.

He lost his button-up, then his slacks. His erection tented his boxers. Dallas needed to feel him, taste him. She dropped to her knees, snatching his boxers down with her. Taking his manhood into her mouth, she suctioned him in, licking the head, then slowly gliding up and down his shaft.

"Damn, Dallas," he moaned, giving her the confidence she needed to please her man.

She was drunk off lust, and if he hadn't pulled her up and carried her to the bed, she would have tasted him all night.

Smoothly, he climbed on top of her body, licking his way up her legs and stomach, stopping to circle each breast before finding her mouth. He kissed her hard while holding her hands above her head.

"You don't run shit. This is about me and what I'm about to do to you."

"Nah, this is about us. I want to please you, too," Dallas panted, wanting to skip the small talk.

"Oh, I'm going to get mine," Trent smirked, softly flicking her nipple.

Then, he took it into his mouth, swirling his tongue around it. His kisses traveled down her body and landed on her lower lips. Her body jerked as his tongue and lips pressed against her swollen clit, sending sensations to her g-spot. Her breathing picked up speed as he settled between her thighs. A slight flick of his tongue nearly sent her over the edge.

Their eyes met as he opened her with his thumbs and blew on her pussy. Dallas couldn't take it. His tongue plunged inside her—teasing, pleasing, and fucking her. One finger, then two, invaded her walls. As Dallas felt herself nearing the point of no return, she clutched the sheets, bracing herself for the orgasm brewing. However, Trenton's lips pulled away just before she reached her peak, and she was delirious.

"I didn't say you could cum yet," he growled, grabbing her legs and aggressively pulling her to the edge of the bed. He stroked his long, thick rod as he stared at her intensely. Dallas couldn't even recall when he grabbed the condom and rolled it on. She was too excited as his dick found her slit and went spearing into her ocean.

They both cried out. He was huge, and her pussy was tight. It took a second to find the perfect rhythm, but once they were in sync, his strokes were hard and powerful as their bodies pounded together. Dallas was on fire. Sex with Trenton was like nothing she'd ever experienced. Now that he had officially made her his addict, she didn't know if she'd be able to survive without him. He was her drug, and she was addicted.

"Damn," Trent moaned after they had worked themselves into a frenzy and the orgasmic high had begun to settle down. "Why have you been hiding this from me all my life?"

Dallas giggled. "Whatever. Why didn't *you* find *me* sooner? I wouldn't have wasted so much time with asshole."

Trenton's brows furrowed as his face grew serious. "Nah, what we're not going to do is talk about that man after I just gave you the best dick of your life. Plus, if you didn't go through that, you wouldn't have them babies. We straight. I got y'all."

Dallas turned so she could look him in his eyes. She couldn't help the blush that stained her cheeks. She loved him. In return, she felt his love all over her entire being. Trenton was the forever she had been waiting for her whole life.

ABOUT THE AUTHOR

Danielle Marcus is more than an author, she's a storyteller who gives readers fast-paced, non-stop drama with the perfect love twists. Born in Detroit, Michigan, Danielle uses her inborn senses to motivate her sexy crime-filled novels. Danielle's work has been featured in the likes of Rolling Out magazine, while her independently produced book-to-film hits *"Plug Love"* and *"Young and Reckless"* currently stream on TUBI and Amazon Prime Video. Danielle has also mentored and helped publish other up and coming authors, creating a name for herself in the literary world.

Danielle has a huge appreciation for her readers and loves to hear from them. Please go beyond the book and connect.

Facebook: DanielleTheauthoressMarcus
Instagram: @authordaniellemarcus